House of Dating Disasters

the

ANGELA PEARSE

For my sisters

Chapter 1

Hi Aster, it's Richard. I'm at The Devil's Advocate.

My attention shifts from the hot kilt-wearing guy who's strolling ahead of me, to the message on my vibrating phone—*Richard?* I thought I was meeting Ryan. Or is he tomorrow night? Then again, there are two Richards I've arranged dates with recently on Soul Connexon. Damn, I'm nearly there, I better check:

Are you RBS Richard or graphic designer Richard?

He doesn't reply immediately and I wince on his behalf. Way to go, Aster, that'll make the guy feel special. Then I get:

RBS Richard.

Ah, yes, the banker. God, I need to start putting these guys in Google Calendar with accompanying notes. From what I can recall he's Richard McAllister, Senior Personal Banker: five-foot-eleven, thirty-four, blond hair, hill runner, addicted to espresso.

Great. I'm two minutes away.

He shoots back:

Hope you haven't double-booked your Richards.

Shit. Me and my big messaging mouth. Now I'm going to have to boost his ego, otherwise this date is going to flop before we've even clapped eyes on each other. I cringe but force myself to type:

Nope, you're the only one. Will be great to meet you F2F.

Damn you, Richard for making me say nice things to you that I may regret later.

U 2!

Phew, he's back on track. I shove my phone into my handbag and look around. But Mr Kilt is nowhere to be seen. Typical.

I suppose I should be feeling nervous about meeting Richard. But I don't get the queasy stomach and clammy palms anymore. Online dating for a couple of years in Edinburgh, and before that in Bristol, has given me a certain level of confidence and a few strategies. I find having a certain level of cynicism works particularly well; before, during and after the date. And even if, miracle of miracles, there's actually a spark and he seems interested, I arrange dates with other people because, inevitably, he won't contact me again. If he does, bonus, but trying to figure out why a guy who was giving off *all the right signals* hasn't messaged is a waste of my valuable time and mental energy. Once I got really depressed because this guy I was into ghosted me. It took at least a couple of weeks to get over him. Two whole bloody weeks! The fucker. I could've had six more potentials lined up during that time.

It's amazing, even after all the players, weirdos and shitheads I've met online, I still haven't given up on finding Mr Right. I've just had to lower my expectations. Markedly. Currently, my expectations are subterranean and scuttling with the rats in the boarded-up closes underneath the Royal Mile.

The bar Richard has suggested is halfway down Advocate's Close, a dank passageway with steep narrow steps and the stale odour of a men's urinal. A wooden board propped outside the doorway declares the Devil's Advocate offers "Over 300 Scottish and World Whiskies". I've never been here before and the out-of-the-way location strikes me as a strange choice for a first date.

Inside, a modern rustic aesthetic greets me: brick walls, a white marble-topped bar counter, and warm light pooling from low-hanging silver lights. There's a muted weeknight ambience. Couples converse in hushed tones while nursing their drinks. I spy a tallish blond guy perched on a wooden stool at the bar checking his phone. I gather that's him, as there's no one else fitting his description.

I stride over and open with, 'Hi, are you Richard? I'm Aster.'

He nods, and brown eyes flick briefly over my face; his expression registers surprise. I'm surprised too. He's a strong eight, possibly even a nine, and that's without gin goggles.

Soul Connexon is a blind dating site, so I have no clue what a guy looks like when I agree to meet him, apart from the basic description he's given in his profile. I've been using it for a couple of weeks now after my flatmate Dee tried it and met a stonkingly hot aged-care nurse with this description: six-foot-three, thirty-two, brown hair, kind and loves the elderly. She was lucky; the guys I've met so far have been ... well, let's just say they didn't inspire a deeper connection. Richard is the first to make my libido sit up on its hindquarters and take notice.

We do the necessary "nice to meet you" pleasantries. His handshake is warm, dry, and confident. No first date nerves for him either. 'What would you like, Aster?' he asks, gesturing at the bar.

He has a divine Scottish accent with a light rolling r, so my name sounds incredibly sexy coming out of his mouth. Cue upper thigh tremor.

'A vodka martini thanks,' I reply.

He smiles. 'Very James Bond.' I hitch a shoulder in response and smile back.

Despite my cool, calm demeanour, I pay a lot more attention to Richard when he's talking to the barman. I hop up onto an adjacent bar stool, and with one elbow on the counter and chin in hand, do a surreptitious eye swivel to check him out.

It's an after-work date, so he's suited and booted; nice, I like the clean-cut look. His white shirt is unbuttoned at the neck, showing smooth skin with a sprinkling of golden chest hairs. Hmm, too revealing for the workplace, so he must've undone it at the bar. His hair is short and flaxen-blond, casually swept to the side with a fresh undercut; sexy, and shorter than mine, bonus. He has a pouty mouth; that's intriguing. Suggests he's used to getting his way. Strong jaw. My gaze drops to his hand as he holds his credit card against the machine. Ooh, lovely and big. Great.

'Sláinte,' Richard toasts when the drinks arrive and I echo it. We clink glasses and sip. He's ordered a vodka martini as well. 'You're not what I expected,' he says, giving me a quick appraising glance before shifting his eyes back to his drink.

'Oh?' I wait politely, thinking I'm going to get a compliment. *You're way prettier than I thought you would be. I'm into sexy redheads with green eyes.*

But he just says, 'So, you're a freelance editor? Who likes dogs?'

'Yup. And you're into hill running and drinking espresso.'

'Aye. They don't usually take place at the same time, mind.' I chuckle at this, and he looks pleased.

Ho, he's got a sense of humour. Great. My expectations rise to pavement level. This might actually be a good date and not a mare.

'How often do you hill run?' I ask. Sipping at my martini, I settle back on the stool as best I can without toppling off. If I were wearing a dress, I'd be showing a lot of leg right now, but I don't do dresses, so he's out of luck. Instead, I'm in snug black tailored trousers and my favourite green top that clings in all the right places.

'A couple of times a month,' Richard says. 'But I need to get back into it. I'm out of shape. Too much socialising lately.' My man slut radar beeps. *Socialising* is dating code for *sleeping around*.

'What about you?' he asks, giving me another once-over. 'You look fit. I mean in a healthy way, not the other way. You look nice ...' He sounds flustered and I get the feeling he's trying to say the right things. Maybe he's an online dating newbie.

'Oh, I go to the gym occasionally.'
Like once in a blue moon.

'How long have you been on Soul Connexon?' I ask, hoping it's only been a month or so, and he's not a man slut.

'Two months,' Richard replies. 'I like the blind dating idea. People are way too hung up on appearances. I'm interested in getting to know the person.'

I nod in agreement, relaxing at his admission. 'Though if the person does happen to be good-looking, it's a bonus, right?'

He laughs. 'True.'

We raise our cocktail glasses and sip in unison. He engages me in a meaningful eye lock. My stomach flips. Is Richard giving me the I-want-to-fuck-you look already? I've barely broken the surface of my martini. Usually, they wait until after the second drink at least.

I break the gaze and shift position, feigning disinterest, to see if that puts him off. Instead, he casually leans on the bar still looking at me and angles his knees towards mine. His body language is saying loud and clear: I'm interested.

Woah, OK. He's a bit quick off the mark, but Richard is certainly a possibility if the emotional connection is there. Although I'm starting to think he might be a player.

'Two months ...' I take another sip. 'Have you been on many dates?'

I'm realistically expecting ten, or maybe even fifteen at a push, so when he says airily: 'Forty', I gulp more martini than I mean to, and it burns my throat on the way down.

'Forty?' I rasp, my nonchalance act slipping. I do some quick mental calculations. 'But that's a date every night of the week! Unless you spill over to the weekend?' *One on Saturday night and two on Sunday after church ...*

Richard smiles benignly. 'Let's just say I'm good with numbers and extremely organised.'

I was hoping it was an exaggeration meant as a joke but from the sense of pride he's exuding, I can tell he's serious. My heart sinks. It's not a case of thereabouts or somewhere in the vicinity of forty-one. I am officially number forty-one.

Wow, here I was thinking he was a newbie! Forty dates suggests he's either fussy or sleeping his way through the Soul Connexon database. I'm onto him. He should've lied and said ten so I didn't get suspicious. Maybe the martini has gone to his head, or more likely, he can't resist boasting.

'Um, so if I'm forty-one, what happened to the other forty if you don't mind me asking?' I ask, trying to keep my tone light.

He shrugs impassively. 'Nothing. We met up, we chatted, it didn't work out.'

'You must have very specific criteria if you haven't met someone after forty dates. Are you looking for something in particular? Some elusive quality?'

'I've just got two must-haves: pretty and nice.'

'Oh.' *So much for not being hung up on appearances.*

He gives a choir boy smile and moves closer so one of his knees touches my thigh and I get a waft of his aftershave, which if I'm not mistaken is Dior's Sauvage (or as Dee calls it "Sausage"). As the description says on the bottle, it's "unique in its confident virility", but I'm starting to feel uncomfortable about Richard's virile confidence. *"We met up, we chatted, it didn't work out"* is also dating code for "I *charmed their knickers off, we had sex, I ghosted them."*

Disappointment floods through me. He's a player. He's not looking for a bloody soul connection or anything remotely like a relationship. It's purely no-strings-attached, physical. Damn, he was so promising.

I lean back out of his Sauvage aura and say witheringly, 'Richard, you're on a dating app without photos. Surely if 'pretty' is one of your two must-haves, you'd be better off on a site *with* photos.'

Richard guffaws. His shoulders shake with mirth. Gosh, OK, I didn't think it was that funny. I suppose most women enhance themselves in some way, whether by make-up or a beautifying app, so their profile photos don't give the true state of affairs. I can only imagine that Richard has had some interesting beauty-and-the-beast encounters.

'I like you, Aster,' he says now, edging even closer.

You just want to sleep with me, Richard.

'Why don't we finish our drinks and head to my flat for a nightcap? It's not far away, on Cockburn Street,' he suggests.

Hello! His bar of choice suddenly makes perfect sense; it's a mere five-minute trot to his lair. Before I can say anything, he reaches out and grasps my hand, and starts massaging my palm with his thumb.

And there it is. A clear-cut offer. No-strings-attached sex with a good-looking guy. The mini thumb massage is arousing and I'm tempted. My fortress of cynicism is fully intact; I'm not going to get hurt if we sleep together and he ghosts me.

But it would be breaking my self imposed "no sex on the first date rule" and ultimately, he's just wasted my time. I don't want a player who's after a one-night stand, I want someone who's interested in a relationship. Once I may have fallen for Richard "Sausage" McAllister's smooth moves and gone back to his Cockburn flat. But that's all in the past. He's three months too late; I've raised my standards.

Chapter 2

Scroll. Read. Hmm, possibly. Save to favourites.

Scroll. Read. Nope.

Scroll. Read. Nope.

Scroll ... I peer closer, that's not what I think it is?

Scroll away from the image quickly.

The trouble with online dating sites that do have photos is that you need to be open-minded. You have to give all the guys a fair go. If you scroll too fast because you don't think they're attractive, you might miss a vital piece of information in their profile. The *thing* that connects you. There might be a hidden nugget in there. Like, I don't know, that he adores Ferrero Raffaello and so do you. And then it's too late. You've scrolled past, so you miss out on your only chance at happiness.

The sad thing is, when you're desperate, you look for anything that suggests a connection. Even something as mundane as the shared love of white chocolate balls with coconut flakes.

Speaking of white balls ... I snap my laptop shut with a shudder. I'm not sure what's worse, being on Soul Connexon, where I can't see anything, or Hearts of Fire, where I can see everything. I'm seriously thinking about cancelling my subscription to that site, the number of males that post body parts as profile photos seems to be increasing.

Dee says: "You have to wade through the mud to get to the hog". But sometimes I wonder how much more mud I can take. And do I really want to view the hog's privates?

As if she's heard me, right on cue my phone buzzes.

Aster, I've had a mare of a date! I hope you're home for a debrief. I'm bringing wine and chocolate.

I cackle. It sounds like Dee's hot aged-care nurse is about to, or has been, dumperoonied. I had a feeling he was too good to be true.

Another pops up:

Just remembered you're on a date. If you're naked and having rumpy pumpy, ignore this message!

I sigh and reply that I'm at home. Technically, if I'd agreed to Richard's offer, I would be naked right now. A vision of us going at it like the clappers, dances in front of my eyes. Ah, well ... He'll be onto number forty-two in less time than it takes to order a bacon butty. I press my thighs together tightly as my nether regions twinge in regret ... and guilt. The end of my date with Richard wasn't as clear-cut as I would've liked. Now I'm trying to forget about him.

I flick on Netflix and watch *Bridgerton* until, all of a sudden, Dee appears in the doorway with her long blonde hair in disarray. She's got a bottle of wine gripped in one hand, and a Waitrose bag in the other. I open my mouth to ask about Mr Nurse but before I can say anything she announces, 'He's no more! I vamoosed him to the ether. He's just like all the other shitheads I've met this year!'

She flumps onto the opposite couch, with her coat half unbuttoned and starts unscrewing the wine, while upending the Waitrose bag. King-size bars of Cadbury chocolate, Freddos and Yorkies slither out all over the coffee table, a couple of creme eggs bounce out last.

'I'll take some of those, thank you very much,' I say, reaching for a handful of chocolate Freddos. Wine now opened, Dee takes a long slug from the bottle, then another. She then stuffs a whole creme egg into her mouth and chews dejectedly.

I eye her, amused. Dee is naturally theatrical so I can never tell if an actual disaster has occurred, or if we've just run out of toothpaste.

'What happened? Not another Sam?' Sam is always used as the benchmark for the worst dates.

'Urrrgggh,' Dee mumbles through a mouthful of a creme egg. She takes a slurp of wine to wash it down and bursts into tears.

'Oh God, Dee ...' Instantly I'm up and throwing my arms

around her and she lets loose with a volley of sobs against my chest.

After much hoo-ha and sniffling, I get the whole story about Dee's date at Bella Italia on North Bridge. It turns out Mr Nurse was lying when he wrote in his profile that he was kind. When she ordered tiramisu for dessert, he told her in not so many words, that she needed to lose weight. Then tried to make out like it was a joke. Hah bloody hah. Dee isn't stick-thin, but she's hardly Ten Ton Tessie either, and I have no patience for men who think they have a right to comment on women's bodies. 'Who does he think he is? You've got a lovely curvy figure, don't take it on board. Stupid fucker.'

Dee sniffs and unwraps a Yorkie bar and nibbles at it. 'I thought I was looking OK until he said that. I haven't been to the gym for a while but, I don't know, it was like he was trying to make me feel bad about myself. He seemed so nice on the first date ...' Her lip quivers and I hug her again.

'He was no doubt on his best behaviour, and then the veneer of niceness slipped. Nasty gaslighting prick. Forget him. Bella Italia isn't even high-end Italian. He was too stingy to take you somewhere decent.'

'True.' She shudders. 'Anyway, how was your date? You're home—which either means it went well and you're saving yourself for the second date, or it crashed and burned and you've been sitting here scrolling through guys on Hearts of Fire.'

I look at her. Then at my laptop pointedly.

'Ahhh …' she says quietly, heaves a sigh and takes a big bite of Yorkie.

'He was a player,' I say, 'I was onto him before we'd even finished the first martini.'

'What are we going to do, Aster?'

'I think we should give up on Soul Connexon,' I say, thinking pragmatically. 'It's a good premise, but we've both had bad dates and two data points make a trend. It's attracting the shitty good-looking guys who have slept their way through the photo sites.'

'No, I mean … What are we going to dooooo!' Dee wails. 'We have to face facts, there are no nice guys out there. They've all been snapped up and we've been left with the dreeeeggggs!!!'

I flinch. Her anguish is hitting a nerve. It's what I've secretly been fearing for a while now. That it's too late. That, at the ripe old age of mid-thirties, the odds of meeting an agreeable mate for marriage and reproduction are nearing zero. It's why we've been pouncing on the new members of Hearts of Fire like hot chocolate sachets at a cheap hotel. So far we've had plenty of offers for "a good time" but no one we'd want a relationship with. Dee almost thought she'd nabbed Sam. He was good-looking, funny and incredible in bed—she was gutted when she found out he had a girlfriend. I'm starting to wonder on a daily basis: where are all the good men hiding?

'We must be on the wrong sites,' I insist. 'I refuse to believe there are no nice guys out there.'

'I'm glad you've still got a smidgen of optimism. I think we should just buy a cat and be done with it. Sod the lot of them. Their loss.'

I sense another onslaught of tears welling beneath the surface. 'Don't give up,' I say, trying to inject some positivity into her. 'Maybe we just need a different approach.'

Dee is silent and I think she's mulling over which breed of cat to buy, but then she says, 'It's a good idea. Actually ... it's a bloody brilliant idea.' She tosses the half-eaten Yorkie onto the coffee table and sits up straight, animated. 'We ditch Soul Connexon and stick to Hearts of Fire, since it's the most popular site and everyone uses it. But we upload new photos and rework our profiles to attract a better quality of men. Our photos should show us in everyday life: working, cooking dinner, drinking coffee, reading or something like that. We need to showcase ourselves as intelligent, natural, wholesome women that want a relationship, not as tarts who live for nightclubbing.'

'Riiigght,' I say, not sure I do look like a tart in my photo but going with it.

'And ... oooh ... oooh!' Dee is on a roll now. 'We should screen them somehow, maybe a questionnaire they have to fill out before we agree to go on a date. And definitely no sex until they've proven themselves worthy.'

'Ah, steady on,' I protest, visions of my only side-pleasure of online dating going out the window.

'And the pièce de résistance to make us stand out from the rest,' she announces triumphantly, 'We go bare-faced!'

'What!' I'm aghast at that suggestion. 'But my make-up is usually minimal. They're not getting anything different when they see me in real life.'

I know it's the fashion to use bronzer three times darker than your skin tone and magic marker in your eyebrows, but I refuse to look like an Oompa Loompa.

'The no make-up look, à la Gwyneth Paltrow, is trending right now, Aster. Besides, you're disgustingly tanned and it's not even summer,' Dee says mock accusingly, staring at my arms. They're still golden brown from my two-week holiday in the South of France in September.

'I can't help it. Blame my Italian great-grandmother, bless her wee dead genes.'

Dee is still musing. 'If they make it through to the third or fourth date and it's looking promising, we need to be across their socials sooner rather than later. Not accepting a request is a red flag. That's how I discovered Sam wasn't single, remember?'

I do remember—Dee was a mess for weeks. She's never admitted it, but I think she was in love with him. Even though they'd only been seeing each other for a couple of months he'd broken through her barrier with his charm, witty banter, and smooth bedroom moves. But when Sam didn't accept her

Facebook friend request, Dee became suspicious and checked his profile photos more carefully.

Sure enough, the evidence was there, a loved-up photo of him smooching a pretty girl. Dee confronted him and he admitted he had a long-distance girlfriend who lived in Berlin. He said Dee and him could keep seeing each other and the girlfriend didn't have to know—what a shithead. Sam was instantly dumperoonied.

Dee's enthusiasm, the annoyance about our latest dating disasters, and the Freddos I've eaten, are beginning to swirl and combine in a way that's softening me up to the whole idea. What have I got to lose? 'Fine,' I say. 'I'll agree to the no-makeup photo, but sex is still on the table if they pass the screening.'

Chapter 3

'Can I at least do my hair?' I moan as Dee flits around like a Vogue photographer—angling her iPhone left, right, high, low. I have short hair, naturally red with a few dyed blonde highlights, but since I'm overdue for a haircut, if it's not styled properly, it just looks messy. What with bed-hair and no make-up, unsurprisingly, I'm not feeling particularly attractive or enthusiastic about this impromptu morning photoshoot.

'No, it's great! The sun is making it look all glossy and fiery. Just smooth down that bit at the back that's sticking up like a duck's tail. Look at me, look away, now look at me again. Not like that, too severe. Smile! No, subtly, like you've got a secret! See, you look really natural.' Dee shows me her phone.

'Naturally boring,' I say sarcastically, and she giggles.

I suppose I don't look too bad, it's just casual in comparison to the photo I currently have on Hearts of Fire: tanned and glam, in a gold top, at a restaurant in the South of France.

For this one, I'm posing in my bedroom chair by the window, with my legs crossed, and holding a book. The room is bathed in the soft morning sunlight, and through the window, you can just see Calton Hill in the distance. I'm wearing grey track pants, a faded green t-shirt with *University of Bristol* plastered across the front, and the pièce de résistance according to Dee: smiling coquettishly like I've got a man tied up in the wardrobe.

'I'll just do a bit of tweaking,' she says busily cropping and brightening the images. 'Trust me, I'm used to making dull things look good.'

'Gee thanks, I think!'

Since she's the front-of-house manager for a boutique hotel, I know she's got marketing experience. Although, prettying up hotel rooms is somewhat different from promoting my wares.

For her photo, Dee insists on an outdoorsy shot, so she can model her new hiking gear. She's had it for a month and this is the first time she's worn it. Unfortunately, it means going to Salisbury Crags before Dee has to be work at nine. As she tells me after we get out of the Uber, which has dropped us off at the bottom of the hill, 'This is brilliant, it will make me look like a go-getter.'

'Aren't you being fake though, acting like you hike all the time when you don't?' I query when I'm photographing her posing in black lycra leggings and a turquoise tank top on the edge of the cliff, her hair swirling becomingly around her pinkened cheekbones. 'At least I do read. I can't remember you going on a hike in the two years I've known you.'

'It's a hobby I've been planning to take up,' she says with a shiver, peeling off a strand of hair sticking to her clear lip gloss. 'Can you get a shot of me looking over my shoulder without my hair all over my face? Then let's get out of here, it's fucking freezing.'

Despite the gooseflesh, I have to admit she is rocking the bare-faced, outdoorsy look. But Dee is naturally beautiful without make-up; she has an English rose complexion, azure eyes, and a winning smile. Along with the blonde hair and the Marilyn Monroe figure, I'm surprised that Mr Nurse was being such a picky prick. She is quite short though, and didn't put her height in her profile, so maybe he was wanting a skinny supermodel, who knows?

After lunch, I head up to the nearby WeWork in George Street to do some editing for a client and upload our new Hearts of Fire photos and profiles. I rewrote both of them last night, with Dee looking over my shoulder and making suggestions. They're now more intellectual and serious and make it clear we want a relationship and are *not* interested in a casual fling. The originals were a lot heavier on the socialising aspect and, on reflection, may have made us come across as party animals.

I've added a note at the bottom that says anyone who wants a date will need to answer the questionnaire, otherwise they'll be deleted. I have to admit it does make me sound rather mysterious and exclusive, if a little precious.

I grit my teeth and click "submit" before I can change my mind. Then I do Dee's since she's given me her login and password.

Luckily, the two girls I've met here, Stacey and Fleur, also freelancers, aren't around today. There's a chance one of them could walk behind me and peer over my shoulder. Not that I'm ashamed of my online dating habits, but I don't particularly want to get into a long-winded discussion about it. They might see me as a serial dater. I'm nowhere near Richard's league of forty in two months, but I have at least two dates a week, sometimes three if there's a bank holiday weekend.

I've been trying not to think about him but he sent a message in the Soul Connexon app about meeting up again. So far I haven't replied. I knew this would happen. Saying "no" to sex has marked me as a challenge.

And, I'm ashamed to say, despite all my high and mighty posturing about not touching him with a barge pole—we snogged in the close after leaving the bar. So I'm not surprised it's given him mixed signals.

It just kind of … happened. After I politely turned down Richard's offer to go back to his flat and extricated my hand from his grasp, there wasn't much more to say. The conversation died a sudden death; on Richard's part since he knew he wasn't getting into my knickers, and on mine, since

I'd guessed he wasn't interested in a relationship. We knocked back the last of our martinis and headed outside.

After a few stilted pleasantries about the mild weather and not quite looking at each other, it was decidedly awkward and time to leave.

'Where's home?' Richard asked. His voice had an undertone of petulance which suggested he wasn't best pleased with the way the evening had ended.

'New Town, Frederick Street.'

After a few more stairs, Advocate's Close turns right into a passageway and then pops out onto Cockburn Street. It's the quickest way to get back to the New Town but the lamps were dim and who knew what was lurking in the depths? I hesitated, considering walking up the stairs to Royal Mile and going the long way round. Richard sensed my dilemma. 'Scared of the bogeyman? Want me to walk you to the end?'

'Yes, thanks,' I replied, relieved.

When we reached the yellow street lights, we stood side by side silently. Richard bumped his shoulder against mine. 'Sure you don't want a nightcap?'

'I'm sure,' I said.

'Right. Well, it was good to meet you, Aster.'

God, why did my name have to sound so sexy when he said it? He went in for a peck on the cheek. And then a hug. This was surprisingly nice, even though I was enveloped in Sauvage, so it may have gone on for longer than I intended.

Then he murmured 'come here' and guided me back into the shadowed archway, and was gazing down at me brooding-like in the gloom, which fired up all six of my cylinders. When he kissed my cheek again, and then brushed my lips lightly with his, I didn't bother resisting. Before I knew it, we were snogging with abandon and he was squeezing my arse. I was hot and cold at the same time, literally. My breasts were pressed up against his warm, firm abs, and my back was exposed to the chill air as he lifted my top and ran a couple of fingers under my bra strap.

My toes started to curl as his tongue expertly caressed mine. If he'd suggested we went back to his flat again, I would've gone willingly. But he didn't. He just gave me one last lingering smooch, walked me back to the street, and whispered 'goodbye' in my ear, as if to say 'duh, big mistake, see what you're missing.'

'Well, uh, yeah, goodbye then,' I said breathlessly, staring at him dazedly; everything was askew, including my brain. I tucked my top back in and pulled my handbag back onto my shoulder. He nodded, we shook hands, and both stalked off without a backward glance in opposite directions.

Bloody hell, Richard, I thought, as I headed towards Princes Street, lips on fire and blood boiling like a kettle. He'd completely caught me off guard and I was shocked at how good a kisser he was, and that thought led to—what else is he good at? I came straight back to the flat, spent some quality time with my vibrator, made a strong cup of tea, and sat on the couch scrolling through Hearts of Fire, cursing at myself for being weak and succumbing to his tactics.

Attractive men who just want sex and are extremely practised at getting it, like Richard, are bad news. He's never going to be potential boyfriend material and I don't want to be notch number forty-one on his bedpost. Besides, I doubt he'll pass Question Six on the screening test we've just devised. I stare at my newly uploaded profile photo and wonder who on earth this homelier version will attract.

As if he's in tune with my thoughts, another message from Richard arrives. Reluctantly I open it. He's sent a meme of an old-fashioned typewriter with a piece of paper inserted.

Written on it is something that I assume is his way of trying to connect with me on a deeper level by wittily tying in my job: **DON'T ~~RIGHT~~ WRITE ME OFF.**

Actually, it's funny. And cute. Grrr.

Chapter 4

I'm in Bon Vivant's Companion shortly after, scanning expensive wine labels and wondering which to buy, when Dee calls me.

'I'm getting it right now,' I tell her. 'I'll be home in ten minutes.' She's cooking coq au vin using a recipe the chef at the hotel gave her. It demands a list of ingredients as long as my arm, including a bottle of good red wine. We only have white in our stash.

'Can you get some brandy too, or Cognac, either one,' Dee says.

'This is all a bit fancy for a Tuesday night, isn't it?'

'I need to work on my cooking skills. My profile says I'm practised in the art of French cuisine.'

I sigh and eye the bags of corn chips. French cuisine equals slow cooking. I'm going to need something to stave off my hunger. 'All right.'

There's a silence and I think she's hung up, 'Hello? Are you there?'

Dee's screech nearly takes out my ear drum.

'Jesus!' I jerk the phone away. 'Why'd you do that?'

'Oh. My. God!' She sounds like she's hyperventilating.

'What?'

'I just got a bunch of notifications from Hearts of Fire.'

'Ah, yes, you should expect a few to trickle in. I just uploaded the new profiles.'

'I've got fifteen messages.'

'*What?*' I splutter.

'Check yours!' she gasps excitedly.

I open the app and stare in disbelief at the number of messages clogging my inbox.

'I've got twenty-four ...' I say, feeling slightly faint. 'Jesus. It's only been half an hour!'

Dee screeches again. 'It's working! It's fucking working! The men of Edinburgh are rising to the challenge!'

'Don't get too excited,' I say, trying to calm her down, 'This isn't the Hunger Games, they still have to pass the screening ...' But Dee's not listening.

'Come home, we need to talk tactics!' She hangs up abruptly and I giggle. She sounds like she's in the war office.

I buy a bag of corn chips, a cheap bottle of red, and an even cheaper bottle of brandy, and hotfoot it back to the flat.

Dee's in the kitchen slicing onions with tears pouring down her cheeks and Dua Lipa's *Be the One* blasting from her Spotify. Hopeful energy radiates from every pore. I feel a rush of affection and protectiveness. There's nothing I'd like more than to see her waltzing down the aisle towards the man of her dreams—geez, I want that for myself—but I've been internet dating way longer than she has, so I'm a little more wary about this plan working.

I dump the goods on the counter. 'Thanks!' She gives me a beaming, albeit watery, smile.

'What time will it be ready? I'm starving now.'

'Around eight.'

'Right.' I resign myself and break open the corn chips while Dee stretches up and brings down the largest saucepan we own. She's put her hair up into two twisted cones, and is wearing a blue-white-striped t-shirt and her Gordon Ramsay apron which has a picture of him scowling and the caption "My Gran Could Do Better and She's Dead!"

'So that's good news about the messages,' I say tentatively, nibbling on a corn chip, and leaning on the island counter. 'I didn't expect so many guys so quickly. I guess we could use a spreadsheet to keep track of them ...'

But Dee is way ahead of me. She turns down the volume on Dua Lipa.

'I considered that, but I think we need something more sophisticated—a project management tool where we can enter their details, attach a photo, and add comments on how they did on the date. That way we can keep track of them.'

'Good idea. I use Trello for work, so I'll just create another board and share it with you. I think maybe just three columns each: "Potentials", "Rejects" and "Seeing", to keep it simple.'

She nods. 'Are you sure there are enough questions?'

'Yeah, I think we're good. Don't want to scare them off.'

Dee stares at me. 'How many, if any, do you think will make it through?'

'Oh, I'd say five per cent.'

Dee snorts. But I'm deadly serious. The men who make it through will be rare beasts indeed.

The six questions we've agreed upon took us two hours to come up with. Initially we had eight but I vetoed two of Dee's: "Where do you buy your clothes?" and "Which do you prefer: Tesco or Waitrose?" because I thought they were snobbish. If she's worried about that that she can ask them on the date.

A couple of the questions could be seen as too personal, but we feel anyone who's looking for a relationship will answer honestly. And it's better to find out anything nasty upfront, rather than three dates in when you're getting that mm-I-quite-like-you feeling. The questions are:

1. Are you definitely single?
(Be honest because we will find out if you're not.)

Dee and Sam. No explanation needed here.

2. Do you smoke or use recreational drugs?

This one is based on a date Dee had with a guy who

mentioned he smoked a joint every morning with a cup of green tea. He thought it made him sound cool. Fail.

3. Are you a legal resident of the UK?

There's nothing worse than meeting a guy you like, only to discover he's an illegal immigrant and is only after a visa. I learned this the hard way.

4. What are you currently reading?

This is another one of mine as I feel it shows a certain level of intelligence. Whether it's car magazines or Tolstoy, at least we'll know what we're dealing with.

5. Do you have a favourite joke or funny story?

We both agree a sense of humour is a high priority in a man, so the object with this one is that if he can make us laugh on paper, chances are he'll be funny in person.

6. How many women have you slept with in the last month?

This last one is rather controversial, and we debated for ages on whether or not to include it. But after my date with Richard, I think it's pertinent. I know we're liable to get, "it's none of your business" replies, but we haven't given any indication of what is an acceptable number. For all they know, ten might be OK.

If a guy makes it past the first date, there are a few more tests he'll have to pass before he can be considered a viable prospect for the "Seeing" category. We're calling these tests "The Dealbreakers".

To any outsider, the lengths we're going to may sound extreme. But finding a decent man for a boyfriend, let alone to marry and have babies with, isn't an easy mission nowadays. Especially when you've reached a certain age and you're staring down the barrel of being permanently on the shelf.

I stretch out on the window seat and steadily plough my way through the rest of the corn chips, while Dee hums and stirs something in her saucepan. Taylor Swift's *Red* is now on in the background, but softly. Dee knows I don't mind her, but that too much Taylor, too loudly, gives me a headache. I'm flicking through my twenty-four messages, and hoo-wee, judging from the photos, there are some guys that I'm hoping will make it through the screening. One, in particular, is catching my eye. He reminds me of Gareth (or was it Garrett?) whom I had a date with a few months back.

'Dee, check it out. Doesn't he look like that guy Gareth?'

'Who?' Dee comes over and I hand her my phone.

'Oh yeah, from the shower-sex incident.'

I cough, embarrassed. 'I wish you wouldn't call it that.'

'Sorry, I'm just not sure what else to call it.'

'You make it sound tawdry.'

'Well, it did make Emma move out.'

I cringe. 'Don't remind me.'

Dee zooms in on the photo and scrutinises it. 'I don't think it is him, you're safe.' She scrolls through my messages. 'Hey, some of these guys are the ones who messaged me, they've said exactly the same thing!'

'Figures ... They've probably just copy-pasted the same message to fifty women.'

'Ugh. Ooh, you just got something from Soul Connexon. Can I open the message?'

I shrug. 'Sure.'

'Oh, this is cute! He sounds nice.'

She shows me my phone.

Since I haven't replied to the typewriter meme, Richard has now sent through a GIF of a baby goat butting a knee, in time with a flashing message:

I WANT TO GOAT TO KNOW YOU

I have to laugh. He's a trier.

'That's Richard. The player who inspired controversial Question Six. He wants a second date. I'm resisting his advances.'

'You should send him the questionnaire,' Dee says, handing me back my phone and returning to her saucepan.

There's an angry bubbling noise coming from under the lid.

'I could, I suppose. But I doubt he'll want to do it.'

'You never know, he might surprise you.'

'My instincts are saying it's not a good idea. Besides, he's a great kisser and I'm not sure I can resist him.'

Dee pauses stirring, sauce dripping from her wooden spoon. 'I thought you were going to tone things down and not do anything on the first date?'

'I couldn't help it,' I say, feeling guilty.

'Hmm, well, if you're attracted to him, you shouldn't write him off.'

'Hah, that's what he said.'

Dee considers and then brightens. 'You could have dinner at the hotel so I can keep an eye on you. If you're feeling tempted, just send me a signal at the end of the date and I'll swoop in and save you from yourself.'

God this "no sex until they're worthy" rule is going to be even more difficult than my "no sex on the first date" rule. I think I'd better stock up on batteries for my vibrator.

'Fine. But the chance of him being worthy is zero. At least we can test it. He can be the guinea pig.'

Before I can change my mind, I send it with a preface:

If you want a second date, you'll need to answer these questions. It's a new online dating method I'm trialling.

But it's not until Dee and I are sitting down to a late dinner at the kitchen table that my phone buzzes. Sure enough, Richard has completed his questionnaire. The accompanying message he's sent says:

Done. If you're playing hard to get to make me hard, it's working.

I swallow a partially chewed lump of dry chicken and it goes down painfully. 'He's answered them.'

I read his message again and shift in my seat as some of my body parts start twanging. Just imagining him saying my name—Asterrrrr—brings to mind us kissing in the close. Yikes, he knows exactly what to say to make me want him.

'That was quick,' mumbles Dee through a mouthful of food. 'He must be keen.' I notice she's pushed aside her chicken and is only eating the mashed potato and gravy.

I've deemed it wise to keep mute about the coq au vin apart from nodding when she asked if it was OK. I'm not sure a guy with cordon bleu tastes would approve of Dee's French cooking skills, but she might be able to slip them by a meat and veg man.

'Aren't you going to look at what he's written?' she asks me with a quizzical expression.

'I want to but ...' I lower my fork as I get a sudden realisation. 'God, there's a small part of me that's hoping he turns out to be a nice guy. But I just know he's not. I'm afraid to find out that I'm right because I want to be wrong. Does that make sense?'

Dee rolls her eyes. 'You ninny. This is why you shouldn't do anything physical with a guy until you've got to know him. Now you're emotionally invested! He's making it difficult for you to flick him.'

'I don't think I am. I'm pretty sure I can flick him. But oh, I don't know ... I'm like you, tired of meeting shitheads. I want to meet someone I can connect with on a deeper level. But I don't think Richard is that person.'

'Only one way to find out. Give it to me, I'll check them.' Dee waggles her fingers for my phone.

Silently I hand it over.

She opens the message and starts reading. Her eyebrows raise at one point and she smirks. I'm jigging my leg madly.

Dee keeps reading. God, has he written a thesis? Then at last she gives me a look bordering on amusement.

'Well? He's given a whole load of run-of-the-mill answers to pretend he's a nice guy, hasn't he?'

'Oh, Aster,' she says, 'He's perfect for you.'

It turns out Richard is my male doppelganger. He's shared a shower-sex incident for the funny story question.

In his words: "My flatmate's girlfriend broke up with him because she said she preferred girls. I decided to see if this was true or just an excuse to dump him. So, when she came round to collect the rest of her stuff, and my flatmate was out playing squash, I made a move on her. One thing led to another, and we ended up having hot shower sex. Literally. There was an issue with the cold water and the water turned scalding making us scream, but not with pleasure. Then my flatmate got home from squash early and walked in on us, just as we burst out of the shower, naked and red as lobsters. Not only did I have to find another place to live, but I had first-degree burns for a week."

It's what I would expect of him, and it did make me snort—once. But is it funny enough to waste my time going on a second date or just reaffirming what I already know? The other thing is, it's making me uncomfortable because I'm starting to perceive Richard and I are somewhat similar. It's like he's inadvertently drilled into my psyche.

All his other answers are fine; he's single, he doesn't do drugs, he's a British citizen, he's reading Barack Obama's memoir and he's slept with only three women in the last month (I don't believe that for a second, but I'll give him the benefit of the doubt).

It's Dee's fervent insistence, 'He's the male version of you! You have to give him a chance!' along with her reassurance that she'll stop me from going home with him that pushes me over the edge. There may be more to him than meets the eye. Perhaps sleeping with every woman in Edinburgh isn't his main objective?

Me
OK, dinner tomorrow night, 7:30 pm, Liberty Hotel in Rothesay Terrace.

Richard
Great. You won't regret it.

Uncannily I can almost hear his thoughts *'I've got this one in the bag'.*

Dee has helped me get out of nightmare dates in the past. Usually, it involves me messaging: *Help, I'm stuck on the date from hell,* from the loo then receiving a surprise "emergency" phone call from her when I'm back at the table. This is always the part I love the most because it means I can leave guilt-free without looking like a callous bitch. I just throw in a few heartfelt apologies and a 'can we take a raincheck?' and then I'm out of there. But if Dee is on a date herself and doesn't see the message, I'm stuck. I have to endure further conversation that is either excruciatingly boring, full of egotistical preening or worse, non-existent.

To my way of thinking, Richard is bordering on egotistical preening. I mean telling a girl you've just met that you've had forty dates and then showing off about getting it on with a lesbian? The guy is up himself. Good looks aside, he's only barely managing to hold on because of the Barack Obama memoir.

When I arrive at the Liberty, there's only Dee stationed at the front desk. She usually manages a couple of underlings but she must've given them the night off to attend to me personally. She's dressed in her uniform, navy pinstripe trousers, a matching jacket with a white shirt, and a light-blue silk scarf knotted around her neck. She hates it but I think it looks smart. I like the crisp clean look when it comes to clothes; no flounces or frills for me. Since I'm wearing a similar get-up (minus the silk scarf), I almost blend in with the hotel staff.

Pinned to her jacket is a gold name badge with her full name—Edie Crowley-Smythe—engraved on it.

'Is that new? I don't remember you having that before.'

'No, I just don't normally put it on. I'm supposed to, but I always forget. I thought it might look more official in case he gets stroppy.'

I glance over her shoulder into the restaurant area but I can't see Richard.

'Speaking of which, is he here yet?' I ask in a low voice.

'Yes, he's having a drink in the bar. He was ten minutes early,' she says and gives me a meaningful look which I brush off with, 'He was probably just bored at home.' I know what she's trying to intimate: he's early because he's into you.

'He's cute. If you decide you're not interested you can throw him my way.'

'Nope, it'd be like introducing an innocent lamb to a wolf.'

Dee giggles. 'Oh, come on, he sounds fun.'

'Not a chance.'

Sometimes I go overboard with the protective sister act, but Dee is a couple of years younger than me so I guess it comes naturally. And I don't have any sisters, only a brother who lives in Australia.

Looking at Dee's hopeful face now, all of a sudden, I've got cold feet. I need to be going on dates with nice guys, not wasting my time on ones like Richard. 'Maybe this is a bad idea ...' But she gives me a shove towards the lounge bar. 'Just go and talk to him, get to know him better. Ask him about his family or his hobbies.'

'I know what his hobbies are,' I mutter under my breath.

But I dutifully walk into the bar where Richard is seated on a red leather banquette nursing a tumbler of amber liquid and ice, doing something on his phone.

He looks up as I approach the table and gives me his angelic smile, 'Hello again.'

'Hi yourself.' He taps the tumbler with his finger. 'Want one of these?'

'What is it?'

'Scotch on the rocks.'

'Ah, maybe not. I might just have a glass of wine. It's too early for the hard stuff.'

'Suit yourself.' He looks away and I notice that his jaw tightens.

It occurs to me then that perhaps he's nervous. Maybe he doesn't do second dates. It makes me feel sorry for him, just a little, so I soften. 'Actually, I will have one. Why not?'

Richard catches the barman's eye and holds up an index finger, and he nods in return.

'So,' I say, sitting down in the turquoise chair opposite. 'How are you getting on with Barack Obama?'

Richard sips his drink and looks at me. 'I was surprised you're using that questionnaire thing.'

'Why?'

'It just seems easy to get around. If you're trying to find a husband, you might want to add that they have to take a lie detector test.'

'Er, who says I'm trying to find a husband?'

'Aren't you?'

I shift uncomfortably. Gosh, this is getting serious straight off the bat. Nobody expects the Spanish Inquisition.

'I think doing some groundwork is a good idea. It's a waste of my time if I find out after three dates he overstayed his visa and just wants a route to citizenship.'

'Hmm.'

'Anyway, you managed to get a second date, so you must've said something right.'

'I think I know what it was.' He gazes at me steadily with smouldering brown eyes, and I feel a little zing in my solar plexus. Oh, not the eyes. No fair.

'It was the goat. I thought it was cute,' I say hurriedly, averting my eyes.

'You didn't find the shower story funny?'

'It was, ah, mildly amusing. I have a similar story,' I admit.

Just then the waiter brings over my drink. 'Your table is ready if you want to come through?'

'So I have to hear this story,' says Richard, after we've given our orders for starters and mains. The lighting is muted thanks to the low-lit wall sconces and it's creating more of an intimate atmosphere than I would like. It's the sort of atmosphere, where after a few scotches, you end up telling someone your deepest, darkest secrets. Then going home with them.

But he seems like he wants to know, so I say, 'A previous flatmate walked in on me and a guy when we were at, er, a critical point in proceedings.'

Richard's eyebrows lift slightly, but he doesn't seem phased. 'You left the door unlocked?'

'Yeah, stupidly. I planned it so we were the only ones home that night. But my flatmate came back from her movie early because she wasn't enjoying it. She thought I was ill because she heard groaning noises and came in to check. She did knock, but I didn't hear her because I had water in my ears ...' Richard laughs. 'Anyway,' I say hastily, feeling like I'm giving away too much information, 'It was a highly embarrassing situation for everyone involved.' Not strictly true as Gareth/Garrett thought it was funny.

Our starters arrive, and there's a pause while we sort out who's whose. I've got the Salmon Fishcakes and Richard's ordered the Cockburn Haggis Fritter, which I'm amused by. I'm going to have to start calling him Mr Cockburn at this rate.

'So what happened after that?' he asks.

'We ended up having a showdown,' I say between mouthfuls, 'Voices were raised. Insults were flung. She moved out.'

'That's a bit harsh,' Richard replies, spearing a pickled turnip and peering at it curiously before popping it in his mouth. 'I mean, it's not like you were sleeping with her boyfriend or even her ex-boyfriend.'

I hesitate, wondering if I should say more. It's going to put me in a bad light. 'Well, let's just say, it wasn't the first encounter she'd had with a strange man I'd brought into the flat.'

It was usually the next morning, in the kitchen, making a cup of tea in their underwear.

Richard crunches his turnip slowly and stares at me with a knowing glint in his eye. 'Are you a bad girl, Aster?'

My heart rate speeds up at hearing him say my name and I swallow. 'I wouldn't use the word *bad* exactly, I just went through a phase of sleeping with guys on the first date. Things are different now.'

'What's so wrong about sleeping with someone on the first date?'

When you go through them so fast, you can't remember their names ...

'It's just different for men. You sleep around and you're seen as a stud. Women do it and we're accused of being sluts.'

Emma's words still sting like a slap in the face. I can see her standing there, face screwed up in disgust, and shouting righteously: *'I'm sick of it. You're a bloody slag, Aster!'* Gareth/Garrett was the strawberry blond dude that broke the camel's back.

'I don't sleep around.' Richard puts on a mock offended tone.

I take a breath and try not to roll my eyes. 'Come on, we both know you've slept with more than three women in the last month.'

'There's sleeping with someone, and there's other stuff. I presumed you just meant intercourse,' Richard says blithely. 'I could give you a more detailed breakdown if you want.'

Oh God. 'Maybe we should talk about something else,' I say quickly. If we start discussing *other stuff*, I'm going to have to make a quick trip to the ladies'. I touch my small chain handbag on the chair's back to reassure myself it's still there. Along with my phone, lipstick and house keys, there's a mini vibrator hidden within its depths. It's my secret weapon. I thought I could gird my loins between courses and head him off at the pass if he tries any sneaky tactics.

Richard smirks. 'Getting hot and bothered?' He stretches out a leg so it presses against mine under the table. 'I don't have a problem with first date sex. Besides, this is the second date, so you're off the hook.'

I smile thinly, 'I thought you wanted to get to know me?'

'I do. The naked you.' He smiles encouragingly, and before I know what's happening, he's doing that thumb massage thing on my palm again. Damn, it feels good. Desire starts blossoming in my loins. Shit. I can't let him win. Snatching my hand away, I grab my bag and say desperately, 'I'm going to the ladies'. If the mains come before I do, start without me.'

Richard's determined to get me into bed and I'm determined not to let him. Nothing is getting past this fortress, even if a quickie in the loos isn't exactly ladylike.

Dee's not in reception, so I send her the agreed-upon message:

Red alert, red alert, the viper is about to strike!

But there's no reply. Oh well, needs must. I go into one of the three empty stalls and get to work. Things are going well, and I'm getting close, until I inadvertently let out a tiny groan and a woman's voice calls out, 'Hello, are you all right in there?'

Shit, shit, there's someone else in the loos! I quickly switch off the vibrator (which I've set to whisper-quiet mode) and sit up from my sprawled, legs askew position on the toilet seat. I must've been so caught up in what I was doing that I didn't hear them come in. 'Ah, yes, I'm fine,' I call back airily, zipping up my pants. 'Just ate some gluten, it goes straight to my gut. Bad cramps.'

I flush the toilet, tuck in my shirt and peer out. There's a blonde woman in a tight black dress at the counter touching up her bright red lipstick. She gives me a sympathetic glance in the mirror. 'Poor you. I've got a friend who's gluten intolerant, she has a terrible time of it.' She hands me a tissue. 'You might want to mop up.'

I glance at my face in the mirror. She's right. Yikes, sweaty betty. I look like I've been having a heavy workout and now I'm horny as hell. This was an epic fail, it's going to make things ten times worse! Still no reply from Dee. Where the fuck is she? She's supposed to have my back.

The woman chatters away about the best gluten-free restaurants in the New Town while I nod absently and run my wrists under the cold tap, trying to think what to do. I could just skip out of the hotel and avoid Richard altogether. But it's a cowardly custard move to leave him sitting there with two mains when the date was my idea. I'm just going to have to eat fast, make my excuses, and leave.

'What did you order? Just so I know to tell my friend to avoid it,' continues the woman, fluffing her hair and pouting her lips at her reflection.

'Huh? Oh, the fishcakes ...' I say distractedly drying my hands. Right, let's do this. I square my shoulders and push open the door.

The woman follows me out into the reception area still talking about my issues.

'There must've been breadcrumbs in them or something.'

'Mmm, yes, maybe.'

'I would ask to talk to the chef if I were you.' She sounds agitated.

Lord, she's getting annoying. Maybe I should tell her the real reason I was groaning. That would shut her up.

I walk fast back to the dining room, knowing that I've been gone a suspiciously long amount of time. But she's hot on my heels. Thankfully, she heads across to the other side of the room and I see her talking animatedly to another woman. They look over at me with concerned expressions. God, don't tell me she's here with the gluten-free friend. Shit, I hope she doesn't complain. Back at my table, the Sous Vide Lamb Rump I ordered is waiting and looking decidedly lukewarm.

Richard is munching away on his Sirloin Steak and Hand-cut Chips. He's also ordered another scotch on the rocks. 'Hey, you've been a while. You OK? I was going to send a search party. Sorry to start, but you said to.'

'No, no, that's fine. I got caught up with this woman. She was chatting to me and I couldn't get away.' I cut into my lamb and take a bite. It's pink and buttery soft, just the way I like it.

'Oh, which one?' He looks around the room.

'Don't stare, but it's the blonde in the black dress.'

'The one who's gawking at us?'

'Yes, that sounds like her.'

'The one that's also coming over?'

Shit, what?

Sure enough her voice materialises by my elbow. 'Look, I'm sorry to interrupt your meals, but my friend says you shouldn't eat that because it may have gluten in it.' She points at my parsley potato purée accusingly. 'And after the fishcakes gave you cramps, well ...' Richard is listening to this with his lips twisting in amusement.

'Right, thanks,' I say nodding up at her. 'I won't eat it.' Jesus, just go away, woman!

'Are you gluten-free?' says Richard when she's left in a self-satisfied haze of do-gooderness. 'You didn't mention that.'

'No, but tonight I am. It's a long story.' I turn my full attention to cutting up chunks of lamb and getting out of here. But as I'm sawing vigorously, I accidentally knock my bag with my elbow where I've hung it off the back of the chair. To my horror, it sets off the vibrator and it's not on whisper-quiet mode. My bag is juddering so much against my arm, it feels like it's on double-strength mode. I risk a glance at Richard hoping he hasn't noticed, but he's staring at it.

'Why is your bag making that noise?'

'It's nothing!'

'It's not nothing. It's moving around. Is there a gerbil in there?'

In desperation, I yank the bag off the chair and stomp on it. The vibrations are now going directly up my leg to my groin, which isn't helping matters.

'Is that what I think it is?' he asks.

I'm trying to eat and act nonchalant, but I'm blushing madly, which is a dead giveaway. Richard chuckles. 'Aster,' he drawls, rolling out his r's, and I shudder along with the vibrator. 'You don't need that. Just come back to mine. I'll sort you out.'

I fork the last bit of lamb into my mouth and look longingly at the dollop of purée. Better not. It might set off a gluten-free alarm or something.

'No,' I tell him, trying to sound more decisive than I feel. 'I know what will happen. We'll have sex. You'll ghost me.'

'I won't ghost you. I like you. If the sex is as fantastic as I think it will be, then I definitely won't ghost you.'

He's looking at me with sultry bedroom eyes which, combined with the shockwaves travelling up my leg, throws me into a whirlpool of weakness. The. Viper. Is. Striking. *Where the fuck is Dee!*

'We can have dessert at mine,' he continues. 'I've got this fun game—it's called Ben & Jerry's Caramel Chew.'

'W ... what does that involve?' I ask shakily. Is it hot in here or is it just me? I take a long swallow of water, then another, until my glass is empty.

Richard smiles complacently watching me. I get the feeling he's toying with me, like a lion circling its prey. 'Well,' he says at last. 'I dig out all the chocolate caramel chunks and place them strategically over your body. Then I eat them off—

slowly. The one between the legs is the best. I leave that till last and by the time I get down there, it's gone all melty.' He leans in for the kill. 'I have to spend a lot of time licking up all the chocolate and caramel. It's quite enjoyable by all accounts. Once you've experienced it, you'll be begging me to play it again.'

I groan inwardly. My crotch is throbbing just imagining it. I want to play the Caramel Chew game. *Now*. Fuck.

'OK, I'm in.'

A smug look crosses Richard's face. 'I'll get the bill then.' He looks around for the nearest waiter. But then, like a saint summoned by my impure thoughts, Dee appears at the table. She's even holding a frosted jug of holy water.

I stare at her in amazement. She chooses now to show up, just when I've decided I'm going home with him. There's nothing she can do to stop Richard's tongue from lapping between my thighs. It's a foregone conclusion.

'I trust everything was good with your meals? Can I offer you dessert or coffee?' she enquires.

Richard assumes she's a waitress. 'It was great, thank you,' he says pleasantly. 'But I think we'll have dessert at home. Can I get the bill please?'

Dee smiles enigmatically. 'Of course, Sir. I'll be right back. I'll just top up your water while you wait.'

She takes a step forward to fill my glass and catches my eye, and in that split second, I know exactly what she's going to do. I grab her forearm and there's a small wrestling match, but she's got a better angle because she's standing up. She upends the jug and a waterfall of iced water, complete with ice cubes, cascades onto my chest and crotch. It's so freaking cold, I scream like a banshee causing every head in the dining room to turn in my direction. Instantly Dee is all apologies. 'Shit! I mean, I'm so sorry, Madam!'

My white shirt and River Island pinstripe trousers are soaked through, and a pile of ice cubes perch in my lap. Chilly water trickles down my calves and drips onto the carpet. I'm too shocked to do anything but gasp while Richard gawps at my see-through shirt with his mouth hanging open.

Dee is still apologising. 'I'm so terribly sorry. Please come with me, Madam, I'll get you a towel at once.'

I let her drag me away squelchily before Richard has time to say anything.

'What the fuck?!' I hiss between gritted teeth when we reach reception. 'That wasn't the plan! You were supposed to ring me and say a beloved aunt had died and I was needed urgently at home for the funeral!'

'Sorry, I had to improvise. But it worked, didn't it?'

It's true, my desire has been shocked into hibernation. Then I notice she's limping. 'What's wrong with your leg?'

'I was sorting out a woman's issue with her friend's order; the chef was getting irate because she kept insisting there was gluten in it and he said there wasn't. When I finally got to check my phone, I saw you'd sent the message. I tried to ring, but you didn't pick up. So I panicked and ran to grab a water jug, but then I twisted my ankle.'

I've started to fade throughout this longwinded explanation as cold seeps into my flesh.

'Here!' Dee hands me my bag (which has thankfully stopped juddering) and a white fluffy bath towel emblazoned with the Liberty logo. 'I called a cab. It should be here in a few minutes. Wait for it outside in case he comes looking for you.'

'But ...' I look back towards the dining room.

'Just go, now! I'll tell him we ordered you a complimentary cab straight back to your flat because we were worried you might develop hypothermia.'

So I'm thrust out in the cold night, huddled in a towel, with a glacial wind blowing. My wet trouser legs flap like wet cardboard against my calves, and my chest is slowly starting to freeze solid. I whimper miserably. If I've thought it once, I'm thinking it again, *Online dating sucks balls*.

Chapter 7

By the time I get to the flat, I'm shivering uncontrollably. I run a hot bath, peel off my wet clothing and leave it in a sodden mass on the floor. Sinking into the steaming water is heaven and my brain starts to thaw out. That was close. Too close. Richard nearly got his paws into me. I feel a mixture of shame and relief. But also annoyance that I can't just sleep with him and get it over with. Three months ago I would have, but Emma's done a good job of making me feel bad about my behaviour.

I'm still sitting in the bath giving myself a hard time when Dee arrives home an hour later. I hear the thwunk of her handbag being dumped on the hall table and her footsteps out to the kitchen. A few minutes later, she knocks lightly, 'Are you in there?'

I hug my knees up to my chest in the tepid water. 'Yeah.'

Dee pokes her head round. 'How are you?'

'I'm OK.'

'You don't look OK. You look wretched.'

'I'm sure I'll laugh about it ten years from now,' I say in a brittle voice. Then I can't help blurting what I've been thinking. 'There's something seriously wrong with me.'

Dee frowns. 'There's nothing wrong with you, Aster.'

'I thought I could handle Richard. But he had me right where he wanted me. If you hadn't shown up, I'd be at his flat right now, letting him do what he wanted. No qualms. Emma's right. I'm a slag.'

'You're not a slag!' Dee exclaims. 'She was totally out of order to call you that. Can I come in?' I nod and she sits on the edge of the tub. 'You have a high sex drive. So what? You just need to find someone who can fulfil you mentally *and* physically. Forget about Richard. You're right, he's just after one thing. I'm sorry, I shouldn't have pushed you to go on a date with him.'

I feel better hearing my libido described so matter-of-factly. Not in a derogatory way. High sex drive. That sounds almost like a medical term.

'So what happened after I left? Was he pissed off?'

'No, he was fine. I said you'd gone home and I'd take care of the bill.' Dee answers smoothly. But I notice she's picking at something on her trouser leg with her fingernail and seems distracted.

'Just fine? No other repercussions? I thought he may have messaged me but there's been nothing.'

Dee gets up abruptly and walks over to the sink, I assume, to start her nightly five-step routine, which always starts with eye make-up remover. 'I offered him another scotch, but he said no. That he'd had enough and he was going to the gym tomorrow, so he didn't want a hangover. And then I asked him what kind of workout he did so we talked about that.'

'Oh. Sounds like you had a right old natter.'

She shrugs, 'It's all part of the job, keep the customers happy so they don't sue you.'

I watch curiously as she grabs her toothbrush and spreads a generous amount of toothpaste on the bristles. Strange. She never starts her routine with teeth brushing.

'So then he left?'

'Yummph!' She gestures with one hand while brushing madly with the other. But the rest of what she's saying is unintelligible and I have to laugh. She's put so much toothpaste on her brush, she's like a rabid dog foaming at the mouth.

The next few weeks pass sedately enough. Still nothing from Richard, which is odd, seeing how he was chomping at the bit to fling me into bed. I suppose I should be grateful he's leaving me alone and not pestering me for a third date whilst stocking up on Ben & Jerry's. He must've put me in the "too hard" basket ... Or maybe he's had an accident? He could be in a hospital right now with broken fingers and unable to type. Not that I care. I've been busily going on dates with the guys who've passed the screening test. I had high hopes, but to be honest, they've all been—slightly weird.

There was the environmentalist guy who ate my leftovers

directly off my plate because he couldn't handle food waste. *Cringe*. The IT guy who boasted about the chatbot he created to talk to his ex-GF because he was too busy. *WTF?* The journalist guy who conducted the date like an interview, and even asked if he could record it. *Balk*.

Don't get me wrong, I like quirky guys but what sounds interesting on paper, often translates to creepy in real life.

Speaking of dating, Dee's got her eye on a likely prospect who isn't one of the fifteen messages she received (newsflash: none of those made the cut); he isn't from Hearts of Fire at all. Her ankle was still sore after twisting it, so she made an appointment with a local physiotherapist for a few sessions. After the first one, she came home full of enthusiasm and said that apart from giving her a bunch of exercises and a painful myofascial massage, the physio was cute and funny, but possibly not single. The second involved her balancing on a small rubber ball whilst holding onto his arms and there was great hilarity. He still hadn't mentioned a girlfriend, but I told her not to get her hopes up.

I'm getting ready for a date when she comes home and reports that the third session involved her lying face down on the table and him massaging her calf muscle with oil. She has a dreamy look on her face and I know she's reading more into it than she should be.

'That's what physios do, Dee, they have to touch people to heal them. It's his job. It doesn't mean anything.'

'He was checking out my butt,' she insists.

'How do you know if you were lying face down?' I ask.

'I could just *sense it*, you know. I'm pretty sure he's single. He never says "we" when he talks about stuff, it's always "I".'

'That's not a conclusive argument for him being single. He's not going to talk about personal stuff in a professional setting.'

'There's only one session left. I'm going to ask him out for a drink. Why not? I've got nothing to lose, I never have to see him again.'

Despite thinking it's a bad idea, I'm impressed at her bravery. At least with online dating, the guys are primed to do the asking. With this physiotherapist, she's going in cold, and the chance of rejection is high.

'OK, well, good luck,' I say, not expecting it to end well.

A few days later I'm at WeWork editing a bunch of blogs for a client when Dee rings me. She had a lunchtime session with the physio, so I've been on tenterhooks waiting for her to call, feeling empathetically nervous because she might be rejected.

'I did it. I asked him out! He said yes! We're going for a drink!' She sounds ecstatic.

Since I was expecting a mournful tale of being politely turned down, I can breathe again. 'Wow, go you! How do you feel?'

'Relieved! My knees were practically knocking together, but I didn't have to worry. He was really nice and said that he'd love to.'

Now that she's done it, I'm more interested in hearing about this physio.

'So he's cute? And funny?'

'Yes! I've been telling you.'

'What's his name?'

'TJ McKelvie. I don't know what TJ stands for. I guess I'll find out.'

'I still can't believe he said yes.' I feel slightly envious. He's nice, cute *and* funny. The holy trinity when it comes to men.

'I know, me too.'

'What about the screening test? Are you going to make him do it?'

'I'm not sure. He's an exception, isn't he?'

'He could still be a player or a dweeb.'

'I don't want to scare him off by subjecting him to it.'

'Fair enough. But be on your guard.'

'I think he'll be fine. I've got a good feeling about him, Aster.'

'OK.' I'm not convinced.

I know when my cynicism about men began. It was when I was thirteen years old. I'd been steadily consuming a diet of happily ever after books up until that point. Cinderella was my heroine. Who doesn't love a good rags-to-riches tale with a hot billionaire trope? But boys of thirteen are not princes. They're little shits.

At the time, I attended a co-ed school in Oxford. We lived some distance away in a neighbouring village and there wasn't a direct bus. I'd have to get up at some ungodly hour so my mother could drive me there before heading back to her job at the local dry cleaners. Then in the afternoon, I'd wait outside the gates for her to pick me up to repeat the whole performance.

The school was incredibly cliquey, but luckily a girl called Lulu had befriended me early on. She was my gateway into Penny's little gaggle—Penny Worthington: the richest, most popular girl in school. Posh, pretty and perfectly groomed; I was in awe of her. I knew where she lived, everyone did. The converted eighteenth-century farmhouse with its red-brick gables, rolling lawn and sweeping driveway, was hard to miss since we drove past it each morning.

When I was invited to Penny's for a birthday sleepover, along with Lulu and eight other girls, I was over the moon. We had the entire detached annexe to ourselves. Her parents didn't care what we did as long as everyone was still alive the next morning. Imagine ten teenage girls in shortie pyjamas, smeared with an overabundance of lip gloss, gyrating around to Britney Spears' *Oops I Did It Again*.

When we'd exhausted ourselves and collapsed giggling

into our sleeping bags, the birthday girl decided it was time to play "True Confessions" along with a filched bottle of sherry from Mummy's liquor stash. This basically involved admitting to everyone which boy in school you liked. Most of the confessions elicited 'Ews' or rolling of eyes but when it came time for my turn, I hesitated. I'd been crushing on the best-looking boy in school for the past year—Christian Parker with his jet-black hair and green eyes. The way he laughed and casually tossed back his floppy fringe made me ache in ways I was yet to understand. Of course, he didn't know I existed. No one else had said they liked him, so I was unsure what that meant. Was he too popular to realistically aim for?

'Aster, it's your turn!' exclaimed Penny, which set off a slow chant of *As-ter, As-ter, As-ter* with everyone staring at me.

'I don't like anyone,' I mumbled blushing. But that set off *Li-ar, Li-ar Li-ar*.

'She does too,' said Lulu, whom I'd told in the strictest confidence. I gave her the evils to let her know that she was dead meat if she said anything. But the chance to be in the spotlight overtook Lulu's loyalty (if she'd had any, to begin with). 'She's in love with Christian Parker!' I sunk into my sleeping bag, face aflame, as squeals of approval rose from the group.

Somehow, during this commotion, Penny came up with

the idea to play fairy godmother and help Cinderella get her handsome prince. At the time, I totally trusted her and believed that she had my best interests at heart. But what occurred isn't the kind of happily ever after story you'd want to read to a child.

Chapter 8

The New Town flat Dee and I live in is a three-bedroom maisonette with a private entrance onto Frederick Street. We have another flatmate, but she's hardly ever around, and sometimes I forget she exists. Her name's Rosie and she's a stewardess for EasyJet. When we interviewed her, she warned us that her schedule was unpredictable and she couldn't be relied upon for flat dinners, group grocery shopping, or anything remotely resembling a friendship. She said she was more of a breeze-in breeze-out flatmate, and if we weren't comfortable with that, then she would understand. We snapped her up. She was exactly what we wanted.

Dee and I have a symbiotic relationship which is something that can be difficult to join in on. We're sort of like twins, I guess, even though we look nothing alike. We just *get* each other. I think that was another reason why Emma moved out, she felt like the third wheel. We don't have to worry about that with Rosie. She's either up in the air or living out of a suitcase in a hotel somewhere exotic.

Sometimes I'll stumble into the kitchen half-awake on a weekday morning, and find her sitting at the table drinking coffee and reading her Kindle. There's always that moment of utter surprise and 'who the hell is this?' before I realise with a jolt that it's Rosie, and she lives here. We'll exchange pleasantries while I potter about making toast and tea. Then I'll sit at the table with her and enquire about where she's been—Morocco, Hungary, Amsterdam, New York—or some other far-flung destination. I'll laugh at her stories of crazy passengers, sympathise over her lack of sightseeing time, and gently suggest she look for another job. Then I won't see her again for another month. She's the perfect flatmate.

Well, she would've been during my 'dating with reckless abandon' phase. My bedroom and hers are on the top floor next to the kitchen, and we share a bathroom, which can be awkward if you're trying to *entertain* as Emma discovered. Dee's bedroom is on the level below, along with the lounge, and she has her own en suite, so there was no danger of her bumping into anyone.

The great thing about Dee is that she wouldn't have minded. She'd probably just tease me about it afterwards. And she used to quite happily chat away with whatever guy happened to be in the kitchen making a cup of tea in the morning, without batting an eyelid. There was no rolling of eyes and insults like 'Jesus, you go through them like a packet of macaroons.' Even now, if she's encouraging me to tone it down, it's because I've said that I want to and she's being supportive. She never thinks badly of me, no matter what I do.

So, because I'm usually the one entertaining men, I'm not expecting to see a dark-haired stranger lounging at the kitchen table on Sunday morning, scrolling on his phone. For one surreal instant, I think it's Rosie and she's had a run-in with an enthusiastic hairdresser. But Rosie's locks aren't as dark as these. She also doesn't have stubbled cheeks, or narrow shoulders and doesn't prop one leg up sideways on the other. Rose is taller than me and can reach the overhead bins with ease, but she doesn't have this person's height, and she wouldn't be seen dead in lycra.

'Um, hi. Who are you?' I ask from the doorway.

The guy looks up from his phone and I get a dèja vu. I feel like I've stood here before and asked him this same question. Weird.

'TJ,' he supplies. Ah, the famous Mr Physio.

'You must be Dee's flatmate,' he says.

His eyes flick over my nightwear, and I thank God that I'm wearing boxers, a t-shirt and a pale green cotton robe, albeit untied. If it was the height of summer, I'd be in a see-through camisole and skimpy knicker ensemble. *Shit, Dee, you could've warned me.*

'Yeah. Aster. Nice to meet you.' I tie the cord of my robe firmly round my waist and pad over to the fridge in my bare feet. I need something frosty, fruity, and vitamin-infused asap.

Thanks to a raucous date last night at The Cauldron, I

may have drunk too many homemade cocktails. All I can remember is mixology, wearing a wizard cape, and a lot of dry ice. It was a fun evening, though my head is now pounding. I vaguely recall that my date, Scott, was pleasant, reasonably attractive, and easy to talk to. But nothing special. I've had a few dates like that lately and they're all blurring into one.

After a few long gulps of strawberry and cherry Energiser smoothie straight from the bottle, I feel more human.

'Fresh air and exercise are better for a hangover than sugar,' TJ informs me in an *I'm a physio, I know stuff* tone which instantly irks me. Great, I bet he's one of those health gurus who only drinks tonic water and lemon or half-pint shandies if he's celebrating.

My grip tightens on the bottle. 'Um, why are you here at this ungodly hour?'

TJ checks his phone and arches an eyebrow. 'It's after ten. Hardly ungodly. I'm ...'

But he's interrupted by pounding footsteps on the stairs. Dee bursts into the kitchen resplendent in her black lycra leggings and turquoise tank top, and clutching a pair of titanium hiking poles. 'Sorry, sorry. I couldn't find my sticks!' She stops short when she sees me. 'Oh, Aster! Morning.' She looks from me to him. 'This is TJ.'

'We've met,' I say, and deliberately take another swig of sugar-laden Energiser smoothie. In your face Mr Physio. 'So you two are going hiking? Nice day for it.'

'Yes, we're doing Arthur's Seat,' says Dee.

'Is that wise with your ankle and all?'

'Well, it was TJ's idea at the pub last night ...'

TJ stands and collects a small black backpack from the floor, which I hadn't noticed, and walks over to Dee. I now have a chance to check him out on the sly. He's tall, wiry, with incredibly good posture. I wouldn't call him a ten in the facial department, more of a strong seven, perhaps an eight if you've had a few. His black hiking shorts and long-sleeved red top look well worn. His runners are mud flecked. He definitely exercises in his gear, not just poses for profile photos in it.

'I thought it would be good for Dee to start exercising her ankle,' he says. 'Light walking should be OK and Arthur's Seat isn't too strenuous. Should be fine since she's an experienced hiker.' He smiles down at her, the first time he's cracked a grin, and it makes him look more approachable, less severe. If he were a woman, I'd say he had a resting bitch face, but I'm not sure what the male equivalent is.

However, *experienced hiker*? I stare at Dee. She's been laying it on a bit thick. Dee avoids my steady gaze, her cheeks slightly pink. She smiles up at TJ. 'I'm ready. I'll just fill my drink bottle.'

'Fine, I'll wait outside.' When he's gone, with a curt 'bye' to me, I lay into her.

'You could've messaged me he was coming round!'

'Sorry, I forgot! It was a last-minute thing we arranged at the pub. He was supposed to be here at ten, but he was early.'

'Humph. So you're getting on well then?'

'I guess. I'll let you know after the hike. If I make it back in one piece. He was very enthusiastic when I told him it was a hobby of mine, and well, you know ...' She shrugs.

'I do know. Good luck, you might need it. He looks like a fitness freak.'

Dee starts walking towards the stairs and I call after her. 'Just tell me. What did he drink at the pub—tonic water and lemon?'

She looks back at me and frowns. 'Huh? No, he had a small shandy.'

Aha, I knew it.

Chapter 9

From my position on the couch, I can see Dee's mouth moving as she unlaces her hiking boots in the hallway. Removing my headphones, I pause the YouTube video on my laptop. I'm supposed to be watching a two-hour series on how to be a more efficient editor. But it's boring, and I've been distracted by a clip on how to apply make-up, so it doesn't look like you're wearing make-up.

'Sorry, what?'

'I asked what you thought of TJ.'

'Oh, he seems OK. I didn't talk to him that much.' I wrinkle my nose. 'Are you sure he has a sense of humour?'

'He has a dry wit. He loosens up when you get to know him.'

Wit as dry as a desert, and a personality as grating as sandpaper ... I prefer my men to be more convivial.

'Well, as long as you like him. That's the most important thing. How was the hike?'

'Exhausting. I don't think I'll put my hand up to do that again in a hurry.'

She plops on the couch next to me and peels off her grey wool hiking socks to reveal pink, swollen feet, with a pulpy blister on the back of one ankle.

'Yikes. Maybe you should've broken in your boots. You know, being an expert hiker and all.'

She jabs her elbow into my arm. 'Sometimes you have to make sacrifices in the pursuit of true love, Aster. I'll have you know it was a successful date. I'm moving him onto The Dealbreakers.'

'Really?'

This is news. So far, none of my men from Hearts of Fire have even made it past the first date, let alone be considered for The Dealbreakers.

'Sure.' Dee checks off her fingers. 'He's single—his girlfriend broke up with him a year ago, and he lives alone with his dog. He doesn't smoke or do drugs—he said he's into healthy living. I even asked him if he was British, which he thought was odd since he's Scottish, but he said he's lived in Edinburgh all his life. Oh, and he's working his way through a list of indie authors. I thought you'd appreciate that since you've edited novels for a few.'

I grudgingly admit that's cool. 'And the joke or funny story?'

'He told me he took his dog for a walk in The Meadows one day and some people were barbecuing. It got a whiff of the meat, broke its lead, ran over and started chomping on their sausages. TJ was mortified.'

I stifle a snort. That is quite funny.

'Is he on any dating sites?'

'No. I asked him.'

'I don't believe that!'

Not one site? Is the guy a monk in disguise?

'I may be the first woman he's been out with since the breakup,' she adds, with an air of pride.

'Seriously?' I'm flabbergasted.

Dee nods wisely. 'Not everyone's into online dating and he seems like a bit of a loner. That's the only thing that's slightly concerning. But he has two friends, at least, because he mentioned going on a ski trip to France with them. So I don't think there's any chance of him turning into a weirdo stalker.'

'Having friends is good, as are outside hobbies. It's when they say they're into John Paul Satre, and playing all-night sessions of *Call of Duty*, that you have to worry. I wonder what happened with the girlfriend.'

Dee hitches a shoulder. 'I didn't want to pry too much. All I know is that it was a long-term relationship and she left him.'

'Well ...' I don't know what else to say. For someone who turned up in the kitchen only this morning, it's annoying that I now know all these facts about TJ McKelvie. And some of them are making me more disposed to like him. I mean, it must've been a bad break-up if he's been too distraught to even go on a date.

And it's not that I dislike him exactly, I just think he could just potentially rub me up the wrong way. I was hoping that Dee might decide he wasn't her type and ditch him, but it seems the opposite is now happening. She wants to spend even more time with him if what she says next is anything to go by.

'I think we should have a Scrabble evening, it's the sort of thing TJ would be into.'

I perk up. 'Oooh, Scrabble.'

Dee grins. She knows it's my favourite game. 'It would be good if it were a double date, so you're not a third wheel. You've got someone you could ask, haven't you?'

'Oh, er, I guess I can find someone.' Richard's face materialises in my mind but then warps like a TV screen with dodgy reception ... No, I can't ask him. He'd probably use it as an excuse to spell out sexy words to tempt me. And I feel funny about asking him since he hasn't been in touch. It would be like I was the one doing the chasing. And I never do that with good-looking guys I want to sleep with. Ever.

In the end, I ask the mixology guy, Scott. He's harmless enough, I'm not particularly attracted to him, and we did have fun on our date at The Cauldron—what I can remember of it. He accepts the invite and so does TJ, so it's all on for Saturday night.

Dee, in her usual attention to detail, has the evening all planned out including the seating arrangements and the snacks she'll serve. Thankfully, it's nothing too complicated; just opening a bag of truffle crisps and assembling smoked salmon on fancy crackers. I'm tasked with the drinks, which is fine by me since I want to try out some of the cocktail recipes from the night at The Cauldron. I also have to buy a new Scrabble set as the current one is missing the Z, an F and a G.

On the morning of the Scrabble soiree, Dee decides she has nothing to wear and hauls me down to Princes Street to go shopping. She's after, of all things, a blue dress. Of course, the stores are full of this season's trending colour—lime green.

'It's just a casual evening,' I say, trying to hide my impatience as she rifles through H&M's sale racks because she thought she saw an elusive flash of blue. 'Can't you just wear jeans and a t-shirt like me? You were the one who said we needed to look more natural.'

'I know but I want to make a good impression on TJ. Blue is my colour; it matches my eyes.'

'You're overthinking it. If he likes you, he won't care about what you're wearing. Besides, if anyone's going to be getting swoony, it will be because they've had one too many of my vodka cocktails.'

'Oh, Aster, you haven't got a romantic bone in your body.'

I pull a mock hurt face. 'I do too. My little toe on my left foot. It twitches uncontrollably when I hear Celine Dion's *My Heart Will Go On*.'

The door buzzer goes when Dee's still getting ready, so I head downstairs to answer it. It's TJ, the first to arrive. I'm sensing he's one of those people who stake their life on being punctual. He looks surprised to see me when I open the door but swiftly arranges his face into a placid expression. Hmm, could it be I rub him up the wrong way too?

'Hello,' I say. 'We meet again.'

'We do,' he replies. His eyes do a quick reconnaissance of my white Mango t-shirt featuring a pineapple wearing sunglasses and black skinny jeans. 'You're not in your pyjamas this time though.'

'Haha. No. Come in.'

As he passes by I get a whiff of something light and musky. Not Sauvage, something else I haven't come across. It smells nice. I almost ask him what it is so I can add it to my aftershave catalogue, but I don't want to embarrass him. He's obviously wearing it for Dee.

I show him into the lounge where we've got everything set up. The new Scrabble board with its accoutrements is laid out on the coffee table in front of the couch with our two 1950s armchairs pulled up opposite. And I'm quite pleased with my efforts on the makeshift bar. I've brought down the hall table from upstairs and placed it in front of the bookcase, the shelves of which I've lined with various bottles of spirits. On the table, I've spread a black cloth and set up jars of lime, lemon, an ice bucket, a cocktail shaker and several containers of fruit: oranges, lemon, pineapple, strawberries, some mint, plus grenadine and chocolate syrup for good measure.

'Have a seat, Dee won't be long,' I tell TJ. 'What would you like? Cocktails à la Aster are the speciality of the evening.'

'Just a juice, thanks. With some ice, if it's not too much trouble,' says TJ. He hands me a Waitrose reusable tote and I look inside. He's brought his own carton of orange juice and a bag of crinkle-cut crisps.

'Oh, come on. I'm dying to try out my cocktail skills,' I urge him. 'Have a mocktail at least. I'll do you a Tequila Sunrise sans tequila.'

'Fine.'

I roll my eyes inwardly. Jesus, he's hard work.

TJ perches on the couch and watches me make his mocktail without saying anything. I decide to have one too—with tequila. But when I pour in a generous measure, I get the feeling he's itching to put his two-pence in about it being the devil's drink or something. However, he just says, 'I haven't played Scrabble for years. I don't even remember half the rules.'

'I'm sure it will come back to you,' I reply reassuringly.

He shifts uncomfortably. The couch sinks a bit.

'Sit in the chair if you want.'

'No, no, I'm fine. Is Dee around?'

'I'll check in a minute. You're kind of ... early.'

He smiles ruefully 'Aye, sorry. I hate being late.'

I notice then that he's wearing black suit trousers and a blue shirt the exact colour of Dee's dress, and I have a quiet giggle to myself. She'll love that. But honestly. The amount of effort these two are going to. It's supposed to be a casual evening, not the bloody Oscars. Scott better not be in a suit.

The buzzer goes again, and I hand TJ his mocktail and beat a hasty retreat to answer the door. I do a detour via Dee's door at the end of the hallway and discover her putting her hair into some complicated plait thing. 'TJ's here. He was early,' I hiss, resisting the urge to add 'again!'

'All right, I'm nearly finished,' Dee mumbles through a mouthful of bobby pins.

'Good, I'm hosting a one-woman show here!'

'How do I look?'

She does a hip shimmy and her cornflower blue shirtwaist dress flares around her thighs. She remembered she'd bought it last summer and poked it into the back of her wardrobe. So we didn't have to go shopping after all.

'Gorgeous. You two are made for each other.'

'Huh?'

'You'll see. Just hurry up. I have to let Scott in.'

So much for a relaxing Scrabble evening, my nerves are all strung out. It must be TJ's presence; for a physio, he's got a very disturbing bedside manner. Dee seems to be immune, but I wonder if he makes any of his other patients feel like this?

Chapter 10

Thankfully, Scott is a good conversationalist and he manages to smooth over the awkward vibes I've been getting off TJ. He's also turned up in jeans and a hoodie, so I'm not feeling underdressed either. He's like the human equivalent of Polyfilla, I've decided. It's a pity I'm not remotely attracted to him, and that he's utter shite at Scrabble. He's put down an inordinate number of three-letter words which is making it hard for anyone else to lead off.

'Any joy, Aster?' asks TJ, as I move tiles randomly around on my rack. Dee's put down POSY and there are two triple letter squares right next to the 'S'. I've got a 'Q' and a 'U', but the other letters aren't cooperating and I can't make a word.

For someone who hasn't played for years, TJ is proving surprisingly good at Scrabble, and he's beating me by twenty points. Either he's getting all the good letters or he reads a thesaurus for fun. I wouldn't put it past him. But this is my game. I consistently beat Dee, my family, and everyone else, hands down, when we play.

I sigh and concede the triple letter square and get a measly twelve points for a mediocre four-letter word elsewhere. Boo. I take the last four tiles out of the box. Three of them are an A, a C, and a K, and I brighten. Now I can make QUACKS and the Q and the K can go on the triple letter squares. Fantastic.

It's TJ's turn and he starts putting down his tiles methodically one after the other in the space I've earmarked. He keeps going until there's nothing left on his rack. Oh my God. He's. Used. All. His. Tiles. And he's taken my triple letter squares.

'Well done, TJ!' Dee exclaims admiringly.

I stare in disbelief at his seven-letter word: INCUBUS.

'Fuck,' drops from my lips before I can help it.

'Not the rock band,' he says, 'it's a male sex demon.'

'I know what an incubus is,' I snarl.

TJ triumphantly tots up his score which sends him soaring into the lead because he also gets fifty points for using all his tiles. It's the end of the game. There's no way I can win now. I'm stuck with a full rack, including three high consonants, so I get that taken off my score and he gets it added onto his. Plus what's on Dee's and Scott's too. His total score is three hundred and twenty-four points, to my two hundred and thirty-six. My face flushes with ire. I'm trying not to feel annoyed but arrrgh, it's so annoying. I grip the edge of the chair and glare at TJ who's lounging back on the couch, looking delighted, and basking in his win.

'You obviously had good letters,' I say, voice tight.

Dee throws me a warning look. 'Why don't you have another cocktail, Aster. Scott, can you make her one? Add lots of ice.'

An hour later, I've calmed down considerably. The fact that I've had another couple of strong cocktails is helping. We've abandoned the Scrabble on Dee's insistence that we should just chill and chat. I'm now feeling pleasantly woozy and finishing off a Pineapple Daiquiri. Dee and TJ are sitting in the chairs and Scott and I have moved to the couch. Scott has snaked his arm around me, which I'm not too happy about, but since his cocktails are great, I'm letting it fly.

TJ is telling us about his dog Maxie who gets into all sorts of mischief on a daily basis. And Dee is hooting with laughter.

'Oh, he sounds so cute, I'd love to meet him.'

'You can,' says TJ with a smile. 'Any time you like.' He takes a swig of orange juice, and I notice his eye swivel to her bare knee which is barely touching his. I still haven't worked out if he's attracted to her but checking out her legs is a good sign. I'll have to mention that later in our debrief.

'It's funny how some people treat their pets like children,' says Dee lightly. 'But, I guess, caring for a pet is like training wheels. You know, if you don't kill it, you should be OK with a child.'

Woah, I think. Go, Dee. TJ doesn't realise it, but she's steering the conversation towards the "Does He Want Kids?" Dealbreaker.

But TJ just shrugs nonchalantly. 'Maxie is definitely a dog.'

Hmm, I'm not too sure what to make of that.

Dee must not be sure either because she persists with it. 'But just think. In five years' time, we might all have kids. Can you imagine it?' She laughs a little and cocks her head in a thoughtful manner like it's only just occurred to her.

I watch fascinated to see what TJ will say: is he *for* or *against*? My money's on *against*. He doesn't seem the fathering sort.

But, after a moment's silence, TJ says softly looking down. 'Yeah, with the right person and all that.'

Dee's eyes flick to mine and widen. Her facial features are perfectly still but I *know* she's mentally punching the air right now. Wow, she's taking this guy by storm, it's like poetry in motion.

Then Scott chooses that moment to chime in. 'Urk, no, thanks! Crying, shitting, little monsters. Anyone who wants kids needs their head read.'

Oh no. That's not good for morale.

'Does anyone want a cup of tea?' enquires Dee abruptly.

'Yes, please,' I say.

'Yes, please, white, no sugar,' echoes TJ.

'No, thanks,' says Scott.

'Scott—you can help me carry them,' Dee commands in a no-nonsense tone.

'Oh, er, sure.' He sits up straight, surprised to be singled out since he doesn't actually want tea. I know what's going on. Dee is removing the interloper before he causes TJ to change his mind about wanting kids. I think if TJ has strong enough convictions, what Scott says shouldn't make a difference but Dee isn't taking any chances.

Scott goes off dutifully with Dee and I'm left alone with TJ. An awkward silence brews. When there are other people in the room it's not as noticeable, but when it's just us two I feel the discomfort acutely.

'So what type of dog is Maxie?' I ask when the silence gets too much to bear.

'I thought I'd said,' says TJ frowning. 'He's a Cockapoo.'

'Ah. Sorry, I must've missed that bit.'

TJ says nothing, just chews his lip. Which annoys me. He thinks I've had too much to drink. I'll have to show him I'm a responsible human being.

'That's a Cocker Spaniel and a Poodle, right? I used to be a house sitter in a previous life and I've looked after a few of those. They're lively.'

'Where did you house sit? In Edinburgh or ...?'

'Mostly in the UK, but some in Europe too. It was a good way to keep costs down when I shifted into freelancing.'

TJ looks thoughtful. 'Do you still do it?'

'No, not really, why?'

'I need someone to look after Maxie when I go to France next week. I usually rely on a family friend, but she messaged me this morning to say she's away. I was going to book him into a kennel, but if you're interested, it's up for grabs. I'd pay you, of course.'

'Oh.' Oh, indeed. I was just attempting to make conversation. Now he's leapt on my house-sitting skills. Shit. I love dogs but I'm not sure I should do it since it will involve staying at his flat.

'Um, how long are you away for?'

'Five days. Wednesday to Sunday.'

'Where do you live?'

'In Gardner's Crescent. Near Haymarket.'

'How many bedrooms do you have?'

'Just the one. Plus a lounge, a kitchen, and a bathroom,' TJ says in an amused tone. 'It's not Buckingham Palace but it's big enough.'

'No, I didn't mean ...' Sheesh, he thinks I'm being fussy about his flat now. I was just asking to see if he had a spare bedroom. Awkward.

'What are we talking about?' says Dee, coming into the room with two mugs of tea and a packet of Hobnobs tucked under one armpit. 'Is someone going to London?'

'No, it's the ski trip to France. I need a house sitter to look after Maxie.'

'Aster can do it. She loves dogs. And she used to be a house sitter,' says Dee instantly.

'Yes, she's just been telling me.'

I look from TJ to Dee.

'You don't mind?' I ask her.

'Why would I mind?' she replies, holding out the biscuits to TJ.

I open my mouth but I can't exactly say *because I'd be sleeping in your potential husband's bed*, so I zip it. 'No reason.' Well, if she doesn't mind ...

'OK,' I tell him. 'But you don't need to pay me. I'm happy to do it for free.'

'Och, I think it deserves compensation, but we can sort something out. Great, thanks. If you give me your email, I'll message you the house sitter PDF.'

So it's sorted. Somehow I'm now staying at TJ's flat, to look after his dog. And, it hasn't been mentioned, but I guess sleeping in his bed? How come Dee is OK with this?

Then I realise Scott still hasn't made an appearance. 'Where's Scott?' I ask Dee, who's pouring herself a gin and tonic.

'He left,' she says flatly, screwing the lid tightly on the gin bottle.

'What do you mean, *he left*?'

'Just that. He left the flat. He remembered he had some stuff to do at home and told me to say goodbye to you.'

'Are you sure? I didn't hear the door shut or anything?'

'Yes, I saw him go.'

'Oh.' I feel irrationally wounded by this behaviour. I mean, I know I wasn't that into him, but it's rude to just up and leave without even saying goodbye. I sigh. Cross another one off the list. I'm not sure this new screening malarkey is good for my ego. Not only am I not having sex with anyone, I can't even get them to stick around for a cup of tea.

Later, when TJ's gone home and Dee and I are in the kitchen washing up the teacups, glasses and whatnot, I pump her for more information. 'So did Scott say anything else?'

'Like what?'

'I don't know, like he'd message me or something? It's weird that he just left.'

'You didn't like him so why do you care?' she replies in a terse voice, handing me a plate to dry. Hmm, she's hiding something.

'Edie Crowley-Smythe,' I say, in a warning tone.

She sighs. 'Look, it's not a big deal. I tested him all right? And he didn't pass.'

'What do you mean you *tested him*?'

Dee looks uncomfortable. 'We were waiting for the kettle to boil and he was standing there, where you are now,' she gives a nervous laugh when she sees my grim face. I'm not liking where this is going.

'And ...?'

'And I made a flirtatious comment and touched his hand to see what he'd do and ... and he responded.'

'Responded ... How?' I ask slowly, staring at her.

Dee avoids my eyes. 'He kissed me. We kissed.'

I shake my head like I'm clearing water from my ears.

What the fuck?

'Why?' I ask her, feeling numb. 'Why did you do that?'

'For you. Now you don't have to waste your time. You didn't like him anyway. I just moved things along to get him out of the way. You know, the Dealbreaker about cheating? He didn't pass. He was all apologetic afterwards and begged me not to tell you which was soooo much worse. I told him it was better he left and to not bother contacting you.'

I stare at her amazed.

'You're not mad, are you? Honestly, I did you a favour. It's a good thing, Aster, don't you see that? Besides, he was a terrible kisser.'

'But, Dee, what about TJ? I thought you liked him.'

She shrugs. 'This has nothing to do with liking him. It's a separate issue. I was helping you out.'

For the life of me, I can't think of anything to say to that— I'm lost for words.

Chapter 11

When Dee interviewed me for a flatmate, she never hid the fact that she came from a rich family. It was one of the first things she said: 'My parents bought me the flat so I had somewhere to live while I pursued my degree in hospitality management.'

However, she didn't say it in a way to make me feel inferior, she almost seemed a little embarrassed about it.

'They bought you a three-bedroom flat?' I exclaimed wonderingly, looking around. It seemed outrageous at the time.

'I know. They're generous, but it's extreme even for them. It's an investment really,' she admitted.

'So why do you need flatmates?'

'Well, they don't want me to be *lonely* ...'

In the two years, I've been living here, I've never once met Dee's mysterious, wealthy parents, but I've heard enough about them. They live in Chiswick and her mother, Isadora, seems to have a ton of ladies' lunches. She's just discovered Instagram so she's been posting selfies in cafés around London. Dee showed me her account. It's all cups of tea in delicate china, tiered cake stands, and colourful macarons.

Dee's father is the owner of a five-star hotel in Soho. I

looked it up online and it's pretty swish; trendy artwork, designer fittings, a massive indoor heated pool, and exorbitant spa treatments that only celebrities can afford. He doesn't seem to be around much, maybe because he's always working. But I can tell he's a respected presence because Dee calls him 'Daddy' in reverential tones when she's speaking to her mother on their weekly catch-ups. It's also his name on the account I pay my rent money into: Michael Crowley-Smythe.

They've made the trek north a couple of times to visit her and to 'check on their investment' in Dee's words, but I was away on both occasions. The first time I was visiting my parents who now live in Bristol. They decided to move there when I was in my twenties because I attended Bristol University. The second time Dee's parents came up I was on holiday with a uni friend in the South of France.

Usually, it's Dee who makes the effort, catching the train down to London every couple of months to see them.

'It's easier,' she says, 'They have busy schedules.' From the looks of her mother's Instagram account, she's up to her eyeballs in lunches.

Isadora seems a little overbearing to me, but Dee's pretty good about standing up to her. She told her mother in no uncertain terms that she was sick of London and wanted to live in Edinburgh. By all accounts, it was a family crisis that involved intense discussions for months, and many tears on her mother's part (Dee being their only child). But, according to Dee, Isadora had suddenly accepted it, rallied, and convinced Michael that they needed a property investment in Edinburgh. The upshot: Dee got her independence and her own flat. She hasn't told me the ins and outs of the mortgage, but I suspect she's paying family rates for rent, while Rosie and I pay the going rate.

I don't begrudge her any of it. She can't help coming from a wealthy background, and I respect her for wanting to make her own way, apart from her parents.

But there's being headstrong and overstepping the boundaries of a friendship. What she did with Scott was out of line. Fair enough that she removed the interloper from the lounge, but snogging him in the kitchen and then telling him to leave? I'd never in a million years dream of testing TJ behind Dee's back, even if I knew she wasn't that into him. Because I'd let her make her own mind up. I wouldn't decide what was right or wrong for her.

The worst thing is because it's so out of left field I have no clue what to do. I'm an equal mix of fucked off and disconcerted. In the words of Catherine Tate: *I'm bovvered.*

For the next few days, I manage to skirt the issue by changing my schedule. I leave earlier in the morning and have breakfast at a café, before heading to WeWork. For dinner, I grab a chicken salad from the Co-op and eat it in the WeWork lounge area while watching YouTube videos.

But by Wednesday afternoon, it's obvious I'm avoiding her, so I'm not surprised when I get a message.

Dee
Are you OK?

Me
Yup

Dee
Did TJ email you about house sitting?

Me
Yup

Dee
Are you going to his tonight?

Me
Yup

(A five-minute gap. Then *Dee is typing* appears.)

Dee
Are you sure you're OK? Are you mad about Scott? I'm really sorry. I took things too far.

My bad attitude ebbs away and I decide it's easier to just forgive her. I can't keep sending her one-word replies or finding excuses to stay away. She feels bad about it and she's apologised. Why make a big song and dance? There's no need for any confrontation. The last thing I want to do is lose my temper because that can be permanently damaging. It cost us a flatmate the last time it happened.

Me
I'm OK, I was just surprised you did that.

Dee
I was surprised at myself. Maybe I'm taking this dating thing too seriously.

Me
Maybe

Dee
Are we all right? xx

Me
Yes. I'll message you from TJ's xx

Dee
OK. Have fun with Maxie xxx

After that, I go into the loos and have a bit of a cry. It's a mixture of relief and PMT. I've been thinking all sorts of bad things about Dee and now I know it was just a slip-up on her part. I can still trust her. I don't have to put her in the same basket as Lulu and Penny.

When I return to my desk, I pull up TJ's email. He sent it on Sunday.

Hi Aster,
Thanks for doing the house sit and looking after Maxie, I appreciate it. I've attached a PDF with general instructions. Are you OK to come round on Wednesday afternoon at five?
TJ

Since I just replied to his email and haven't looked at the attachment, I suppose I'd better check it to see if there's anything special I should know about Maxie's routine.

I'm expecting a one-page list, so I'm confused when I encounter a photo of a golden Cockapoo holding up a paw and red text plastered across the top that says: *Hi, I'm Maxie and This Is My House Sitter Cheat Sheet.*

I check the number of pages in the PDF and my eyes nearly bulge out of their sockets. Twenty goddamn pages! For looking after one small (but admittedly cute) dog? Surely not. I start scrolling and discover that it's mostly screenshots with text and arrows, pointing out things that you'd have to be an imbecile not to know. Like photos of Maxie's dog bowl and text saying "in case you think it's a human bowl!"

There are five screenshots on how to work the washing machine, at least another five for the TV remote control, and more ... so much more.

By the time I've reached the end I'm crying again—but this time with laughter. Actual tears are running down my cheeks and plopping onto my laptop. If this is TJ's humorous side, then he's got me hook, line and sinker. It's the funniest thing I think I've ever seen.

Eventually, I pull myself together and wipe my face with my hand, and take some deep breaths. But I get a glimpse of the front page with Maxie and "Cheat Sheet", and it sets me off again.

Stacey has been working at a desk nearby and walks past to go to the loo. She must see my shoulders shaking and wonder what's going on because she comes over.

'Are you laughing or crying?' she asks, sounding concerned.

'I can't ... Just look,' I gasp, gesturing at the screen. She swivels my laptop towards her. 'Cute dog!' she exclaims, then starts scrolling through the PDF.

She laughs out loud when she sees all the oven screenshots and the accompanying arrows and text about which food to cook on each level. She keeps scrolling and peers at the six-screenshot collage depicting the shower controls. 'Who made this? Are they funny or mad?'

The genuine confusion in her voice causes fresh waves of mirth. I take a deep lungful of air to try and calm down.

'Just a friend of my flatmate's. I've been roped into house sitting for him and looking after his dog. I wasn't expecting the instructions to be quite so ... detailed.'

'Yeah,' Stacey says. 'I guess he's making sure the house sitter doesn't call and bother him on holiday. But I think he might have ... *issues*.'

'Just don't, please. My stomach muscles can't handle it.' I snap the laptop shut so I don't have to look at the PDF anymore. Oh no, how am I going to go round there and say I've read it without cracking up?! Hopefully, TJ's meant it to be funny because if he hasn't and it's deadly serious, then I'm in big trouble.

Chapter 12

TJ lives in a ground-floor flat midway along Gardner's Crescent, a sleepy Georgian row with a lush strip of green lawn out the front. I assume he's been watching for me because when I reach the stoop, he instantly pokes his head out the door. 'Hi!'

'Hi yourself.' There's yapping going on behind him so I gather it's Maxie.

'Someone's excited.'

TJ grins. 'He's desperate to meet you.' He opens the door wider, and a ball of golden fur rushes out between his legs and leaps up at me. Eager front paws scrabble on my thighs. 'Hello there!' I bend over to pat the waggling head and get my cheek thoroughly licked in return.

'Maxie, *down*,' says TJ sharply.

'That's OK. My face needed a wash.'

'Come in, I'll give you the tour. I've got an hour before I need to leave for the airport. I like to give myself a decent buffer,' he says, trying to shepherd Maxie inside without much luck.

'Oh, yes. It's good to do that,' I reply politely. Of course, TJ would be organised. I'm usually running around like a headless chicken when I go on holiday.

I take a step inside, but Maxie runs around behind me and grips the bottom of my bootleg jeans with his teeth. Growling softly, he tries to pull me away from the door.

'Maxie, stop that! Aster's going to be looking after you!' Giggling, somehow I manage to shuffle inside; yanking him along without my jeans ripping. This dog is personality plus.

'Sorry, he needs a firm hand,' says TJ apologetically, grabbing Maxie's collar.

'He's fine. It's funny.'

'Come through.' TJ leads the way down a narrow hallway with dark polished wood floorboards. The white walls are bare, apart from a lone abstract artwork of blue and green triangles. He swings off to the left into a small but bright kitchen with a bay window.

'Do you want a cup of tea?'

'Go on then.'

I take off my backpack to sit down at the table but he says, 'I'll give you the tour while the kettle boils. It won't take long. Bring your bag, you can put it in the bedroom.'

'OK,' I pick up my pack and follow him dutifully, with Maxie snuffling at my heels. When we get to the lounge, Maxie takes a flying leap onto the couch and starts upending all the cushions, looking for food titbits, I assume.

'Maxie no—off there!' exclaims TJ. Maxie looks up when he hears his name and gives a small yap. Then continues bouncing all over the couch.

TJ gives an exasperated sigh. 'I should've enrolled him in puppy training, but I thought I could do it myself. As you can see, the results haven't been great.'

'He's certainly lively,' I say, trying not to laugh. 'How old is he?'

'One and a half.'

'He'll probably calm down when he gets older.'

'God, I hope so. Anyway, this is the lounge. It may still be intact by the time Maxie's finished with it. Feel free to browse the bookcase. There are a few DVDs.'

'Great.' I look around briefly. It's spacious but it doesn't have much furniture. There's just a mustard yellow couch, a coffee table, a decent-sized TV, and a bookcase which is half-filled with books, CDs and DVDs. It could do with a fluffy rug to cover the polished floorboards or some knick-knacks on the bookshelf to make it look more homely. But perhaps the dog has torn the rug to shreds and smashed the knick-knacks.

'Do you rent or own?' I ask him as we leave the lounge.

'Own.'

'Ah, cool.'

'Are you looking to buy?'

'One day. I had a healthy deposit, but I've dug into it since I started freelancing. I'm trying to build it up again. But I'm happy flatting with Dee for the meantime.'

I decide not to mention Dee's parents own the flat, she can tell him if she wants.

'Do you enjoy freelancing?'

'I do, but it's taken a few years to turn it into a viable business. I was living on pot noodles at the beginning.'

'Yeah, I've got a couple of freelancer friends and they haven't found it easy. Um, so, this is the bedroom. The sheets are clean. I changed them this morning.' We hover at the doorway and I peer in at the queen bed encased in a pine wood slat frame, it has a plain blue-and-grey duvet and matching pillows. It feels weird that I'll be sleeping in TJ's bed when I hardly know him, but it's not like he's going to be in it. And where else am I going to sleep? The bath?

I nod in a business-like manner. 'Cool.'

He doesn't say anything, so I go in and dump my backpack on the floor by the bed and look around. Like the lounge, it's devoid of any bits-and-bobs or homely touches. The only personal effects are a stack of books on the bedside table, and a rack of neoprene hand weights of varying sizes over by the wardrobe. Above them, thumbtacked to the wall, is one of those medical posters that details the various muscles of the anatomy.

'The bathroom's next door,' TJ says.

We stop in there briefly and he opens the cupboard to show me a stack of white towels and packets of Dove soap.

Everything's super clean and there's an overpowering

smell of bleach coming from the toilet; like he's scrubbed it thoroughly for my benefit and dumped in the rest of the bottle for good measure.

'Lovely,' I say, trying not to breathe in bleach fumes.

'Er, so, that's the tour. Tea?'

'Sure.'

TJ leads the way back to the kitchen and when we get there, he takes a couple of mugs off the tree stand and says casually, 'Did you get a chance to look at the PDF?'

Oh no, not the PDF! Luckily, I'm behind him when he says it, so he doesn't see me struggle to keep a straight face.

'Ah, I did. It was very … thorough.' It comes out normally, apart from a slight squeak at the end.

TJ's head whips around.

'Are you laughing at my PDF?'

'No!'

'You are.'

'It was just a bit … full on. Is all that detail necessary?'

TJ folds his arms and stares at me. 'You have no idea how annoying it is to be interrupted, typically when I'm about to ski down the side of a mountain, and the house sitter can't figure out how to turn on the oven or shower. I have to spend half an hour explaining it to them. Believe me, that level of detail is necessary.'

There isn't an ounce of humour in his voice, so I wince inwardly. Yikes, he's sensitive about his PDF as it took him ages to put together.

Kicking myself, I keep quiet and slink into a seat at the table. But when I look up, TJ's grey eyes are sparkling and he's grinning. 'I'm kidding, Aster. It's a piss-take.'

'What?'

'I went overboard on purpose. It's not meant to be serious.'

'Uh ... really?' Wow, he does have a dry wit.

'Of course not.'

My shoulders relax. 'Well, then I have to say, it's hilarious.'

TJ chuckles. 'I know, right? I mean, Jesus, who wouldn't know the difference between a dog bowl and a human bowl?'

'Or need five screenshots to turn on a remote?'

'Exactly.'

'It's pretty funny,' I admit. 'I was in hysterics.'

TJ grins at me and I get the feeling I've passed a test. I guess Dee was right—he loosens up when you get to know him. If she's serious about pursuing him, it's good that we can get along at least.

'So ... is it OK if I ring you about anything that's not in the PDF?' I ask cheekily, testing the water.

'You won't need to. It's a comprehensive document,' TJ says deadpan.

'I'm sure you must've left something out.'

'Aster, if you value your life. You. Will. Not. Ring. Me,' TJ growls, and my insides clutch in mischievous glee. I'm so going to ring him.

But it's TJ who rings me two hours later, when I'm on the couch, three-quarters of the way through a bad sci-fi movie. Maxie's lolling in my lap after wolfing down his dinner (chunks of raw frozen rabbit) in ten seconds flat. Before I can even say hi, TJ takes off at a gallop.

'Our flight's delayed. We're in the Aspire lounge. How's Maxie?'

'I thought you didn't want contact with the house sitter?'

'It's OK if I contact you. Just not the other way round,' he says chirpily.

My stomach flip-flops. *Oh, really?*

'Well, he's good. We're relaxing in a lounge too and he's having a nap, on me. Bummer about your flight.'

'Yeah. So much for getting to the airport early.'

There's an awkward silence. I'm not sure what to say, but I want to keep talking to him, so I settle for, 'Well, you never know about these things.'

'True,' he says. 'So, what are you doing?'

'Just watching a movie on Netflix. It's not very good.'

'Which one?'

'*Passengers*. Chris Pratt and Jennifer Lawrence.'

'The one where the guy wakes up on the spaceship and

everyone else is still asleep?'

'Yeah. Then Chris decides to wake up Jennifer, and tells her that her pod malfunctioned too, and she finds out he's lied to her. But they still get together because he wants to get his end away and make babies. Ugh. Sexist claptrap.'

'Ninety years is a long time to be alone though ...'

'Hah, if I were Jennifer, I'd wake up some other guy. Stuff Chris.'

'Then you'd be just as bad as him.'

'No, because I'd tell the guy the truth from the get-go.'

'Hmm, he wouldn't trust you. He'd just go and wake someone else up.'

'It could go on like that for years.'

'It could. Hang on ...'

There's muffled talking, then he comes back on.

'Everyone's bored, so we're going out to Wetherspoons to get a drink.'

'OK.'

'Enjoy the rest of the movie if you can.'

'Hah. Yeah. Bye.'

Ten minutes later he rings again. From the clinking of glasses and chatter in the background, it sounds like he's in the pub now. Is he ringing me from the table?

'Hi, I forgot to tell you there's a secret treat cupboard. There are dog treats for Maxie if he behaves himself. And human treats too, so help yourself.'

'Oooh, human treats. I like the sound of that. Where is it?'

'In the kitchen. The small lower cupboard, next to the fridge. Just don't let Maxie see you go into it because he'll scratch the cupboard door to pieces.'

'OK. Any update on the flight?'

'They've just announced the gate. We're boarding in half an hour.'

'Cool, well, have a great trip. I may or may not call you when you're on the mountain.'

'Thanks. If I see it's you, I won't answer.'

'Haha.'

I pause the movie, carefully lever Maxie's sleepy head off my knee, and go in search of the treat cupboard. What I discover makes me gurgle in delight. It's a chocolate lover's dream: dark, milk, white, salted caramel, mint, raspberry, coffee, chilli—I have a craving for Cadbury's Fruit & Nut and he's even got some of that. Woohoo. For a guy who's into clean eating with a fridge overflowing with tofu and bean sprouts, it's comforting to know TJ has some bad habits. I wonder what else he's got squirreled away.

I finish watching the movie, breaking off squares of chocolate and giving Maxie his doggy chews; being careful not to get them mixed up. I keep looking at my phone expecting TJ to call back which is distracting. But he doesn't, so he must've boarded and be in the air by now. He told me the name of the ski resort—Courchevel—and mumbled the name of his hotel too when I asked him. It sounded something like Le Strato, so when the movie ends, for the want of something better to do, I look it up on my phone. What the? It's a five-star hotel and the cheapest room is £1,500 a night, so we're talking £6,000 for four nights! Woah. I flick through the photos of the hotel agog. Far out. It's seriously stunning. It has ski-in/ski-out access, a sweeping view of the French Alps from the balcony, a spa with facials and massages, and a huge indoor pool that has me salivating. Add on flights, ski gear, food, drinks and transport, and even if he's splitting it with a couple of friends, the whole trip must be costing a bomb.

How can he afford it? I mean TJ's flat is nice and all but it's not super luxurious and physios aren't paid that much. Maybe he's been saving for a couple of years and he's having a blowout? I know it's none of my business, but I'm bursting with curiosity too.

After I've settled Maxie in his dog bed in the kitchen, I head to the bedroom and change into boxers and a tank top. Now comes the part I've been dreading; getting into TJ's bed and attempting to sleep. I know I'm building it up in my head. But just the thought of lying where he's been lying is making me feel odd. In the end, I clamber over onto the other side, away from the bedside table with the books. I figure that's the side he lies on, so I won't sleep there.

I'm half expecting him to ring me when he lands, so when my phone flashes just as I'm drifting off, I answer and say sleepily. 'You have a serious chocolate addiction, and I need a photo of the pool.'

A female voice replies, 'Huh, chocolate? What pool?'

It's Dee. Shit. I completely forgot about her. I sit upright in bed, now wide awake.

'Ah, I thought you were TJ.'

'I'm about to go to bed soon. You said you'd message me.' She sounds put out.

'Sorry, there was a lot of stuff to go over and I was settling in and sorting out Maxie. Then TJ's flight got delayed ...' I gabble, feeling guilty.

'I know, he messaged me.'

'Oh.'

'Why are you going on about chocolate and a pool?'

I fill her in on the chocolate cupboard and the swanky hotel. 'It sounds like he's got a healthy savings account at least.'

'What's his flat like?' she asks.

'It's nice but stark. He could do with some more furnishings.'

'Maybe I'll subtly suggest we go to IKEA when he gets back since he's got cash to burn,' she muses. 'Can you put me on video? I want to see his bedroom so I can make a list of what he needs to buy.'

I guess it must be weird for her, me staying here when she

hasn't seen his flat. But this whole thing was her idea. So I flick on the main light, put her on video and do a quick scan of the room with my phone.

'Yes, it is pretty boring. It needs some pops of colour, and not just from hand weights,' she comments. I bring my phone back around, and she catches sight of the bedcovers thrown back. 'Oh! You're in his bed.'

'Well, yes, where else am I going to sleep?'

'I know. It's just strange to see.' Dee wrinkles her nose. 'But since you are, how's the mattress?'

I sit on it and do an obligatory bounce. 'Quite firm.'

'Good, I hate beds that are too soft.' I guess she's assuming she's going to be sleeping over at some point. I try to imagine Dee and TJ in this bed together, but the image won't form. She seems out of place here.

'So are there any photos lying around?' she asks.

'What sort of photos?'

'I was hoping there might be some of the ex-girlfriend.'

'If they've broken up, he's hardly going to have photos of her lying around. Can't you check his Facebook page?'

'He's not on Facebook. You could look in the wardrobe or under the bed. There might be a box.'

'Dee, I'm not snooping through his stuff!'

'Oh, go on, just take a quick peek.'

I huff and puff about being an ethical house sitter, but Dee eggs me on. I relent. 'OK, I'll check!'

Even if I do find a box, I have no intention of looking *inside* it. That would just be too nosey and a violation of TJ's privacy. I'd feel guilty every time I saw him, especially since he's been so nice to me and let me raid his chocolate stash and all.

Putting my phone down on the bed so Dee's facing the ceiling, I hang over the side of the bed, hoist up the bedclothes and peer underneath. 'Nothing!' I inform her when I'm right side up and red-faced from all the blood rushing to my head. 'Just one lone sock and some dust. Happy now?'

'The wardrobe. Check the wardrobe too.'

Muttering under my breath, I cross the room and open the wardrobe. There are coats, jackets, shirts, all hanging neatly and, if my eyes don't deceive me, colour coded: black, brown, blue, grey, and white.

'I think TJ might have OCD,' I call over to Dee. 'Either that or he was incredibly bored one weekend.'

'Anything that looks feminine? Dresses?'

I gingerly move the black coats and suit jackets aside. 'Actually, there is a black dress squished right at the end,' I tell Dee, and she squeals 'Oooh!'

'Why is that so exciting?'

'Because now I can see what type of woman he goes for.'

'Huh?'

'If it's low-cut and short, she was a sex kitten. If it's high-cut and long, she was sophisticated,' she explains patiently.

'And this helps you how?'

'I can adjust my clothing accordingly. Ooh, I hope it's sex kitten.'

'Somehow I can't picture TJ with a sex kitten,' I mumble, carefully extracting the dress and examining it.

'Well?' asks Dee.

'It's neither one nor the other. It looks like a work dress.' I check the label. 'It's from Next—short sleeves, a scoop neck, a belt tie thing and a knee-length skirt. It's nice. As dresses go.'

'What size?'

'Ten.'

'Hmm. He likes them skinny.' Dee's a twelve, bordering on a fourteen, and I know she's paranoid after nasty Mr Nurse.

'One dress doesn't mean anything,' I reassure her.

'I guess. Anything else in the wardrobe?'

I do a quick scout in the bottom section.

'No, just an old laptop, black leather shoes and some well-chewed puppy toys. Aw cute, they must've been Maxie's, and he hasn't thrown them away ...'

Dee interrupts. 'What size feet does he have?'

'God Dee, is nothing sacred ...'

'Humour me.'

I sigh and check one of the shoes. 'Size twelve.'

'Bodes well,' she says approvingly, and I have a moment of clarity.

I pick up my phone again and frown at her. 'This was why you wanted me to do the house sit, wasn't it? So I could spy on him!'

'It's not spying as such, it's just information gathering. He's not on Facebook, so I have to resort to other methods.'

'I don't think you've got anything to worry about. At least in terms of basic human decency. From my experiences, if a guy is a shithead, the signs are usually there early on, and I haven't seen anything to indicate that. Though, of course, you'll see a different side of him, being the love interest and all.'

Dee brightens at the words "love interest". 'So, if things did progress, you'd be OK? I mean if TJ and I got together? If he's staying over at the flat, I wouldn't want you to feel like a third wheel or uncomfortable around him.'

'Sure, he's a nice guy. Quirky, but nice. I wouldn't have a problem if he was around. I think we're on the way to being friends already,' I say confidently.

'Brilliant,' replies Dee. 'I hoped you'd say that.'

I spend the next few days working at the kitchen table while keeping one eye on Maxie to make sure he doesn't get up to any mischief. We go for short walks in the morning around the neighbourhood and then I take him to the Meadows in the afternoon. I get a red mark on my hand from him pulling on the leash when he spots any dog within a fifty-metre radius. Luckily, it's not barbecue season, and there are no sausages.

During this time TJ doesn't call or message, and I don't call or message him. I thought about doing it to be cheeky, but I changed my mind after the conversation with Dee. It might be best to keep my distance since she's interested in him and was weirded out about me sleeping in his bed. Besides, I don't have anything to say, it would just be a joke. And it might not be a good idea to have private jokes with him in case it's seen as being flirty.

When Friday night rolls around I'm bored and wishing I was back at the flat so I can do my own thing. I'm also in the mood to go on a date. By unspoken agreement, Dee moved Scott's card into my "Aster-Rejects" column in Trello, so I followed suit and moved Richard's in there too. Now there's a clean slate and I can start adding new cards under "Aster-Potentials". But it feels weird arranging dates from TJ's couch like he's going to know or something, so I put it on hold until I'm back home.

Since I can't find any good movies to watch on Netflix, I check out TJ's selection of DVDs. *Braveheart*—seen it ten times; *The Patriot*—seen it, didn't like it; *Mad Max Anthology*—does he have a Mel Gibson fixation?

I move onto the CDs and idly flick through them. How old school. He must've bought them online or at a secondhand store. The music is eclectic; there's heavy metal, pop, electronica, classical, and weirdly, Swedish folk polka.

The last CD has a plain white cover and I spot a *B*, so I think it must be The Beatles' White Album, but when I pull it out, I see it has **FOR BETH** written on the front. This has to be the ex, and it's a compilation that he's made for her. Was she an old-school CD fanatic too? I open the case but there's just a shiny silver CD, no indication of the playlist.

Why would he keep this? Does he want a reminder of her? From what I know of TJ, it's more likely that he spent a lot of time making the CD, so it's probably a screw you I'm keeping it. I wonder what's on it. A bunch of love songs I assume, hopefully not Swedish folk polka, that would be a good reason to break up with someone. I insert the CD back in the bookcase and go back to the couch for another round of Netflix searching, but give up and lie there, thinking instead.

If one wanted to listen to a CD, how would one go about it? I wonder. I've checked but I can't find a CD player anywhere in the flat. There's the old laptop in his wardrobe but I don't want to go messing around with that. Can you even buy personal CD players anymore? I pull over my laptop and search 'CD players near me' and, surprise surprise, Argos sells them for £15. I shut my laptop again. I am *not* going to buy a CD player just to listen to a compilation of songs that TJ made for his long-lost ex. It's a violation of privacy. Although, technically speaking, he did say I could browse the bookcase.

On Saturday morning, I go for a walk to Shandwick Place, so I can buy magnesium tablets at Holland & Barrett. For some reason, I'm not sleeping well in TJ's bed, so I thought some magnesium might relax me. It's always worked in the past. One tablet and I'm out like a light. When I exit the shop and start walking back, the Argos collection point at Sainsbury's is right there … Funny that.

But then again, I did order a CD player the night before, and it's ready to pick up.

<h1 style="text-align:center">Chapter 14</h1>

It was in the bookcase, so surely it's for public consumption?
It's not like he's going to dust it for fingerprints.
Dogs can't talk, he'll never know.

Back at the flat, Maxie is watching what I'm doing with interest and I'm feeling like a massive snoop. But it doesn't stop me from inserting the CD and plugging in my headphones. The console displays 1/1. Weird. A whole blank CD dedicated to one song? Maybe it's *their song*. I press "play", then prop myself on a couch cushion with Maxie's head on my lap, not sure what to expect. When it starts, I recognise Bryan Adams' raspy vocals but I haven't heard this one.

Woah it's full-on lovey dovey ... aww, sweet ... yikes that part's a bit sad ... making love oooh nice ... oh no, sad again ... geez, these lyrics, is this song meant to be happy or sad? ... it's like an emotional rollercoaster ...

I play it three times without stopping and I'm wrecked. To the point where I end up crossed-legged on the bathroom floor, breathing in bleach and bawling into an enormous wad of toilet paper. Bryan going on about being transported to heaven after a life-changing night of rumpy pumpy and in no doubt that it's love, has hit home—TJ was besotted with Beth, and she smashed his heart to smithereens. I'm really regretting having listened to that CD because I never thought I'd cry this much over a freaking Bryan Adams song!

Afterwards, I lie on TJ's bed feeling emotionally drained, as if I've just broken up with someone myself. *Well, that was a downer.* Maxie jumps up and tries to lick my face, so I end up hugging him and burying my head in his furry chest. The metal tag from his collar is digging into my neck, so I grip it to push it aside, then look at it properly. On one side it says: *Max.* On the other: *I belong to TJ and Beth*, and a mobile number underneath.

'So Max is your real name,' I say to him. 'Did Beth call you Maxie?' At her name, Maxie gives a sharp yip. Oh no, not only did Beth leave TJ, but she also left her puppy! Is this woman for real? They're two lost boys. And ... I'm crying again. God, what's wrong with me? I must have seriously bad PMT this month.

The next day I take Maxie for a short walk to clear my head, then do some hoovering. But Maxie follows me around whining and keeps trying to chew the cord. It's like he knows I'm upset about something. In the end, I shut him in the kitchen. Hoovering does help expend some nervous energy, though I'm still feeling out of sorts. I've got to pull myself together. TJ's due back at three and I said I'd stay until he arrived. I have to act normal around him, not spaced out, otherwise, he'll know something's up, and there's no way in hell I'm admitting I listened to his private CD. He should've just chucked it away. That thing is an emotional menace. I put it safely back in its case on the bookshelf last night, making doubly sure it's in the exact position I found it in. He'll be none the wiser.

I'm sitting at the kitchen table with my laptop and backpack when there's the sound of a key in the lock and Maxie runs to the front door, barking his head off. *He's back*, I think, feeling relieved. The house sit is officially over and I can go, he doesn't have to take up space in my brain anymore. TJ comes into the hallway and I hear him doggie talking to Maxie, 'Hello, did you miss me? I missed you too. Have you been good for Aster, huh? Good boy, good boy.'

Right, cue normalcy act; cheerful expression, welcoming smile, get ready for friendly banter. But then I remember—*I haven't packed the CD player*. It's still sitting in the lounge on the window sill. I moved it so I could hoover the couch, told myself not to forget about it; then promptly forgot about it.

A slow wave of horror washes over my body.

TJ strolls into the kitchen carrying Maxie in his arms. 'Hi!' he greets me breezily with a grin, wrinkling his nose as he gets a thorough tongue lashing. Over the top of Maxie's fur, he clocks my wide-eyed, unblinking, rictus expression.

'Is everything OK? Did something happen?'

I manage to move my mouth but all that comes out is a gurgling sound.

'Aster, speak to me. Are you ill? Have you had bad news?'

'No, and no,' I manage to get out. 'I've just remembered an important deadline that's due tomorrow. I completely forgot about it.'

'Oh. Well, luckily you remembered now. So, did Maxie behave himself?'

With an effort, I try to act normal. 'He did, he was a perfect angel.'

TJ chuckles. 'I'm not sure I believe that.' He deposits Maxie on the floor, who jumps at him yapping, wanting to be picked up again. So much for 'he's definitely a dog' I think, amused.

'How was the ski trip? Fun?'

'It was great. We had some hassle getting there as you know but och, it all worked out. The weather was perfect.'

During this conversation, I've been thinking three things. One, TJ looks more relaxed and happier than I've ever seen him; two, he's picked up a slight tan from skiing; and three, how the fuck am I going to get to the lounge and grab the CD player?

I'll just say I need to go to the loo and make a detour via the lounge. I half get out of my seat but TJ says, 'By the way, I can run you back to your flat. I'm catching up with Dee, so it's no trouble.'

'Oh, OK, thanks, that would be great.'

'Are you ready to go?'

'Yes. I'll just use the loo.'

'Sure.'

But when I come out TJ's standing in the hall right next to the lounge doorway jangling his car keys, and I can't think of a good enough excuse to go in there. Hell's teeth. So I shoulder my backpack, scruff Maxie's head in farewell, and follow TJ outside to the car. It's a black four-door Audi with a sunroof and, as I find out when I get in, heated seats. Again, I wonder how he can afford it. He must be a dedicated saver.

'Nice car.'

'Thanks, it was a present to myself for a ... tough year.' Whoops, an oblique reference to Beth there, maybe I should just say as little as possible for the journey back. TJ pulls out of the parking space and punches the Spotify app on his phone attached to the dashboard. He jabs at a playlist and I brace myself for Bryan Adams ... but it's a Black Eyed Peas number, so I relax.

'You like them?' I ask, gesturing at his phone.

'Yeah, just this song though. I have a whole lot of random playlists with one song on them. As the mood takes me, you know.'

No kidding.

My gaze drops to his cargo shorts, then his bare knee which is jigging in time to the music. It's lightly tanned with minimal hair. Come to think of it, TJ is quite hairless. I run my eyes over his arms which are tanned too and well-muscled.

'What about you?'

'Huh?' I jerk my eyes back up to the windscreen.

'What music do you like?'

'Oh, er, you know. Anything.'

Maybe we shouldn't talk about music.

'So, yeah Maxie was pretty well-behaved on the whole, but he went crazy in the Meadows. He kept trying to run after other dogs.' I show TJ the red mark on my palm and he grunts in sympathy.

'I know, he's a little horror.'

'The only time he kept still was when we were watching Jennifer Aniston rom-coms.'

TJ snorts. 'Yeah, he's in touch with his feminine side, which is more than I can say for me,' he says self-deprecatingly.

We chat some more about Maxie, then the conversation moves on to Dee. TJ wants to know if we've lived together long. I say two years, but I'm somewhat surprised Dee hasn't mentioned this to him. Have I not come up in the conversation at all?

'You seem to get along well.'

'Dee's great. She's like the sister I never had. I've just got a brother,' I tell him, 'but he lives in Sydney, and I only hear from him once or twice a year.'

When we pull up at the flat, TJ turns to me and says, 'Thanks, Aster. As I said, I think I should pay you.'

I wave it away. 'No, no. I don't want anything.'

'Perhaps I can shout you lunch or dinner sometime then?'

'Honestly, it was my pleasure. He's a sweet dog.'

TJ nods. 'Well, thanks again.'

Dee bounds down the stairs as I'm getting out of the car. She looks amazing in a black coat, lavender jeans, a white blouse and black high-heeled ankle boots. She's wearing her expensive gold E pendant and hoop earrings, and her long blonde hair is carefully styled with side flicks, which I know takes her ages to do. Instantly, I feel grungy and scruffy.

'Hi! You're back.' We hug briefly and her hair smells of Georgio Armani *Si,* her signature scent. She bends down to wave to TJ through the open window, then straightens up.

'We're going to a gastropub near the Botanic Gardens for a late lunch slash early dinner,' she tells me. 'Come too if you want. We haven't booked. It's just a casual thing.'

'Oh, I ... can't.'

TJ overhears and says from the car, 'Aster's got an urgent deadline.'

I know he's just reiterating what I told him, but I feel a sting of rejection nevertheless. I'd be the third wheel. Dee hugs me again. 'We'll catch up tonight,' she says, and raises her eyebrows meaningfully as if to imply, 'I'll see what else I can find out about him.'

'Sure, have fun.'

I watch as Dee gets into the car and says something laughingly to TJ. She waves at me and they drive away. They look good together. The perfect couple.

Chapter 15

When she comes back from the gastropub, we debrief in the lounge over a cup of tea. So far I haven't learned much. All Dee has said is that she and TJ 'bonded'.

'What does that mean?' I ask. *Is bonded a euphemism for snogged?*

'He told me some stuff about his past, but I can't say what. He didn't tell me to keep it a secret, but I would feel like I was breaking his trust.'

Typical, *now* she decides to respect his privacy. Just when I'm burning with curiosity to know what happened with Beth!

'But,' Dee continues, 'I can officially tell you that TJ stands for Thomas Jason. There were three Thomas' in his class at school so they all got called by their initials. It stuck, and he's been TJ ever since.'

'Cute ... So has he made a move on you?' I ask, cutting to the chase.

'What kind of move?'

'Tried to kiss you.'

'No, we're taking it slow.'

'Is that what he told you?'

'It's what I'm sensing he wants.'

'But he's into you?'

'I'm pretty sure he is.' She hitches a shoulder defensively. 'Why all the questions anyway? How're your dates going?'

'They're not. I'm thinking about quitting Hearts of Fire and trying something else. Maybe staking out the men's toiletry aisle in Boots.'

Dee giggles, 'You totally should! Sometimes you have to think outside the box. I mean if it wasn't for your disastrous date with Richard, I'd never have twisted my ankle, and then I wouldn't have met TJ. All these things happen for a reason.'

I raise my mug of tea. 'Here's to Richard! Proof that dating disasters can lead to true happiness. Even if it's yours and not mine.'

We clink mugs and Dee pats my arm reassuringly. 'You'll meet your Mr Right soon, I feel it in my bones,' she says. 'Don't give up.'

Feeling a fresh surge of enthusiasm after Dee's encouraging words, I arrange a couple of Hearts of Fire dates for next week and settle back into life at the flat. But part of me is on tenterhooks thinking TJ is going to message about the CD player. He must've discovered it by now. I've thought of a few explanations if he does, but none of them sound remotely believable:

'I bought you a present to say thank you for the house sit.'
'Oh yes, I always pack my CD player when I go away.'
'I really wanted to listen to your Swedish polka CD.'

However, when he hasn't messaged or called by mid-week, I relax. I'm making too big a deal out of it. Even if he is wondering why I left it there, he's not going to connect it to me being nosey and listening to his private CD. If it was *that private*, he should've locked it away in a drawer.

Then on Thursday night, when I'm getting ready for my date, Dee tells me that she and TJ are going for a hike round Loch Leven on Saturday and asks me along.

'I dunno,' I say noncommittally.

'Come on,' she presses, 'It'll be fun.'

'Well ... OK,' I say hesitantly. The weather has been lovely lately, and I feel like getting some fresh air. Besides, I consider TJ a friend now, so there's no reason I shouldn't go for a hike with them.

'Oh, goodie. It was TJ's idea to invite you, actually. He said you looked stressed out at his flat and he feels bad that Maxie was too full on. I think he wants to shout you lunch at the loch café to say thanks.'

The tension in my neck dissipates. He's been thinking about me—in a good way, not a suspicious way. There aren't going to be any CD player repercussions. 'Oh, that's nice of him. I don't want to be a third wheel though.'

'You're not, but you could invite someone if you want, to even up the numbers.'

'True.'

So I message a few Hearts of Fire guys I've screened, but haven't yet had dates with, and say I'm going on a hike on Saturday with another couple if anyone's free and interested. The guy who reminds me of Gareth/Garrett replies to say he's up for it.

Awesome, now I'm not a third wheel and I get to have a date with a good-looking guy. Win-win.

The plan is to meet at our flat, then TJ will drive us to Loch Leven and we'll have lunch in the café halfway round. The full loop is thirteen miles, but we're planning to walk to the café and back which is only seven, and 'doable' says Dee, the experienced hiker. Unfortunately, it pours with rain on Thursday and Friday night, so there's a chance the loch may have overflowed its banks, although we won't know until we get there.

TJ arrives first and I hear Dee greet him at the door. He says something and Dee replies with 'He's not here yet. We're waiting for him.'

The Gareth/Garrett lookalike is actually called Noah, so I'm training my brain to think of him as that, in case I accidentally call him Gareth or Garrett, which would be embarrassing.

My stomach dips when TJ comes into the lounge, closely followed by Dee. He's wearing his black hiking shorts and a khaki green top that shows off his tan. I smile and say hi but he doesn't smile back. Instead, he reaches into his backpack and brings out the CD player. Uh oh.

'I think this is yours? You left it at mine,' he says flatly.

Dee sniggers when she sees it. 'I didn't know you listened to CDs, Aster. How old school.'

I think rapidly. 'Uh, yeah. I've been wanting to get one for ages to play my CDs, and when I saw TJ had some I decided it was a good time to buy one ...' It sounds fake even to my ears.

'I hope my music wasn't too boring for you.' TJ is gazing intently at me and I feel my face starting to go red.

'The Swedish polka was ... interesting.'

TJ doesn't say anything but he keeps staring at me with a tight-lipped expression. *He knows,* I think, shrinking in shame. He knows I listened to his Beth CD. Not only that, but I went out and bought a CD player especially to find out what was on it. Shit. I feel like I've gone through his underwear drawer and found out he wears flowered jockeys.

Then the buzzer goes and thankfully Noah arrives. So there are introductions to be made, social chit-chat about the hike, the weather, and a discussion on what the path will be like. So I'm saved from any further incriminating looks from TJ. I'm just going to have to avoid being left alone with him on the hike. Which won't be too difficult as Dee's monopolising his attention.

Noah and I are relegated to the back seat of the Audi where we make stilted "getting to know you" conversation. I already know I'm not interested because he's starting to irritate me with his continual references to movies and books which only he seems to have seen or read. Then, when I say I haven't, he exclaims animatedly, 'Oh, you have to. It's fab!'

Dee keeps turning around at intervals to ask him questions and to give me secret thumbs-ups, which is annoying me too.

TJ is quiet and makes out that he's concentrating on the road. But since I'm sitting right behind him I'm getting a strong vibe of *something*. He's either pissed off at me or embarrassed, or a combination of the two. From this angle, I can see the back of his head and a slice of his cheekbone every time he turns his head to check the road. I'm enjoying looking at him without him knowing. To the point where I'm ignoring Noah entirely and he's given up talking to me. The breeze from the partly open window is giving me a decent waft of the aftershave TJ wears and I breathe in deeply. What the hell is it? It's driving me crazy. He turns his head to say something to Dee and I get a full profile view and my heart gives a funny little leap. Why have I never noticed TJ has an adorable nose? It's dead straight and flares out at the end with a tiny ski jump tip.

Until now my libido has been sulking, shocked into

submission by the Richard date, and I haven't felt any desire to sleep with the guys I've been out with recently. But now, looking at the smooth tanned skin on TJ's freshly-shaved cheek, jaw and neck, I wonder what he tastes like. Salty, perhaps sweet, like buttery salted caramel. I watch his lips move and imagine what it would be like to kiss him. Hmm, pretty nice. I don't seem to mind thinking about that at all. The fantasy of the two of us kissing starts getting X-rated, clothes come off, and my brain flies out of control imagining all sorts of things; the twitch and pull in my groin is unbearable. Oh God, he's so freaking hot. As if sensing my private fervour, TJ's grey eyes flick up to the rearview mirror and lock on mine while the Kings of Leon's *Your Sex Is On Fire* pumps through the speakers. His gaze is intense, knowing, and heat zings through my body lighting me up like a pinball machine; my cheeks flame and my scalp tingles. Dee suddenly squeals 'TJ!' and he promptly rights the wheel before the car ends up in the ditch.

From then on, TJ keeps his eyes firmly on the road, and I concentrate on Noah, but inside I'm quivering. What just happened?

Chapter 16

When we pull up to the Kinross Ferry Landing, I announce I need to use the loo, and shoot out of the car before TJ has barely put on the handbrake. The Boathouse Café doesn't look open but, thankfully, it is. It's just early and there're no customers yet.

A woman, who is wiping down the counter with a cloth, looks at me enquiringly as I come in.

'Hi, can I use your loo?' I ask, breathing heavily like I've been on a six-hour hill run.

'The toilets are for customers only,' she says, looking pointedly at my backpack.

'Well, can I buy something?'

'Aye, but we're only serving coffee at the minute.'

'Fine, I'll have one of those. A flat white, double shot.'

'The toilets are through there.' She points to a door and starts opening a new packet of coffee.

In the loo, I do some deep breathing in an attempt to calm down. *Get a grip*, I tell myself sternly. *It's just TJ. He's not that attractive and you have no interest in him whatsoever.* But my brain insists on giving me a replay of the naked fantasy in graphic technicolour detail. There are even sound effects.

I wish I'd never agreed to go on this hike. Now I've got hours and hours of having to watch Dee and TJ together.

There's a knock on the door and Dee's voice. 'Aster, are you in there?'

Speak of the devil.

'Just a minute,' I call.

I flush the loo, splash my hot face with freezing water and pat it with a paper towel. When I come out, I expect Dee to comment on my hasty retreat, but she just says, 'Good idea, I needed to use it too.'

When I go over to the car, I see TJ showing Noah some warm-up stretches and saying something about old hiking injuries.

As I approach, he looks at me with an unreadable expression. 'All good?'

'Yup,' I say, avoiding his eyes.

I lean against the car door, sip my coffee, and tilt my face to the sun to dry my damp skin. It'll be fine. I just have to keep my distance.

This proves more difficult than expected since the path is only wide enough for two people, so TJ and Dee walk ahead and I trail behind them with Noah. But I have a clear view of TJ's back, outlined through his t-shirt, and his thigh muscles when he steps over anything. Now that I've started seeing him as smoking hot, I can't unsee it. It's like I've been wearing a blindfold and it's been rudely whipped from my eyes.

Noah has given up on making conversation with me since I've been responding in monosyllables and has started talking to TJ. Every time TJ glances back and says something in reply, I see his face, and my innards turn molten. What with my heart pumping wildly from the caffeine, enduring a guy I don't particularly like, lusting after one I can't have, plus a blister forming on my little toe—I'm struggling.

After hiking for half an hour, we meet a couple who look like a walking advertisement for Mountain Warehouse, complete with poles and gaiters.

'What's it like up ahead?' TJ asks them.

'It's pretty flooded,' says the man rubbing his beard. 'Do you have waterproofs? Gaiters?'

We shake our heads.

'Och, then you may want to turn back now.'

'OK, thanks, we'll see what it's like and decide then.'

As soon as they're out of earshot, TJ humphs and says, 'He's being overdramatic. I'm sure it's not that bad.'

Once we round the next bend, we can see that the man has indeed painted an accurate picture. The path ahead disappears into a shimmering stretch of loch water, and the neighbouring field is waterlogged too.

'Oh, shit,' says Dee. 'We can't get through that.'

I'm relieved. Now we can just go home. But TJ has other ideas. He walks in part-way and discovers it comes to just over his knees. 'It's fine. We can just wade it.'

'It's fine for you, you've got long legs,' Dee protests, 'The water's going to be up to my waist, and Aster's wearing *jeans*. She's going to get sopping wet.'

Everyone turns to look at me and I hold up my hands. 'Hey, I'm an amateur hiker. You're lucky I'm here at all.'

'Well, Noah and I can piggyback you then,' TJ says.

Noah is shorter than TJ, and not as fit, but he's not a weakling and he's not stupid either. He sizes me up and then Dee, and asks her if she wants to go with him. I assume because she's a lot shorter and it will be easier. After a second's hesitation and a glance at TJ, she says 'OK' politely. I can tell she was hoping to be piggybacked by TJ, but she doesn't want to appear rude. She climbs up on the fence and clambers aboard Noah's back and he starts sloshing through the water bouncing her up and down saying 'you're as light as a feather', so she giggles.

TJ and I look at each other. 'I'll wade it,' I say, and start rolling up my jeans.

'Don't be silly, I can piggyback you.'

'I'm not as petite as Dee,' I point out.

'Are you doubting my manly strength? I do work out.' He holds up an arm and flexes his bicep, and I nearly drool. He has awesome muscles.

'I know, I've seen your collection of Neoprene hand weights,' I say, averting my eyes. *And listened like a pervert to the love CD you made for your ex ...*

'So are we doing this?'

'Fine, if you insist. But if your knees end up buggered, don't blame me.'

I climb up on the fence in an unladylike fashion and do an awkward leap onto his back. He staggers forward, and for a second, I think we're both going into the drink, but he manages to keep his balance at the last minute.

'Perhaps sit higher up,' he suggests.

He hoists my thighs so my arms are around his neck, and our heads are practically touching.

'That's better,' I say, trying not to press my breasts against his shoulder blades. So much for keeping my distance.

By this point, Noah and Dee have reached the other end of the path. Noah waves and yells back at us. 'It's dry here!'

TJ starts sloshing along the path and I keep my legs pointing forward so they don't dangle in the water. I'm thinking we're not going to talk so he can concentrate, but he says, 'Maxie's been missing you.'

'Oh! Has he?'

'He keeps wanting me to watch rom-coms.'

I laugh. 'Well, you'll just have to oblige him.'

'I feel bad that he doesn't get out much during the day. I take him for an evening walk, but I don't think it's enough. He has so much energy to burn.'

Before I can stop myself, I say, 'Maybe I could pop round and take him for a walk every now and again?'

'I think he'd like that.'

'Cool.'

TJ stops for a breather and hoists me up again to get a better grip on my legs. His earlobe is now directly in front of my mouth. My blood quickens and I feel positively vampiric. I have to physically restrain myself so I don't nibble on it. *What the hell is going on,* I think, my heart thundering.

He starts walking again—splosh, splosh, splosh.

'So where did you meet Noah?'

'Online.'

'The same site as that Scott guy?'

'Yeah, Hearts of Fire.'

'He seems OK.'

I make a non-committal grunt.

'You're not keen?'

'He's not my type.'

TJ doesn't ask what my type is. He sploshes along in silence, then says, 'It's funny, and I know I told you not to, but I kept thinking you were going to call me in France.'

My stomach dips. 'Oh, well, I was going to ... but then I didn't.'

'Why not?'

'I was in a sugar coma from all the chocolate.'

The rumble of his laugh reverberates through my chest. 'You can't tell anyone about that cupboard. My reputation will be ruined.'

'It's good to know you have some bad habits. I was starting to think you were a health freak.'

'Chocolate is one of my vices.'

'What are your other ones?'

'Wouldn't you like to know ...'

His tone is light but playful, and I suck in my breath. Is TJ flirting with me? He relaxes his head into mine so my forehead is just touching his temple. I don't say anything, just tighten my arms around his neck and hold on for dear life as he keeps sloshing.

When we reach the others, I don't want to let go of him but I have to. He bends and deposits me on the ground.

'You guys took ages,' says Dee impatiently. 'What was the hold-up?'

'Aster took some convincing that I was strong enough to carry her.'

Dee tsks. 'Of course, you are!' She gives me a flinty look and I make a face at her. What's her problem? Dee and TJ start walking again, leaving Noah and I to bring up the rear.

'She quite likes him, doesn't she?' Noah mutters to me. 'Are they a couple though?' And I hear a plaintive undertone in his voice. Oh no, don't tell me Noah's got the hots for Dee! This is getting messed up.

The screwy dynamics between the four of us become even more apparent when we reach Loch Leven's Larder for lunch. Dee is solely focused on TJ, Noah is staring at Dee, and TJ, well ... he's replying to Dee, shooting me glances every now and again, and chatting with Noah. The equaliser.

I just nibble quietly on my chicken sandwich (which TJ insisted on paying for as a thank you) and survey Dee's behaviour around TJ. She gets on well with him, but is it anything like what I'm feeling: an overwhelming desire to drag him into the bushes and devour him? She must be, surely.

Later that evening her feelings become clearer.

'By the way, I'm moving TJ onto the "Meet the Parents" Dealbreaker,' she says, settling back on the couch. I feel a jolt of unease.

'Really? That's kind of serious ...'

'I know. But I think he's got what it takes.'

'For what?'

Dee stares at me. 'Duh, you know, marriage, babies, the works.'

'He might have different ideas,' I mumble, prodding the huge blister on my little toe. It's sore and it's making me cranky. In fact, the whole day has been an ordeal. Apart from the piggyback ride, I enjoyed that.

Dee smiles unfazed. 'I'm pretty sure we're on the same wavelength.'

'How do you know?'

'When he dropped us off at the flat, I asked him if he

wanted to go out with me, and he said yes.' She smiles dreamily as if remembering. I prod my blister—hard. It pops, sending a jet of watery pus oozing down the side of my foot. Lovely.

'Congratulations,' I say, attempting to sound sincerely happy for her but not quite managing it. From now on, I'll have to try harder to keep my distance from TJ or a blister is going to be the least of my problems. I just have to find a way to turn off the fantasy of me and him that's on replay in my head.

Chapter 17

Dee keeps me fully informed of her plan to introduce TJ to her parents on the following bank holiday weekend, whether I like it or not. I'm also privy to the paranoia about what they'll think. She comes into my room, sits on my bed, and says she needs to talk it out. This usually happens at around ten at night when I'm reading.

'I'm pretty sure Mummy will love him. Daddy might need more convincing. He doesn't trust people in the medical profession.'

'Doesn't he go to the doctor when he's ill?' I ask, laying down my Kindle, foreseeing that I won't be reading for at least the next five to ten minutes.

'Not if he can help it. He says he's quite able to "take paracetamol, get lots of rest, and keep hydrated" as that's all doctors tell you to do.'

'TJ's a physio, not a doctor. He does massages and exercises and stuff.'

'Daddy's even more suspicious of people who give massages.'

I make a sympathetic face.

'It'll be OK,' Dee says, 'I'll talk him round. I might go and read some articles on using persuasive language. '

'Good idea.' I pick up my Kindle again. That was one of the short visits.

Two nights before they're due to catch the train down to London, Dee's stressing out to the max, and in my room again. 'Maybe we shouldn't visit. If they don't approve of TJ, it's going to make things difficult.'

'Are you going to ditch him if they don't?' I ask.

I feel a tiny bead of hope. If Dee gives him the flick, then just maybe ...

She groans. 'God, then I'll be back to square one! I try not to care about what they think, but I can't help it. They have high expectations for their future son-in-law. Mummy even suggested I make him do a DNA test, so they know what his genetic background is.'

I stifle a laugh. 'He's probably got Viking blood. How would they feel about that?'

She pulls a face. 'It's not ideal.'

'Don't panic, it'll be fine. TJ is a good catch.'

'Do you think so?'

I ignore the flare of pain in my chest. 'Yes, definitely.'

On Friday night, Dee bursts unceremoniously into my room and flicks the light switch. 'Aster! Wake up!' she hisses.

'Whasa matter?' I croak groggily, shielding my eyes.

Thinking it's morning, I peer at my phone on the nightstand. 'Jesus, it's 2 am!'

'You have to come too.'

'Huh, come where?'

'To London. Tomorrow.'

'London?' I'm trying to focus on what she's saying. 'But you don't want me there.'

'I doooo! I need moral support. Two positive voices promoting TJ to my parents are better than one.'

'But I've never met them! Why would they trust my opinion?'

'They know *of you*, I've told them you're my best friend.'

'Have you?' I'm flattered. It's nice to know she's recommending me as her best friend.

'So they won't mind if I just turn up at the last minute. Is there room?'

Dee shrugs dismissively. 'It's a five-bedroom house, honestly, they won't care. I'll text Mummy before we leave and fill her in. Thanks, Aster, I owe you one.'

She turns out the light and shuts the door with a bang. Moments later, she pokes her head back in.

'By the way, the train leaves at 10 am, and I've booked you a ticket, 'night!'

But I'm wide awake now. I'm going to London. And staying in the same house as TJ for the weekend. I might pack my vibrator, I think I'm going to need to gird my loins.

TJ looks surprised to see me with Dee the next morning at Waverley Station but, having excellent manners, takes it in his stride when she explains she invited me along for the ride, more the merrier and all that. He even seems relieved that I'm there. Perhaps the thought of meeting Dee's parents this early in the relationship is giving him gip.

Since my ticket has been booked at the last minute, I'm relegated to a second-class carriage, while TJ and Dee are in first-class.

'Sorry Aster, I would've booked a first-class one, but it was full,' she says, handing me my ticket when the machine spits it out.

'It's fine. I've got some reading to catch up on. It's nice of you to pay for me at any rate.'

'If you get bored, come and see us,' says TJ. He checks his ticket. 'We're in carriage A.'

'Will do,' I say, not having the slightest intention of doing so. Carriage J, at the opposite end of the train, away from the lovey-dovey couple, suits me just fine.

We arrange to meet up outside King's Cross station and I settle into my window seat in J, noting that I don't have anyone sitting next to me until Newcastle. Even better. I breathe a big sigh of relief that I don't have to witness any kissy-kissy stuff between Dee and TJ. I've just managed to turn off the explicit movie playing in my head, I don't want to inspire another showing. It should be OK at the house as well since she said her parents are strict Catholics and we'll all have our own rooms. I'm picking the house will be posh, so it could be like a retreat. A Catholic retreat with free food, minus the spa.

Speaking of food, around lunchtime, I start feeling peckish, so I decide to buy some lunch from the snack bar in carriage C.

I'm leaning against the window, waiting for my bacon roll and coffee, and munching away on a bag of cheese and onion crisps, when TJ strolls through the sliding door. I almost choke.

'Hi! Fancy meeting you here,' he says smiling.

'Yeah, I built up an appetite hiking from J.'

The train chooses that moment to swerve and I almost bang into him. He puts out a hand to steady me. But I don't take it. I hold out the bag instead. 'Want a crisp?'

'Sure. Is that all you're having?'

'No, I've got a bacon roll and coffee coming.'

'Sounds good. I'd better order ours. What would she like, do you think?' he asks, sounding unsure. I imagine Dee's told him all the things she doesn't want, then said 'Oh, just surprise me.'

'Hmm, she loves Twix, so one of those, and just a bacon roll and a coffee. Maybe the fruit cake too. She likes having coffee and cake.'

TJ looks relieved. 'Thanks, Aster, you're a lifesaver.'

'No problem.'

God, they're a pair. Maybe I should hire myself out as their go-between.

'So what did you do with Maxie for the weekend?'

'My family friend was back from holiday, so she's taken him round to her flat to hang out with her Scottie. Maxie likes terrorising him.'

I laugh. 'I can imagine. Maybe you can bring him to London next time if it all goes well with the meet and greet.'

TJ's brow wrinkles. 'What do you mean?'

'Meeting Dee's parents. Bit of a big deal but I'm sure you'll pass with flying colours.'

'Why is meeting them a big deal?'

'Er, isn't that the whole point of going to London?'

TJ shakes his head slightly. 'I think you've got the wrong end of the stick. Her mother's friend is having an art exhibition and Dee asked me if I'd come as her plus one. I didn't have anything on, so I said I would.'

I stare at him, my brain whirring as his words hit home. Dee explicitly told me that she'd asked TJ out and he'd said yes! That she was moving him onto the "Meet the Parents" Dealbreaker. From what he's saying, it sounds a lot less set in stone.

I'm reluctant to say anything else for fear of dropping her in it. *Damn, Dee, what the hell are you playing at?* I backpedal clumsily.

'Oh, I assumed that you and Dee, that you, well ...'

'I like Dee, but we've only been out a few times. I'm not ready to jump into anything serious. I'm still finding my feet with the whole dating thing.'

Just then the train goes into a tunnel, the lights dim, and everything rattles madly. There's a loud roaring noise in my ears which seems to go on forever. Then the train pops out into the light and everything is quiet again. Blissfully quiet. A sense of calm washes over me like I've entered a meditation retreat. *TJ is still single.*

TJ hands me my coffee and bacon roll and flashes a smile in my direction. 'I'd better order. See you when we get to King's Cross.'

'Yup, in exactly three hours,' I say and practically skip back to carriage J as if my ankles have wings.

But when I reach my seat, I have to face the sobering truth. Dee lied to me. She better have a good explanation for all this. After eating lunch, I take my phone out of my bag and type:

Edie Crowley-Smythe meet me by the loos in carriage F asap!

She knows when I call her that she's in trouble, so maybe that's why she doesn't reply. Two blue ticks appear so I know she's seen the message, but she's blanking me. Grrrr. I send her another one, less threatening with a smiley face emoji, but there's still no reply, and I don't get one for the rest of the journey.

When we get to King's Cross I'm confused and anxious about her behaviour. What am I doing here if not to vouch for TJ being a great guy? I'm starting to suspect I'm being used in some way. I push my way through the crowds and go through the barriers. When I get outside, Dee and TJ are standing off to the left looking at their phones.

'Hi!' Dee says when she sees me.

'Hi,' I say stiffly. 'I messaged you twice on the train. Did you not get them?'

'Yes, I got them, but TJ and I were playing backgammon on his iPad. Was it important? Why didn't you come up to our carriage if you wanted to chat?' Her eyes are large, querying, innocent.

I glance down at TJ who's bent over rummaging in his bag for something.

'It was private. Can we talk on the Tube?' I say in a low voice.

'We'll catch a black cab, it's quicker. Look, there are heaps waiting. I'll pay.'

Why do I get the impression she doesn't want to be left alone with me? I go along with it, determined to pin her down at the house.

I know Chiswick is an affluent area, but the leafy tree-lined street we turn into has houses that aren't normal-sized;

they're Victorian mansions. I gape out the window as we drive past, resisting the urge to point and exclaim like a working-class tourist.

The taxi drops us outside number thirty-six, a sprawling three-storey red-bricked affair with two bay windows, a gabled roof and multiple dormer windows. There's a tall wrought iron gate and a neatly paved driveway with a parking area and four black shiny SUVs. Are they all theirs or is Dee's mother hosting one of her afternoon teas?

We pile out of the taxi with our luggage and wait on a small tiled porch while Dee rings the doorbell. 'I don't have a key,' she explains. 'They're paranoid I'll lose it and someone will break in.'

After what seems like forever, a woman who looks like an older version of Dee, but with shorter hair and much thinner, opens the door.

'Kiki Dee, darling!' she exclaims in an accent dripping with plums.

I exchange the briefest of glances with TJ—Kiki Dee?

'Was the train positively horrible?' She leans in and proffers a cheek, and Dee kisses it.

'It was all right. Mummy, this is TJ.' He steps forward and says pleased to meet you and she shakes his hand.

'Lovely to meet you TJ. I'm Isadora,' says Dee's mother gazing at him appreciatively. 'And who's this?' She looks at me blankly.

'It's Aster, Mummy, my flatmate. I messaged you that she was coming.'

Isadora brightens. 'Oh, yes, for Teddy.'

Teddy? Who the hell's Teddy?

'Poor bear, he simply can't be left alone at the moment,' Isadora says to me as if I should know what she's talking about.

As we're ushered into the hallway, I whisper to Dee. 'Who's Teddy?'

'Their Saint Bernard. He was knocked over by a car and he's got a broken leg. TJ and I have to go to a thing tonight with Mummy and Daddy and I thought, since you love dogs, you could maybe look after him.'

'Right.'

Everything's starting to make a lot more sense. I'm not here for moral support. I'm here for the dog.

Chapter 18

Isadora gives us a lengthy tour of the house and grounds—'This is the library cum study with several first edition books, this is the kitchen we had extended last year, this is our extremely large and well-kept garden,' etcetera—before I manage to capture Dee in her bedroom. It's on the second floor, in a separate wing, away from the other guest bedrooms, and it looks like someone's had a chintz-on-chintz decorating frenzy.

'Knock knock,' I say at the doorway.

Dee looks up from unpacking her bag. 'Hi, come in. How's your room?'

'My room is fine.' It's on the ground floor with a pink rose theme, twice the size of my room at home, and I have a private en suite with a claw foot bath, so I'm definitely not complaining. TJ, likewise, looked gobsmacked when Isadora showed him a similar guest room down the hall, done up in lavender, complemented with hanging bunches of fragrant dried flowers. 'Wow,' he muttered, looking around and sniffing the air gingerly. I'm not sure what he's doing now—reading a first edition of something, contemplating the well-kept garden, having a wank under the lavender-sprigged duvet—who knows?

I come into the room and shut the door behind me. 'I think we need to talk.'

'Sure,' Dee says distractedly.

She takes out a black dress from her wheelie bag, smooths it down and surveys it. I notice it's rather like the one from TJ's wardrobe, in fact, it could be the same dress but in a larger size.

'This has travelled well. Hardly a wrinkle. Do you think I should wear my hair up or down?'

'Sod your hair. What the fuck is going on, Dee?'

That gets her attention. She gives me a startled deer-in-the-headlights look. 'What do you mean?'

'I mean, you told me that TJ agreed to be your boyfriend. From what he said, it doesn't sound like that's the case.'

'Oh.' She looks guilty. 'When did you talk to him?'

'We ran into each other in the snack car and I mentioned it in passing. He had no idea what I was talking about. I felt like an idiot.'

Dee shifts her eyes from mine and looks uncomfortable. 'He agreed to come to London and stay here, that's practically admitting he wants to take it to the next level.'

I sigh in frustration. 'Dee, you've read too much into that. He thinks you're just friends.'

Dee's face crumples and she sits on the bed, burying her head in her hands. 'Oh, Aster, I just like him so much and I want him to like me.'

'He does like you.'

'But I want him to like me *more*. I want him to fall to his knees whenever I come into the room and be unable to take his eyes off me.'

I sit on the bed next to her, not sure what to say. 'That's a bit of an ask for someone you've only been on a few dates with.'

'But he's *shared* things with me. I know he wants to take things slow, but that's not helping me. It needs to move faster.'

'Why does it?'

'My biological *clock*,' she wails. 'You have no idea of the pressure I'm under to find a husband. Mummy's on my back constantly.' She presses two fingers to her temple in a pained way. I'm starting to see the similarities between mother and daughter. Melodramatics being one of them.

I'm torn between wanting to reassure her that TJ is the man for her and yelling 'keep your hands off him!', so I settle for 'I get it. It's frustrating but you can't rush things. Just be yourself and I'm sure it will work out. TJ likes you, he told me so.'

She leans against me and gives a shuddering sigh of relief. 'That's great to hear. I'm hoping tonight goes well and he gets along amazingly with Mummy and Daddy. I'm sorry I fibbed, I just ... On the hike ... I feel silly now,' she gives a short laugh.

'What?' I prompt.

'I got insecure when I saw him piggybacking you. All that stuff with Sam came flooding back. But you're right, I just need to be myself and we'll get there. If he passes this test, there's only one left.'

She doesn't elaborate, but I know what she's talking about. The "Is He A Cheater?" Dealbreaker. The one that will prove beyond a doubt that TJ is husband material. Dee's already put it into action with Scott and it worked. Too well. I know at some point, before things start getting serious with them, she's going to ask me to do the same for her with TJ. Dread forms in the pit of my stomach. It's a good idea in principle to weed out a cheater, but I'm starting to regret I agreed to it. I also wish I hadn't let Dee railroad me into this trip to London. Now I have to nurse a Saint Bernard with a broken leg while they go out socialising.

Isadora comes up to collect me from Dee's room, so I can meet Teddy in the laundry. On the way down, she gives me a lengthy overview of how to feed him, and then the catch—I have to give him an injection to keep him sedated. 'Otherwise, he thinks he can get up and start running around and his leg needs to heal.'

I balk. 'An injection? I don't think I can do that.'

'You'll be fine,' says Isadora airily. 'He'll only snap at you if you put it in at the wrong angle and Dee said you have lots of experience with dogs.'

Feeding and walking them, not injecting them ...

She adds that Teddy was knocking on death's door only two days ago, and they prayed for a miracle and wonder of wonders, thanks to God, he's now alive and kicking. Apart from the broken leg, which he won't be kicking anything with for at least another two months.

'He may be asleep. We'll tread softly and see,' says Isadora. She opens the laundry door and we creep in.

My eyes take a minute to adjust to the gloom and, at first, I can't see anything. But then I hear a soft woof and a tail slapping.

'He's awake. Hello, Teddy!' Isadora opens the Venetian blinds and a chink of light falls on the most gigantic dog I've ever seen. Teddy is the size of a cow. He even has the hide of a cow, with tan and white markings.

Looking around, I see they've set up a makeshift dog hospital in the laundry for him. When I say "laundry" I mean a room the size of a one-bedroom apartment. The dog bed Teddy is lying on isn't something you'd buy from a pet store either, it's a double mattress.

He lifts his head and gives a baleful 'woof' as Isadora bends down to pat him. But then he sees me and bares his teeth in a Cujo-like snarl and emits a low growl. I take a quick step back. 'Teddy!' admonishes Isadora gripping his muzzle. 'It's fine. He's just a little wary of strangers after the accident.'

'H ... how did it happen?' I ask, staring at his foreleg in the cast, trying to ignore my quaking knees.

'It was a teenage driver out for a joy ride. He won't be driving his car again. It was totalled,' she says with some satisfaction.

I'm not surprised. I can't imagine any vehicle would look too good after a run-in with Teddy.

'What about, er, Teddy's toileting?'

'You don't have to worry about that. Michael will drive him out to the garden before we go so he can do his business. It's somewhat of a mission.' She laughs, nodding towards the back of the room.

I look around. There's a small forklift with a flatbed and, beyond that, a green roller door that must open onto the garden. Jesus wept. I thank my lucky stars that I don't have to drive the forklift to transport Teddy so he can poop on the lawn. Injecting him is going to be bad enough. I may lose a limb. Dee so owes me for this.

Apparently Michael is at his health club playing squash but we'll meet him soon. Sure enough, he makes an appearance about an hour before they're due to go to the exhibition. TJ and I are in the kitchen tucking into ham salad, boiled eggs, sourdough bread and pungent stilton cheese, when he saunters in.

Isadora immediately gets into a flap. She's been on her

mobile sending him urgent messages, none of which he seems to have replied to. 'Darling! Finally! You need to get ready.'

Michael ignores her and nonchalantly strolls to the sink and pours himself a glass of water. He takes a sip and sees us sitting at the table. His mouth drops open. 'Who the bleeding hell are you two?' he asks in a broad South London accent. He looks so astonished that it makes me want to giggle. TJ nudges my ankle gently under the table.

'These are friends of Kiki's darling. We're going to Camilla Sutcliffe's exhibition tonight, remember?'

Michael rolls his eyes. 'That stuck-up bint. Do I have to?'

Oh my God, Dee's father has absolutely no filter. I clench my knife tightly so my fingernails dig painfully into the fleshy part of my palm. It's either that or squawk.

'Yes, darling,' says Isadora patiently. 'Everyone's been waiting for you.'

'Oh, well, where's Kiki then?'

'She's upstairs. Do you want to have a shower and ...'

'I had a shower at the club.' He runs a hand through his damp grey, but still thick, hair. For an older guy, he looks pretty fit. I guess he must spend a lot of time at the health club when he's not barking orders at his five-star hotel in Soho.

Dee waltzes into the room, serene and lovely in her black dress, accessorised by a seafoam pashmina and matching clutch. I haven't seen those, they must be Isadora's.

I've been trying not to gawp at TJ too, but he's wearing a black suit with a white shirt and looks freaking hot. I felt a compulsive urge to leap on him but just said, 'You scrub up well.' He seemed pleased.

'Daddy!' cries Dee and crosses the room to give her father a kiss on the cheek and a hug which he accepts with a smile. 'Hullo, luv.'

'Have you met TJ and Aster?'

He nods at us. 'Are you two together? It's separate rooms in our house when you stay here, I'm afraid.'

TJ coughs and Dee looks mortified. Wow, Michael Crowley-Smythe doesn't mince words. Dee shoots an anxious glance at her mother and Isadora clarifies the situation rapidly, 'No, darling, TJ and Aster are just friends. TJ is Dee's plus one tonight.'

Michael looks at TJ and narrows his eyes. His lips press together and I'd love to know what he's thinking. My money's on: 'Keep your dick in your pants mate or you'll have me to answer to.'

'Darling you really need to get changed,' Isadora tells Michael, trying to shift him, but he just leans against the counter refusing to be hurried and sips at his water.

'What's TJ stand for?'

'Thomas Jason, Sir.'

'Last name?'

'McKelvie.'

He grunts. 'Pure Scots?'

'As far back as I know. Five generations at least.'

Michael grunts again.

I glance at Dee. Her face has gone blotchy pink from her father interrogating TJ. I can see why she's been so nervous. He's a flipping tyrant who isn't going to be easily won over where his little girl is concerned. I feel sorry for TJ who has to spend the evening being watched like a hawk by Michael. Suddenly Cujo-Teddy seems preferable by comparison.

Chapter 19

'Why do your parents call you Kiki Dee?' I ask curiously after Isadora takes hold of Michael's arm and drags him out of the kitchen to get changed while he protests vehemently. Honestly, those two should have their own comedy show.

'Daddy wanted to name me Kiki Dee after the singer,' Dee explains. 'I think he had a thing for her when she was younger. She's ancient now though. Mummy convinced him to name me after Edie Sedgwick instead. But they still call me that as a nickname.'

'I don't know anything about Kiki Dee, but Edie Sedgwick was beautiful,' TJ says and Dee positively glows. 'Bit of an untimely end though,' he adds and her glow fades a little. 'What about you, Aster?'

'My name? It's Greek for "star". My mother was hoping for a boy, but she got me instead. Luckily it's unisex and I turned out to be a tomboy. I aim to please.'

'I think I prefer it as a girl's name,' TJ muses, 'It's pretty. Asterrrr,' and the sound drips off his tongue like liquid honey. I positively shiver. Oh God.

Dee gives a grit-teeth smile and I hurriedly change the subject. 'What time do you think you guys will be back? Should I wait up?'

'We shouldn't be too late,' says Dee. 'Maybe ten-thirty or eleven? It depends on how quickly we can get Daddy out of the house and back again. He always says he hates going to these things but he does seem to enjoy the free drinks.'

'Do you think you'll be OK with Teddy?' TJ asks me. I told him when we were alone in the kitchen earlier that I was terrified I was going to lose a limb.

'She'll be fine. Aster's great with dogs,' Dee replies for me confidently.

'I know, Maxie loves her.' TJ grins in my direction causing a warm feeling in my chest.

Dee gives another of her grim smiles, and my heart sinks. Is TJ not allowed to say anything nice about me at all? I thought she wanted us to get along? *Yes, but not too well.*

They leave the house in a flurry of goodbyes and 'ring us if you need to' and 'we won't be too late'. I wave them off from the porch, as if I'm the lady of the manor, while they drive away in one of the four black SUVs, all of which seem to belong to Dee's parents. I stay where I am, breathing in the night air and enjoying the occasional whiff of jasmine from a nearby climber. Blessed silence. For just a moment I forget I'm left alone in a Victorian mansion with the dog of my nightmares.

Isadora has left written instructions for Teddy on a notepad, headed with the name of Michael's hotel. Her neat, tight script flows onto two pages. With my editor's eye, I pick out the most important bits: the food, the painkillers, and the injection. The rest is waffle.

Darling Teddy is so pleased you're looking after him!

Sorry Isadora but I call bullshit on that. Teddy is not a darling and he is not pleased I am looking after him.

The meat for his dinner is a slab of fillet steak; red and bloody in a plastic ziplock bag in the fridge. I have to slice it into chunks, then crush a couple of doggie painkillers, cut minuscule slits in the meat, and insert small pieces of white pill into the chunks in a way that is invisible to his doggy radar.

Teddy is smart, and will reject the meat if he even suspects a tiny bit of pill!

My plan is to tip-toe over to the mattress and place the dog bowl as near to him as I can without upsetting him. This way I lessen the risk of being mauled. I'm not looking forward to the injection part either, but the actual administering is fairly straightforward according to Isadora.

Just grab the scruff of his neck briskly and stab in the syringe. Press down firmly until it all goes in. It's easy!

Just the thought of grabbing and stabbing any part of Teddy's body is giving me heart palpitations. I could dispense the medicine into the sink, but I doubt that would work.

Teddy needs the full dosage to sleep throughout the night. Otherwise, he'll start barking at 3 am and wake up the whole house!

And everyone will know Aster was a namby-pamby scaredy cat who hasn't done her job. Basically, I'm screwed either way I look at it.

But I'm not a quitter. Four years of eking out a living as a freelancer have taught me that I have quite a lot of mettle. OK, Teddy is big and has scarily sharp teeth but at least he's sedated. I once looked after a Rottweiler who turned feral as soon as the owners left the house. I'm still not sure how I managed to get out of that one alive. The upshot is: if I put my mind to it, I can handle it.

Outside the laundry door, I pause with the bowl of meat in one hand and the syringe in the other, primed and ready to go. It's all quiet within. If Teddy is asleep, then I can sneak in with the bowl, check his water, grab and stab, and get out of there before he knows what's happening.

Hesitantly, I turn the handle and push open the door. It's pitch black inside the laundry. I run my hand blindly along the wall by the doorframe, but there's no light switch. I try again, higher up. Still nothing. I'm afraid to leave the safety of the light-filled hallway and enter the dark room with Teddy in there. Carefully transferring the syringe to the front pocket of my jeans needle side up, I gingerly lower the dog bowl to the ground and use it as a door prop while I get my phone out of my other pocket. I turn on the torch light and shine it into the room.

The first thing I notice is that the double mattress where Teddy was lying is bare. Heart thudding, I do a slow scan of the room with my phone. Nothing. Where the hell is he? Don't tell me he's escaped! I happen to shine the light by the edge of the door and see two huge eyes glinting glassily out of the darkness right in front of me. My heart jumps in shock, but then I realise it's Teddy who has limped over to the door for his food. He's so close to me, I can hear him breathing.

'Good boy. Do you want your dinner, hmm?' I say shakily, holding the door open with one hand and nudging the bowl forward with my toe. Plan B. If I can feed him by the door, I don't have to go in there. Teddy sniffs, catching the scent of meat, and takes a small step growling softly and looking at me warily. I give the bowl another slight nudge. *Come on, Cujo, it's right there.* Then, without warning, Teddy bares his teeth and lets rip with a volley of savage barks that make me jump out of my skin. Screaming, I kick the bowl into the room, slam the door, and pelt up the hallway as if the hounds of hell are after me.

Only once I'm back in the safety of the kitchen do I dare breathe. My hands are shaking. The top of my thigh is also spasming painfully and there's a small wet patch on my jeans. What the? Did I pee myself? Inspecting more closely, I see with horror that the syringe slipped down into my pocket when I ran. Some of the doggy sleeping drug has leaked out causing the wet patch and the needle is now stuck into my thigh with an empty canister. Fuuuuck.

Coffee. That's what I need. Strong coffee to stay awake. My eyelids start drooping and my vision blurs as I struggle to figure out what all the buttons on the state-of-the-art Nespresso coffee maker are. Do these people not have a jar of instant coffee and a kettle like everyone else?! There's no way in hell I'm going to get it working in time ... What else has caffeine? Dark chocolate 85%, surely they must have that ... Frantically, I start flinging open kitchen cupboards trying to locate anything resembling chocolate. All I can find is a small box of after-dinner mints. Grabbing a handful, I fumble with the tiny brown packets and manage to tear open a few, then stuff slivers of minty chocolate into my mouth. But it's no use, I'm swaying on my feet. I need to get to my bedroom pronto, otherwise, I'm going to pass out on the kitchen floor.

Groaning, I stumble out into the hallway which is starting to warp in a peculiar way. By the time I reach my bedroom door I'm crawling on my hands and knees.

Whatever that drug is, it's enough to keep a two-hundred-pound Saint Bernard asleep for an entire night, so I'm not surprised it's knocking me for six. The last thing I remember is staggering into my room and collapsing face-first onto the rose duvet before blacking out.

Chapter 20

I'm having a lovely dream about me and TJ and Maxie in the Meadows. I'm lying on the grass and he's bending over me and saying something nice. I don't know what exactly it is, but he's smiling at me and I'm feeling happy. His beautiful grey eyes are the colour of a winter sky. *He's so nice*, thinks dream Aster. From far away I hear TJ's voice, and I open my eyes to find that he is indeed peering down at me. But anxiously, not smiling, like in my dream. And he seems to be repeating my name over and over like it's going out of fashion.

'Phew,' he says, drawing back as I attempt to sit up. 'You're a deep sleeper. I was calling you for ages.'

Sitting up isn't happening so I clumsily roll over on one side and prop myself up on an elbow and try to focus. The rose-covered curtains are drawn back and bright sunlight is streaming in, making me squint in pain. I feel an overwhelming urge to throw up which would not be a good look in front of TJ.

'Water,' I croak and he goes into the en suite bathroom, comes back with a glass of water and hands it to me. I gulp it down in relief. 'What time is it?'

'Eight-thirty.'

Events from the night before start flooding into my mind. Teddy. The barking. The injection. The blackout. The wet patch has dried on my jeans and I prod my leg; it doesn't feel too sore. The syringe is still in my pocket, I can see its outline.

I run a hand through my hair feeling like shit. I don't want TJ to see me in this state. But hang on. Why is he in my room anyway?

'Um, did you need something?' I ask, trying not to sound accusing.

'I forgot my phone charger. Could I borrow yours?'

I'm confused. 'You woke me up to borrow my charger?'

'I knocked and I thought you were awake. I distinctly heard you say "TJ".'

Oops, that's embarrassing. I must've been talking to him in my dream.

'How come you're still wearing your clothes and why do you have chocolate smeared all around your mouth? Did you find their secret stash or something?'

I wipe my mouth with my hand and it comes away with a brown mint-scented smear. Oh, why not just tell him.

'OK, confession. There was an ... incident.'

I dig in my pocket and hand him the syringe. TJ looks at it. 'You're diabetic?'

'No, it's Teddy's sleeping medication. I accidentally injected myself with it.'

'What?'

'It was an accident. He freaked me out with his barking and I ran away in a hurry. But the syringe was primed in my pocket and some of it went into my leg.' TJ inspects the label on the syringe. 'Jesus, this is heavy shit. Like a horse tranquiliser.'

I groan. 'Tell me about it. It wasn't the full syringe, but I still copped the effects. I tried to find some dark chocolate, I thought the caffeine might counteract it, but all I could find were after-dinner mints.'

TJ's lips twitch but he doesn't laugh at me, just dons his medical hat, and says in a professional manner. 'Let me check your vision.' He peers into my eyes. 'Hmm, are they always that shade of red?'

'Haha.'

'I think you're fine, but take it easy today and let it wear off. I'll get you some more water.'

'Thanks.' I feel relieved that he's making light of it and knows what to say because he's a doctor of sorts. I'm rapidly changing my opinion about his bedside manner.

When he returns with the filled glass, I say 'Please don't tell Dee or her parents. I feel like a right idiot.'

'I won't, don't worry.'

He stands next to the bed while I sip the water. 'The charger's in the front pocket of my backpack.'

'OK.' He retrieves the charger but then sits next to me on the bed again. He doesn't seem in any hurry to go back to his room.

'How was the exhibition?'

TJ screws up his nose. 'It was all right. A bit poncy.'

'Where and what was it?' I've been kept in the dark, then plunged into looking after Teddy, so I haven't a clue about any of it.

'It was in Chelsea. Isadora's friend, Camilla Sutcliffe, is quite a well-known artist apparently. I'm not sure why Dee needed a plus one as there were plenty of single women there.'

Oh, TJ, I think.

'What sort of art?' I ask, to get him off the subject of Dee's asking him to London to be her plus one.

TJ looks down at the duvet and says quietly, 'Feathers.'

'Huh?'

'She'd painted different kinds of feathers onto canvases. Some had single feathers, some had lots of feathers. But yeah, feathers.'

'What was the going price for a feather painting?'

TJ's lips curve. 'A thousand pounds.'

'No way!'

'Uh-huh. I mean the feathers were well drawn and all, but a thousand pounds! And everyone was posh and had intelligent things to say about them. I felt out of my depth, to be honest. I think I would've rather stayed here and helped you look after Teddy.'

'You'd choose Cujo over canapes and champagne? That's

quite a sacrifice.'

'At least you wouldn't have ended up drugged.' He sounds sympathetic. 'I'm sorry you were lumped with him.'

'Me too. Hopefully, he went to sleep minus the horse tranquiliser. I guess I better get up and have a shower, I must look a right sight.'

TJ's eyes flick over my face carefully as if assessing me for injuries. 'You look good. Apart from the chocolate smears.'

I gurgle.

Sunday passes in a post-drug haze. I feel like I'm recovering from jet lag or a hard night on the Pinot Grigio. TJ says that food will help and I should get some protein and carbs in me for breakfast. Luckily Isadora and Michael have gone to church and taken Dee with them. There's another handwritten note on the pad in the kitchen about helping ourselves to anything we want, so TJ and I unashamedly raid the fridge. It's a treasure trove of sausages and bacon from the local butcher, farm fresh eggs, and market-bought tomatoes and mushrooms in paper bags.

'God, it's manna from heaven,' I say to him, my stomach rumbling loud enough to wake the dead.

'Aye, I'm thinking full English,' TJ says, firing up the hob. 'You do the toast.'

He starts whacking strips of bacon in a pan. Soon a delicious sizzling smell is wafting through the kitchen, making my mouth water in anticipation. I discover a whole loaf of golden crusty bread in a bread bin so I saw off some doorstops. It smells amazing and is no doubt from the local upmarket bakery. I'm starting to think Dee's parents don't ever set foot in a supermarket unless they absolutely have to. And then only Marks and Spencer or Waitrose. I can't imagine shopping like that, but if you're loaded, I guess you can buy whatever the hell you want.

'From the amount of tofu and bean sprouts in your fridge, I thought you were veggie,' I say to TJ watching him crack eggs into the pan. He certainly seems to know his way around a fry-up.

'There's a reason the tofu and bean sprouts were in the fridge. I didn't want to eat them,' he says with a laugh. 'Despite appearances, I'm actually not that healthy.'

'So I should take your nutritional advice with a grain of salt then?'

'Aye, a large pinch of it.' He grins, and starts transferring bacon, eggs, mushrooms and tomatoes onto two plates 'How's the toast coming?'

'It would be coming if I could figure out the toaster.' Like the coffee maker, it has an inordinate amount of unmarked buttons that I'm just pressing randomly in frustration. I try one on the bottom and, to my relief, the bread doorstops sink out of sight.

We sit down to eat, and I'm crunching on my first piece of delectably crispy bacon when a mournful howl sounds from the direction of the laundry. TJ and I look at each other.

'Ignore him,' I say, spearing a mushroom. 'He's smelt the bacon and he's not having any.' The howling continues.

'I'm starting to feel guilty,' TJ says, pausing his eating and looking towards the hallway.

'Don't be. I'm sure he's been fed this morning. Besides, Isadora has him on a strict diet of the best steak money can buy. He's not missing out.'

'Maybe I should check on him though. Just in case the howling is for some other reason.'

'Be my guest,' I shrug, not particularly concerned. 'After last night, you couldn't pay me a million pounds to set foot in that laundry again.'

'Aw, surely he can't be that bad?'

I don't say anything, just raise my eyebrows and continue eating.

TJ gets up from the table and takes a piece of toast with a slice of bacon atop, to eat on the way, or give to Teddy, I'm not sure. After a minute the howling stops and there's silence. Then a low guttural whining begins, followed by a loud lapping noise. Whatever is happening in there, at least doesn't sound like TJ is being mauled. When he returns to the table, he's minus the toast and bacon, his hair is sticking up on end, and his face and t-shirt are covered in doggy drool. His eyes look haunted. 'So that's Teddy,' I say grimly and hand him the paper towels.

We've just finished cleaning up and I'm burping away quietly to myself when the others arrive back from church. I do a double take when Dee walks into the kitchen. She's decked out in a frilly white lace dress, white stockings, ivory court shoes and is that a hairband? She looks like Alice in Wonderland attending her first communion. I've never seen her look so—virginal. Isadora and Michael are also dressed up to the nines. Isadora is in a royal purple silk dress with a pearl choker and a matching hat with a veil. Michael has on a three-piece suit with a purple silk handkerchief in his pocket to complement her. They're giving the distinct impression of attending a royal wedding. Talk about wearing your Sunday best for church.

I daren't glance at TJ in case it sets me off into giggles. Sometimes I can tell exactly what he's thinking just with a quirk of an eyebrow or a certain glint in his eye.

'Oh, good, you've had breakfast,' Isadora chirps seeing the frying pan on the hob. 'Did you find anything worthwhile in the fridge? We're running low on supplies I'm afraid, I'll have to call Martha and get her to top it up.'

Martha?

'We did, thank you,' I say, bemused. I guess my idea of an empty fridge is different to hers.

'Excellent. Well, I should go and get changed, Michael is going to sort out Teddy, then we'll do a spot of gardening.'

She whisks Michael out of the room before he can say anything in protest, but he gives us a farewell salute and looks wistfully at the Sunday paper.

Dee sighs, plucks at her dress, and flops down at the table. She rolls her eyes at me. 'God, church was boring. I don't mind going when I'm here, but for Mummy it's more about seeing and being seen than anything spiritual. What have you guys been up to?'

'Nothing much,' I tell her. 'Just having breakfast. Who's Martha by the way?'

'Oh, their maid. She does a whip round the Chiswick specialty shops and the market for them; they like to support local businesses. About a month ago Mummy discovered she was a fully qualified chef and has been getting her to cook meals for them as well. I think she's too reliant on her. Mummy's quite capable of cooking.' She lowers her voice. 'Honestly, I think she just likes the idea of it, and quite a few of her friends have chefs, so they compare notes.'

'Right.' I really do not want to risk looking at TJ right now.

'How did you get on with Teddy last night? I hope he wasn't too difficult.'

'He was, er, fine. You didn't hear him during the night or anything?'

'Not a peep. The injection you gave him must've knocked him out. Anyway, I need to change out of this dress, it's making me itch.'

She tip-taps across the tile in her ivory shoes. I know I

shouldn't be commenting on the absurdity of it all in front of Dee's love interest, but I can't help saying, 'Well ...' when she's out of earshot.

'Yeah ...' TJ echoes my tone perfectly.

Chapter 21

The weather turns dismal in the early afternoon, so Isadora and Michael's gardening doesn't last long. They join us in the library cum study, which is so far my favourite room in the house. It has a wide bay window that looks out onto the lawn, and from my curled up position on a black leather couch, I can see trees and shrubs swaying in the wind. The room has wall-to-wall bookshelves including an entire shelf dedicated to the classics. In my hands is a first edition of Thomas Hardy's *Tess of the d'Urbervilles* which I'm reading with white gloves on. I'm gingerly turning the pages, hardly daring to breathe, terrified I'm going to rip it (a bloody first edition!).

Dee and her mother are playing gin rummy, and Michael and TJ are involved in an intense game of chess. I think Michael was expecting TJ to be shit when he said he hadn't played for ages. But I instantly thought, uh oh, I've heard that before, so I've been watching with barely contained glee as he dominates the board. Michael's face is an interesting shade of puce when TJ says quietly 'check'. Michael manages to get out of it but TJ's too good. My chest swells with pride when he announces 'checkmate' three moves later. It feels like an us-versus-them victory.

'Congratulations, TJ!' exclaims Dee and shoots me an impish grin, as if to say 'Ooops, Daddy won't like that!'

But Michael is as stubborn as a mule and refuses to let TJ beat him. Two hours later, I've almost finished *Tess of the d'Urbervilles* while they're on game five and TJ checkmates Michael yet again. At last, he admits defeat, nods at TJ and says tight-lipped, 'I should check on Teddy'. He stalks from the room with Isadora gazing after him worriedly.

TJ attempts to look suitably sorry, but I can tell he's not feeling too bad about it. He leans back in the oversized armchair and locks eyes with me. 'Fancy a game?'

'Not likely,' I say with a chuckle, placing the book carefully on the side table. 'Besides, Scrabble is more my thing.'

'I think we have that somewhere,' Isadora interjects. 'It may be in the attic.'

'Perhaps another time, Mummy,' Dees says, glancing at me and I wonder if it's bringing up bad memories of her snogging Scott and my negativity about it.

In the early evening, when it starts getting cold and rain pings against the window panes, Isadora suggests we move to the dining room cum lounge for dinner. It's a smaller room, but the oak dining table still seats sixteen. My eye is caught by a cast iron period fireplace set with decorative floral tiles and surrounded by a black marble mantlepiece. 'Wow, I love the fireplace,' I say.

Isadora beams. 'Isn't it gorgeous? I decided to keep it as a character feature when I renovated the room. I'll light it to make us feel cosy!'

I'm expecting her to cobble together newspaper and kindling, strike a match and crouch down with bellows to fan the flame. But it's more a case of standing next to it and pressing a button on the wall. It's one of those clean, no-mess fires that are fed by gas. For an older-style house, it certainly has a surprising amount of mod cons.

Michael appears again when dinner arrives: fish 'n' chip suppers delivered from the local takeaway. But it's not a polystyrene affair with oversized haddock and limp chips dripping with brown sauce. Oh, no siree. The suppers arrive in compostable tureens with bamboo knives and forks, and the responsibly sourced sablefish is buttery and velvety, battered in egg and gluten-free crumbs. The chunky hand-cut chips are fluffy on the inside and crispy golden on the outside. There are even individual organic rocket and watercress salads with radishes fashioned into flowers. It's the poshest fish 'n' chips I've ever eaten.

'It's so important to eat healthily,' says Isadora to no one in particular.

But TJ nods. 'I agree,' he replies. 'I see a lot of injuries that could have been avoided by eating better food and losing weight.'

'That's why you're a connoisseur of tofu and bean sprouts,

right? And chocolate is banned from your flat?' I can't help teasing him.

'That's right,' he says, wrinkling his nose at me with a private grin. A spark shoots between us and my stomach flips. Hmm, maybe best to concentrate on eating my sablefish.

Dee sees an opportunity to promote TJ's medical ability and pounces on it. 'TJ has a lot of important patients, don't you? He even treated Nicola Sturgeon once.'

All eyes turn to TJ and I almost swallow my organic radish whole at the look on his face. 'Did you?' exclaims Isadora in awe. 'What was wrong with her?'

TJ shifts uncomfortably frowning at Dee. 'It wasn't Nicola Sturgeon, it was her friend. And she was having physio for a broken ankle.'

Dee waves her hand. 'Well, it was still connected to her. And she came to you from a recommendation. That's pretty impressive.'

TJ doesn't say anything and I get the feeling he's not pleased Dee's brought it up. He changes the subject and asks Michael a question about the hotel, and we spend the rest of the meal hearing about his plans to open another hotel in Manchester. But then he says 'I'm hoping Kiki will manage it for me.' Now all eyes turn to Dee but she spears her last chip and brandishes it at him.

'Daddy, I told you. I don't want to live in Manchester, it's too *grungy*. I like my job at Liberty.'

'It would be a great career move though,' TJ says to her. 'And it would look fantastic on your CV.'

'Oh ... I guess.' Dee studies her chip carefully with a pained expression, and I know what she's thinking: *That sounds like he doesn't care if I leave*. Ouch.

After dinner, Isadora and Michael say goodnight and retire to their own wing of the house, leaving us to amuse ourselves.

Dee promptly unlocks the well-stocked drinks cabinet and surveys the contents. 'Let's have a drink. Aster, we can have a G&T, and TJ, there are a few bottles of whisky in here.'

'Are we allowed? There may be a reason it's locked,' I counter, though a stiff drink would hit the spot right now; it's been a tough weekend.

'Yeah, it's fine. They just keep it locked on principle.'

'OK then, a gin or two sounds good.'

'Maybe just one, Aster,' TJ cautions, no doubt thinking of the horse tranquiliser.

Dee gives a harsh laugh. 'What are you, her keeper? She can have as many drinks as she wants.' TJ arches an eyebrow at her tone and doesn't say anything.

I let out a breath. Whoa, she's taken his Manchester comment to heart and the claws are out. I interject to diffuse the sudden tension between them. 'Shall we get some lemon and tonic water from the kitchen, Dee?'

She looks like she wants to go in for another scratch but

nods and tosses a blasé 'Help yourself, TJ, glasses are in the cabinet,' over her shoulder as we leave the room.

'That was a bit rude,' I tell her when we're in the kitchen collecting the ingredients for the G&Ts.

She shrugs and grabs a couple of lemons from the fruit bowl. 'He was being a party pooper. I thought you'd appreciate me sticking up for you. Tonic water is in the fridge.'

'There's a reason he said that,' I say opening the fridge and peering in to locate it. 'I ... I'm feeling under the weather, and he was just looking out for me.'

'OOOOH, looking out for you. Sounds like you two have been getting along well,' she says sarcastically.

'Dee ...' I say helplessly. I hate it when she gets all snooty like this, she's hard to be around.

She recovers her decorum back in the lounge and there are no more barbed remarks, but her tone is clipped when she replies to TJ and I can tell she's still smarting from his earlier comment.

TJ doesn't appear to notice, but then again, he hasn't lived with her for two years. I'm quite in tune with her moods, as she is with mine. I know that if she's being sarcastic, then she's hurt.

To take her mind off it, when we're sitting sipping our drinks, I say 'Your dad is a hoot. How did your parents meet?'

'They met at University. Daddy was doing a Law degree and Mummy was in the Arts, it wasn't an easy relationship though.'

'Oh? How come?'

'Well, Daddy was a ladies' man. By all accounts, he had a different girlfriend every week. Of course, he broke Mummy's heart, but she refused to give up on him. After a year of much convincing by her, he realised that she was the one for him.'

'Sounds like a love story for the ages,' comments TJ dryly, taking a slug of whisky.

Dee pouts. 'I think it shows courage and strength of character.'

'Your mum is definitely brave going after the man she wanted,' I say. 'The broken heart sucks though.'

'Yes, I can relate to her on that count. You're lucky you've never had one.'

I stiffen. That's a bit cutting and I can't help retaliating. 'I have, actually, you don't know everything about me.'

Dee looks incredulous. 'I don't believe it.'

'Why is that so hard to believe?'

'Because you've never had a proper boyfriend. Isn't your longest relationship three months?'

OK, this is getting too close to the bone for the company we're in. I glance nervously at TJ who's watching us. I don't particularly want him to hear about my dating past, now that

I'm trying to keep it in my pants, so to speak.

But Dee has got the bit between her teeth. 'Who was this guy, did I meet him?' she persists.

'It was ages ago, at school, all right?' I say tetchily.

'I have to hear this.'

'No, you don't,' I mutter. 'I don't want to talk about it.'

'Oh, go on, tell us, it might help you. You're clearly still hung up on him.'

'She doesn't have to if she doesn't want to,' TJ says but he's looking at me curiously.

Maybe because I've had a decent dollop of gin, or because Dee is being so insistent, I end up spilling the whole painful story of what happened with me, Penny and ... Christian Parker.

When I've finished there's a silence, broken only by the hiss of the gas fire, and rain splatting against the window panes. I can't believe I've told them what happened. No one knows about it. Not even my family.

TJ starts saying 'God, Aster ...' in a solemn voice but Dee interrupts him.

'So, just to recap,' she says. 'You liked this guy, Christian, but Penny, the popular girl, found out, and said she'd help you get together with him. She gave you love notes from him and in turn you sent love notes back. But in reality, his notes were made up by Penny and he had no idea about any of it.

Then one day Penny decided to show her true bitch colours and brought him over to you in the playground. She gave him your notes and he read them and laughed.'

I shudder, remembering how embarrassed I felt; some of them were pretty gushing but I thought he returned the sentiment. 'It was so humiliating. Practically everyone in the school crowded around to see what was going on. And people were reading the notes while I was running around trying to snatch them back. The other girls just watched and sniggered, not even my best friend helped me.' Lulu didn't say a word, she just jeered along with the rest of them and ditched me afterwards because I was the laughing stock of the school.

Dee puts her hand over her mouth, and I think it's because she's horrified at what I've just told her. But then a tiny giggle escapes from between her fingers and I realise that she's ... laughing.

Shock shoots through me, then anger. 'Why is me being humiliated so funny to you?' I say through gritted teeth. 'I believed Christian loved me from the notes Penny wrote. I was traumatised by what happened and then I was teased for months afterwards as well!'

When Dee sees I'm seriously pissed off she wipes the smile from her face. 'It's not funny, not really, it's terrible, poor you. But also, well, it was at school. It was just a teenage thing, it doesn't count as a broken heart story. Not like how it was with me and Sam.'

Not like how it was with her and Sam?

Then I realise, it's all about her; her pain. She doesn't give a fuck how I feel or what happened to me. Not one iota.

I down the rest of my gin in one, get up from the couch and wordlessly leave the room.

Chapter 22

The extent of my anger right now is scaring me a little. I feel like I'm about to explode so I scream into my pillow but it doesn't help. I'm lying on my rose covered duvet quivering with rage when there's a knock on the door. I don't get up. It'll be Dee apologising. That's how it works. She acts like a royal bitch then expects me to forgive her just because she says "sorry" with that innocent "I didn't know what I was doing" face. Bullshit, she knows exactly what she's doing. The knock comes again. 'Aster?' It's TJ. She's sent him to check up on me no doubt.

'Come in,' I growl. Maybe I'm giving off Cujo vibes because he takes one look at me and stays by the door.

'I came to see how you are.'

I grunt. 'How do I look?'

He shuts the door behind him and sits gingerly on the bed. 'Angry.'

I give an acknowledging grunt.

'Dee's gone to bed.'

'Good.'

'I told her off. She was being a bitch.'

Anger lessens and curiosity takes over. 'Did you tell her that?'

'Yeah. She's not too happy with me right now.'

I sit up and look at him. *TJ told Dee she was a bitch!* I would've liked to have seen that.

'Are you OK?' he asks. 'That was some story.'

The kindness in his voice gets me and I can't stem the tears.

'Aww, noo.' He gathers me into a hug and I sob on his shoulder while he rubs my back. Eventually, I come up for air. 'Sorry,' I gasp. 'It's an old wound. I should get counselling or something.'

'Maybe talking about it is the first step. Sometimes we keep things bottled up inside and they eat away at us; cause issues that we're not even aware of.'

That sounds truer than I'd like to admit.

'If I met Christian now I bet I wouldn't even like him, he's probably fat and bald.'

'Yeah, he could be in jail,' says TJ deadpan, 'Or an alcoholic. Or dead.'

I give a hiccuping giggle, 'That got dark quickly.'

TJ smiles and squeezes my arm. 'I've got a free supply of jokes and hugs if you need them.'

'Maybe one more hug then. You're a good hugger.'

During the hug, TJ's hand strays to the back of my neck. 'Your muscles feel like piano wire.'

'I know, I've got computer neck. I've been meaning to get a massage to sort it out.'

'Turn around then,' he says.

'I didn't mean ...'

'I know, it's fine.'

Well, he is a professional and it's a free treatment.

We shift positions so he's propped up against the headboard with his legs apart and I'm sitting cross-legged between his thighs. When he presses his thumb experimentally into the side of my neck, I wince. 'This might hurt. If it gets too much, let me know.'

TJ has such strong fingers that the neck massage is more pain than pleasure. At one point, I gasp and dig my fingers into his thighs without realising. But he tells me to do some deep breathing and I manage to power through. Now I know what Dee was talking about with her calf muscle. The pain does lessen off though and soon he says. 'That's feeling more pliable.'

'Mmm, it's not as sore, thanks.' God that was intense.

He kneads my neck some more. 'I could give you a proper back massage if I had some oil.'

'Pity there isn't a Holland and Barrett nearby,' I joke.

TJ is silent, then says 'I'll be back in a minute.' He leaves the room in a hurry and my heart rate increases. What is he doing? I'm wary, curious, and half-dazed from the blood circulating at a great rate of knots round my body.

He comes back into the room holding a fancy glass jar filled with reed diffuser sticks.

I laugh out loud. 'You can't use that!'

'Why not? It's lavender essential oil, perfect for relaxation.' He takes the sticks out in a bunch and deposits them carefully on the dresser where they lie in a little puddle of oil.

'You're going to be in so much trouble.'

'Isadora will never know. Now take your t-shirt off please, and lie on your front on this pillow,' he instructs in his deep *I'm a physio* voice, which I'm sure gets his lady patients all in a flutter. There are certainly parts of me that are fluttering at the thought of him touching me. I'm not sure it's a good idea, but he seems intent, the overhead light is on and it is a free professional massage after all. So, I sigh and say, 'Fine, just don't drip it on the duvet.'

'I'll get a towel.'

He goes into the en suite, and I peel off my white t-shirt and lie there, listening to the wind rustling the trees outside. Brightness is replaced by gloom as TJ discovers the light has a dimmer switch. *OK*, I think nervously, *we've moved from a clinical setting into a spa scenario.*

The bed dips as TJ kneels next to me and the scent of lavender hits my nostrils. He slaps his palms together to warm up the oil and I can't help giggling.

'What's funny?'

'Just ... lavender oil. The scene from *Outlander*.'

'Never seen it. Or read it.'

'Oh.'

Warm, oily fingers begin firmly stroking my shoulder blades. Despite the oddness of having TJ massaging me, I start relaxing under his expert touch. *Just enjoy it.*

'So, what's the scene?' he says after a while.

'You don't want to know,' I murmur. 'Let's just say it will put you off lavender oil for life.'

He moves his fingers in circles lower down near my bra strap and stops. 'Would you mind undoing it? It's just in the way and I don't want to get oil on it.'

'It's hardly Victoria's Secret, but fine.'

I reach around and undo the strap trying to ignore the sudden fire in my abdomen as TJ runs two thumbs freely down my spine. He pulls my jeans down slightly to stroke the muscles around my hip area and I wonder idly what he'd do if I unzipped them. 'Stop that, it's platonic,' I mumble to myself.

'What?' TJ says, pausing.

'Huh?'

'I thought you said something about stopping.'

I shake my head. 'No, no. Please, carry on.'

The massage continues and it's moan inducing, not that I do moan, but I feel like it. He has the perfect combination of strong hands and great technique. I think it might be one of the best massages I've ever had. Plus, the scent of lavender is soothing and I keep dozing off, then coming to in fits and starts.

'You seriously have magic hands,' I say blissfully.

'Och, not what my patients tell me when I'm making them squawk in pain.'

'Don't you give normal massages as well?'

'On occasion. But it's usually in the clinic, not in a low-lit bedroom on a bed.'

'Oh.' Hope springs inside me, I was right, this is special. A thought pops into my head before I can stop it: *If TJ was my boyfriend, I could get massages on the house. I'd never have to pay for one again.*

It's the first time I've seriously considered him in that way. As my boyfriend. An image of us having a relaxed Sunday breakfast flashes through my mind. TJ making post-sex eyes at me over our poached eggs on toast. It's enough to make me tense up again because: what the hell?

Thinking of TJ post-sex leads to thinking about what we got up to during-sex. What with him stroking my gluteus maximus and imagining him pumping away on top of me, it's getting too much; I have to bite the pillow. I'm just about to ask him if he wants to massage my front, when he finishes up with a final flourish of painful staccato slaps. 'Ow!'

'It's a Chinese thing. Gets the blood pumping.'

Pumping, oh God ...

He goes into the en suite and I hear water running. Next, a hot damp towel is placed on me and his palms press warmth into my skin.

'That was amazing,' I say, when he's wiped up the oil. I do up my bra and reach for my t-shirt and hold it against my breasts. I do a half roll onto my side to look up at him. Is it me or does he seem a little flushed? 'Um, thank you. For the massage, and for the hug and chat.'

'You're very welcome. I'm sure you'll sort it out with Dee tomorrow.'

'Yeah.'

'I should go and let you get ready for bed,' TJ says, gazing down at me.

'Yeah.'

He doesn't move.

'Thanks again.' Without thinking I grab his hand and we have a moment of oily finger entwining and looking at each other meaningfully without saying a word. My heart is pounding; it's intimate, and not that platonic.

TJ breaks the silence by saying softly, 'It's none of my business, but you can do better than those online jerks you've been meeting.'

'Oh, I'm trying, believe me.' I smile at him. 'I have pretty high standards these days.'

He nods. 'Well, good night. I'll see you in the morning.'

'Yeah, see you,' I say, not expecting him to leave since we're still holding hands.

But he gently withdraws his fingers from mine, and leaves the room, taking the bottle of oil and the reed diffuser sticks with him. OK, that was odd. It felt like something was going to happen. And what was that last comment about? Is he giving me dating advice now? I need to take a shower, I'm too tired though, so I crawl under the duvet. But then I feel hot and confused and can't sleep.

My mind replays the feeling of TJ's strong fingers on my bare skin and the way he looked at me at the end when we were holding hands. My heartbeat starts getting erratic the more I think about it. After tossing and turning for an hour, I give in to the sexual tension and sneakily set my vibrator to whisper-quiet mode. If TJ's feeling anything like I am right now, I'm sure one of his oily hands is coming in useful.

The next morning, I wake to the sound of birds chirping in the dawn light and lie there thinking about last night's massage. I'm sorely tempted to visit TJ and slide under his lavender-sprigged duvet. But I have to keep some self-control even if I'm still mad at Dee. Maybe it's better if I go for a walk in the garden instead, to get some space. I dress in tracksuit bottoms, a hoodie, and a puffer jacket, thrusting my feet into runners.

The house is silent as I pad downstairs and into the kitchen. There, I let myself out of a side door and into the chill morning. The garden is substantial, and mostly consists of lawn, bordered by shrubs and trees to keep the neighbours from looking in. I don't want to walk too far, and there's a wooden arbour next to the patio covered in a flowering creeper, so I slink in there. The bench is damp with dew, but I sit on it anyway. Now that I'm out of the house, I can breathe more deeply and think about the situation.

I'm majorly into TJ and it's not like Dee and him are an item, he told me that himself. But then again, I know she's set her sights on him. TJ is Dee's territory, and even if I am seeing him as boyfriend material, there's not a lot I can do about it. This is crazy, after a gazillion online dates, I've finally found a guy I want, but I can't have him. I chew on a ragged piece of fingernail in frustration. What the hell am I going to do? Dee's voice comes through loud and clear in my head giving me my answer, 'Back off, Aster. TJ's mine.'

As if I'm channelling her, I hear Dee's voice floating around the garden. For a minute I'm confused, then through the leaves of the creeper I see Isadora striding up and down on the patio talking on her mobile and glancing up at the house. She's wearing a brown tweed coat, UGG boots, a purple knitted hat, and hang on ... Is she smoking *weed*?

'Yes, he's very nice,' Isadora says, taking a deep drag on her joint and puffing smoke into the cold air. 'A physiotherapist. Scottish.' She sits on the arm of a garden chair and smiles in satisfaction. 'Dee said he didn't give her an exact figure, but he indicated around a million. An inheritance, I believe.' She listens and nods. 'I know, darling, it's ideal. And such a relief. I didn't want her ending up with someone who was *poor*. Of course, we'd support them, but it's better if he has his own money. Less dependency if things don't work out. Especially if there's children involved ... Oh, I know, darling, I look much too young to be a grandmother, it's all the antioxidants I eat. I abhor free radicals. Anyway, I must go, mwah mwah, enjoy your stay in Nice!'

Isadora, the health nut who only buys organic and who abhors free radicals, looks around furtively, then squats down and buries the rest of the joint in a potted plant.

Chapter 23

I sit in the arbour after she's gone trying to make sense of it all. The smoking weed is hilarious, what she was telling her friend is not. Either Dee has been feeding her mother some bullshit about her and TJ or there is something going on with them. It also seems TJ is stonkingly rich, which would explain the France ski trip, and in Isadora's eyes, he's an ideal catch. But besides all that, where do I fit into the picture? After last night's massage, I'm pretty sure he's feeling something for me. Unless he's stringing both of us along? But I squash the thought immediately, I can't imagine TJ would do that, not consciously anyway, he's no Richard.

When I head back into the house, I have an excuse ready about being down the back of the garden, but Isadora isn't in the kitchen. She must've just sneaked out for a quick pufferoony and gone back to her bedroom. From her cagey behaviour it appears she's hiding her habit from Michael, but how does she disguise the odour? Weed reeks, you can smell it a mile away. She must have some odour zapping perfume or he knows and just blithely ignores it, which seems more likely.

It's still too early for breakfast so I have a leisurely soak in the bath, then hang out in my room and read my Kindle. I'm engrossed in my indie rom-com when I hear a soft tap on the door. My heart leaps, maybe TJ has come to check up on me again? The expectant smile on my face drops when I see it's Dee. She looks shocking. Dark puffy circles bulge under red-rimmed eyes, which she's tried to hide with concealer, but it's gone all cakey. Her blonde hair is tangled, and she generally looks a wreck.

'Can I come in?' she asks uncertainly. I nod. As soon as I shut the door, she launches into her spiel. 'I'm so sorry, I don't know why I acted like that. I've been up all night feeling awful about it.'

'Oh, Dee.' I'm not sure if I feel like forgiving her just yet. 'You really hurt me. It just seems like it's all about you sometimes.'

'I know, I'm a selfish bitch. TJ is fucked off at me too. I've ruined that, I think. Now I've got to spend five hours sitting next to him on the train.' Her mouth turns downwards at the corners and a tear rolls down her cheek. Grrr, not the self-pity act, it always twists my heartstrings and I cave in.

'Anyway, that's not your problem,' she continues. 'I just came to say I'm sorry and I hope you'll forgive me. You're my best friend, I don't deserve you.'

'I'll think about it,' I say. What I've just heard from Isadora is making me waver.

Dee's bottom lip quivers and she looks like she's going to

have a meltdown.

'OK, I forgive you,' I tell her, sighing. 'Just be a little more sensitive in future.'

She gives a small smile. 'I will, I promise. God, now I've got to go and make it up with TJ. That's going to be fun. Wish me luck.' She rolls her bloodshot eyes. 'By the way, Mummy's roped in Martha to make us a healthy breakfast before we leave for the station. I told her not to bother, but she insisted. So, see you downstairs in half an hour?'

She reaches out to hug me and I let her, but she sniffs at me like a lap dog. 'Your hair stinks of lavender. Phew.'

Damn, I didn't think to wash my hair. 'Uh, it's a new organic shampoo I'm trying out.'

She wrinkles her nose. 'It's overpowering. You should check out UOrganic, they've got some good ones. You're going to attract a swarm of bees with the one you're using.'

I shut the door after her and wish Isadora wasn't insisting on a formal sit-down breakfast. Mainly because of TJ. I feel vulnerable after the broken heart admission, crying on his shoulder and then grabbing his hand after the massage. I don't usually let guys see me like that. He's punched through my emotional retaining wall and I haven't had time to brick and plaster it up again. There's also weird shit going on with Dee and her mother and it's confusing the hell out of me.

It's with some trepidation that I enter the kitchen and find Martha cooking up a storm on the hob. She's a slim woman with dark shiny hair pulled back into a thick ponytail, and is wearing a pink t-shirt and black Juicy tracksuit bottoms. Isadora hovers nearby, to assist I assume, but not doing anything as far as I can see. Dee and TJ are sitting at the kitchen table, which is set with a white cloth, plates, cutlery, red and white napkins. There's a colourful fruit salad in a clear glass bowl.

I glance at TJ who's reading something on his phone with an elbow propped on the table. He's wearing the white shirt from the exhibition night, cuffs rolled back and casually unbuttoned at the neck, and faded jeans. He looks good enough to eat and my body temperature rises a notch.

He glances up when I come over and gives me an eyebrow raise and a nod. 'Hi,' he says. 'Sleep well?' His eyes glint mischievously.

'Yes, thanks,' I reply, sitting down and studiously avoiding his vortex of hotness. I check out the activity over at the hob instead.

'Martha's making lactose-free, sugar-free pancakes,' says Dee before I can ask.

'Um, OK. Sounds good.'

We don't have to wait long before Isadora plonks the first steaming plateful on the table.

'Help yourselves!' she exclaims. 'We're onto the next batch!'

Though it's Martha who's doing all the work and wiping

her sweaty forehead with a paper towel. She looks over at us and gives me a wave and a smile. She seems nice. Dee takes a couple of pancakes which are pale, floppy, and strangely shiny. 'There are toppings,' she says 'Fruit, honey, yoghurt, Nutella ...'

Basically items that contain lactose and sugar, which have been removed from the pancakes, so why bother making them that way in the first place? I can feel hysterical laughter threatening to escape and it takes a superhuman effort to control it. TJ nudges my thigh under the table with his knee, willing me to look at him, but I can't. I just can't. I'll explode.

'Where's your Dad?' I ask Dee, when I've managed to get myself under control. I lever a couple of pancakes onto my plate and give them a generous helping of sugar and lactose. Despite appearances they actually taste OK, and I admire Martha for putting up with Isadora's demands. I'm not sure I could have such patience.

'Oh, he had to go into the hotel. Some plumbing emergency.'

Dee seems a lot better; calmer. Her eyes are clear and not so puffy. She's also put on make-up and brushed her hair. She appears to have made up with TJ. I watch as she shovels pancakes onto his plate, insisting he eat more because he's a 'growing lad', and he grins at her amiably enough.

After breakfast Dee orders a black cab to take us to King's Cross. Isadora is apologetic that she can't run us in since someone has to be in the house to look after Teddy, then makes a performance of air kissing each of us goodbye in turn. When it comes to my air kiss, the scent of an expensive floral perfume swirls in my nostrils and, underneath, because I know it's there, is the faint tinge of marijuana. 'It was lovely to meet you, Aster,' she says. 'You're welcome back any time. Now that Teddy knows you and trusts you, perhaps you can look after him when we go abroad?'

I say something polite but noncommittal whilst praying to God that never happens. Over her shoulder I see Martha walking down the hallway carrying Teddy's dog bowl. She disappears into the laundry. Shortly after, just as the taxi pulls up, I hear the beep beep beep of the forklift reversing out. Oh God. Poor Martha.

At King's Cross, the platform isn't showing on the departure board yet, so TJ strides off to Starbucks to grab a coffee while Dee and I sit on the station concourse with the luggage. Dee is doing something on her phone.

'How did it go with TJ?' I ask.

'It was fine,' she replies, putting her phone away. 'We had a good chat and sorted things out.'

A good chat about what?

I try again with a more direct line of questioning. 'Did he say anything about me?'

Dee purses her lips as if considering. 'Nooo? Not that I

can recall. We just talked about what a bad girl I was.'

Her mouth quirks in a self-deprecating smile and she straightens up scanning the departure board. Why do I get the sense she's not willing to tell me what they talked about? I suppose it's none of my business but, for God's sake, are they together or not? And what the hell was Isadora going on about to her friend in Nice?

I screw up my courage to ask her but Dee nudges me. 'He's back.'

'I got you a hot chocolate, Dee,' TJ says breathlessly when he arrives, and hands it to her.

'Oh, thanks, that's sweet of you,' she dimples up at him, taking a sip. 'And marshmallows too, yum.'

I look over, expecting him to say, 'Here's yours, Aster' but it's not forthcoming. Oh, he bought her a hot chocolate, and not me, nice. TJ takes the empty seat next to Dee and they sip at their drinks while I prickle and glower, feeling like a third wheel.

'What carriage are you in this time, Aster?' asks Dee after a pause.

'I'm in F. Further forward than J this time. You?'

'Carriage A again. Remember if you want to chat just come up and see us. I'll check my phone from time-to- time but I may not hear it if we're talking or playing a game. I'm determined to beat TJ at backgammon. He's going down.' She nudges shoulders with him.

TJ grins. 'Not if I can help it.'

Wow, they're so buddy-buddy. The third wheel feeling worsens. Something's going on. But what exactly?

I sit on the train in carriage F and stare unseeing out the window as the suburbs of London flash by. Maybe I'm reading too much into TJ giving me a massage. It felt intimate but as I told Dee when she first met him: It's his job. It doesn't mean anything.

Maybe we've both fallen for TJ's magic hands because we're so desperate for a man to touch us and he's oblivious to all of it. Even Dee's mother is in on the act. I feel like I've been transported into *Bridgerton*. I need to get a grip. Whether Dee and TJ are together or not together is none of my business. I need to start going on some more dates and find my own Mr Right.

So when Dee messages me to say 'Hi, how're things in carriage F?' and sends through a selfie of her and TJ pulling silly faces I send back without a qualm:

Just enjoying the scenery, looks like you two are having fun.

And when I head along to the snack car to buy lunch, and I don't bump into TJ when I'm there, there's no staring longingly at the sliding door, wishing he'd walk through at any moment. My wall is bricked and plastered up again. It's surprising, even to me, that I can recover so easily. But then again, it's what I do.

Chapter 24

When we arrive back at the flat after the London weekend, Dee announces brightly, 'I think that all went rather well!' Was she even on the same trip that I was? It's a mystery.

Over the next few weeks, I keep my distance from both of them and throw myself into work instead. I need some new clients so I can start building up my flat deposit. Getting a place of my own has jumped up the list of priorities.

It's not that I'm looking to move out of the flat right this second, but if Dee and TJ start getting serious, then it's going to make my life uncomfortable. Just saying. I have visions of them bonking in her room downstairs while I sob quietly into my pillow. Or chancing upon them in the kitchen having post-sex brunch in their underwear; or coming home from a disastrous date to find them smooching on the couch while a Jennifer Aniston rom-com plays in the background.

Thoughts like these are great motivators for getting a foot on the property ladder. And for hanging out more with Stacey and Fleur from WeWork. I'm much too reliant on Dee for company and besides, they're both intelligent, interesting, likeable women, so why shouldn't I? Stacey has a successful Etsy shop where she sells artwork, jewellery and homeware by indie artists around Edinburgh. Fleur is an English translator who mainly works with French clients, although she sometimes gets Italians and Germans too.

I don't make it too obvious; just ask how their weekends have been, suggest a coffee and a chat outside on the rooftop terrace, that kind of thing. They know me enough that it doesn't feel unnatural so they start sharing more about their personal lives.

One afternoon, when we're having a coffee break on the loungers, enjoying the view of the castle and soaking up a smidgeon of sun that's peeping through the clouds, I find out that Stacey was married. She had a messy breakup with her husband last year and hasn't had the courage to date anyone else. 'I keep thinking men I see on the street are Simon, so I don't think I'm quite ready yet.' She bites her lip and gets watery eyes at the mention of his name. The guy dumped her for a work colleague he'd known for two months. Personally, I think she needs a good shag to get over him, but I keep my opinion to myself.

Fleur says she's "stoically single" but has recently signed up to an online dating site to give it a try. 'What about you, Aster?' she asks.

'Oh, just online dating. Trying to find Mr Right.'

'I'm sure you don't have any trouble meeting guys. I bet they're lining up.'

My ego gets a nice little boost hearing that, so I open up about my online dating woes. 'I do OK. But it's a fucking hard slog. Even after the screening.'

'What screening?' Stacey wants to know.

'Oh, it's a set of questions my flatmate and I came up with to weed out the time wasters. It works to some extent, but even with the ones who pass, I'm still having trouble meeting anyone I connect with.'

I've been racking up the Hearts of Fire dates since we got back from London in an effort to stop myself from thinking about TJ. There was the guy who said he was looking for something 'extraordinary'. He never messaged me asking for a second date, so I assumed I wasn't it. Then there was the guy who insisted on pinching my chin like I was a five-year-old until I told him that if he touched my chin again, he'd be getting a black eye.

'You're brave, I had a quick look around on the site I'm on the other day and saw multiple penises,' says Fleur shuddering. 'Why do men do that?'

I resist the urge to ask her what site it was ... I've had sex on the brain lately and my old habits are proving hard to break. But they don't need to know about that.

'Beats me. Maybe we need to add that to our list of questions. 'How many dick pics have you sent in the last month?' I quip, and they giggle.

'We should have a girls' night,' says Stacey. 'No talk of men allowed, no picking up men or even looking at them. In fact, maybe we should go to a lesbian bar so they don't bother us.'

'That sounds great,' I say perking up. 'Just what I need for a palate cleanser.'

'Invite your flatmate too, if you want. More the merrier.'

'Oh, er, she's seeing someone, so I don't think she'll be interested.'

Stacey looks like she's going to ask questions, so I quickly change the subject back to when we should do the girls' night to avoid having to talk about it.

I know Dee's seen TJ a few times since we got back but, so far, I've been able to avoid hearing any details. I have a feeling if she does pin me down, I might put my hands over my ears and chant 'Na na na na na' so I don't have to hear about her blossoming relationship, which is extremely immature of me.

But then my luck runs out. A few days later on Friday night, she knocks on my door, pokes her head round and says 'Can we talk?'

Since I'm reading in bed, I can't get away. My heart drops to my stomach. Oh no, I don't want to hear about how great TJ is because a) it's going to make me start thinking about him, b) if I start thinking about him I'm going to want him, and c) I can't have him.

I give a small smile then a big yawn. 'Sure, but I'm going to sleep soon, it's been a long week.'

Dee comes in and perches on the edge of my bed. 'Did you go on a date tonight?'

'Nah, couldn't be arsed. I just had a quiet one at home. You?' I ask conversationally.

She plucks the material of my duvet covet. 'I was out with TJ. We just went down to Leith, to a pub. It was nice, relaxed.'

I nod robotically. 'Cool.'

'I haven't seen much of you lately.'

'Yeah, sorry. I've been up to my eyeballs with work. I've taken on some extra clients.'

It's the truth. The new clients have a backlog of work they need doing, so I'm going to be busy. So busy that I won't be around to hear about her dates with TJ.

'Ah. Well, I'm glad you're home because I wanted to let you know ... I'm ready.'

I'm not registering her meaning. 'Ready for what?'

Dee takes a deep breath. 'For the final test. I want to take it to the next level with TJ, but I can't until I know it's *safe*. After Sam ... Well, it was bad and I don't want to go through that again. I've thought about it a lot and it has to be now, because if I get in any deeper and he turns out to be a cheater, I'm going to get hurt.'

Fuck. The final test. The "Is He A Cheater?" Dealbreaker! I should've known this was coming.

I stare at my Kindle and the words blur. My brain starts processing what she's asking me. It's madness.

'I can't do it, Dee,' I say gently.

She nods. 'It has to be you. No one else would understand what the hell I'm asking. Besides, you owe me. Scott, remember?'

I scrunch my toes and shrink further under the duvet. There's no way I'm doing it.

Dee leans forward intently. 'Aster, I wouldn't ask you if I didn't think it was fine. What do you take me for?' Her tone is disdainful.

'What do you mean?'

She shrugs, 'I mean I'm 99.9% sure he's not going to respond. It'll just be like ticking a box. He's not a cheater, done. We can move on.'

Wait, what?

'Um ... why are you so sure he won't respond?' I ask slowly.

'You're not his type. He likes petite blondes.'

'Really. He told you that.'

'Not in so many words, but he's into me, so the chances are practically nil. It's just for peace of mind.'

'Right.' I'm not sure if Dee realises she's stoking a fire.

'So have you held hands?'

'Yes.'

'Kissed?'

'No.'

I stare at her. 'No?'

She shakes her head. 'I get the feeling he wants to, but I

haven't encouraged anything more than hand holding.'

I breathe in, then out again, and the knot in my stomach relaxes. No kissing yet. Have I been worried about that? I must've been if I'm relieved.

'Have you got any ideas for the set-up?'

'Not yet, I wanted to run them by you.'

I consider. It's fucked up but if he responds I'll know he likes me; if he doesn't then it will be so awkward that I have a good reason to never hang out with them as a couple again.

'So, will you do it?' she persists.

He's being handed to me on a platter; trussed up with an apple in his mouth, how can I resist?

'Yeah, I'll do it,' I tell her.

It's time to find out if TJ does indeed prefer petite blondes.

In the kitchen the next morning, munching on toasted muesli and almond milk, we go over the plan. It's strange, but this is the closest I've felt to Dee in a long time, it's like the old days. We're bonding; back on track; in touch with the grass roots. This is why we devised these tests in the first place. To make sure we get the good guys.

'It has to be a casual meet-up,' Dee says, taking a banana from the bowl and peeling back strips. 'If you message him out of the blue and say 'Let's go out to dinner', he'll instantly be suspicious because I'm not there.'

'Yeah, plus there'd be alcohol involved,' I agree. 'If you

have wine goggles on, anything looks attractive. We need him clear-headed, so he knows what he's doing. Otherwise, he can use the old chestnut, "I was drunk, it's not my fault, she took advantage of me".'

'Riiight.' Dee gives me a hard look.

'What I mean is that if he is a cheater, and I'm not saying he is, it will be second nature to him. He'll be that way inclined.'

'Ah, yes,' she brightens. 'Like with Scott. God, he couldn't keep it in his pants making a cup of tea.'

'Scott and I weren't together,' I remind her.

'I know, but he was invited as your date. He had a certain obligation to you. He could've said 'I'm flattered but I'm here with Aster' and I would've backed off. He didn't though, he took the opportunity presented to him.'

She's right and I feel a stab of indignity. The fucker couldn't even be faithful to me on a second date.

'I told TJ a while ago that I'd be happy to help him out with walking Maxie when he's at work. I could arrange it, so I'm still there when he gets home.'

'Perfect!' she exclaims. 'Then what?'

'Er, I say something flirtatious?'

'Like what?'

'I don't know, tell him his butt looks good or something.' I smirk, imagining TJ's face if I said that.

'He does have a great butt,' she says dreamily.

I almost say, *I know*, but bite my tongue.

'So what reaction are you expecting from him here?' I ask.

'I'd be happy with an abrupt 'thanks' and then him changing the subject. Indignation is even better.'

I scoff at that. 'I'm complimenting him on a body part, surely he's going to be flattered not indignant? He's not a monk.'

'It's just important he doesn't *respond*.'

'Respond how?'

She sighs as if I'm thick. 'Come onto you!'

'Oh, well, the chances of that are practically nil, as you said.'

Dee surveys my old baggy t-shirt, make-up free face, and messy bed-hair. 'If you go over to his place looking like that, I suspect the chances will be non-existent.'

Chapter 25

Me

Hi TJ, if Maxie needs walking, I'm happy to do it one day this week. Let me know. Aster

TJ is typing ... TJ is typing

TJ

Hey Aster, yeah, thanks, that would be brilliant. He ripped into the couch cushions last week. I had to order replacements from IKEA. What day suits?

Me

Lol, oh no! What about Thursday afternoon?

TJ

Great, I'll leave the spare key with my neighbour Eileen McPherson. She's in the basement apartment. His new lead is hanging up behind the kitchen door, he broke the other one. You know where the treats are.

Me

Yup, and the human treats.

TJ
Haha, help yourself!

And so it's done. I tell Dee I'm going round to TJ's on Thursday afternoon and we settle into an anticipatory waiting period for the next few days. I can tell she's apprehensive by the running stream of chatter she keeps up whenever we're in the same room.

'I don't have to do it,' I say finally, after she's repeated a work story for the third time while we're chopping ingredients for a stir-fry.

Dee gives a brittle laugh, instantly knowing what I'm talking about. 'I'm fine. Don't mind me. It's just a weird situation. I'm trying not to think about it.'

'Have you spoken to TJ lately?'

She starts at his name, then continues slicing a carrot. 'No. Not for a few days. But that's normal for us. We don't message or call each other just to chat. Only to arrange stuff or relay information. But I like that, it means I'm not always checking my phone.'

'Oh.'

I think about TJ ringing me from the airport when I was house sitting. He didn't have to get in touch; there was no reason I needed to know his flight was delayed. It felt like he was calling just to chat.

I kept thinking you were going to call me in France ...

On Thursday afternoon I walk over to TJ's flat. Eileen is pleasant enough and hands me the key when I tell her who I am and why I'm there. 'Oooh, you're brave walking that Max, he's a naughty doggie. I took him for walkies once but never again. He almost pulled my arm out of my socket.'

'I know, he's a handful. I thought I might do a run with him, so he can burn off some energy.'

Eileen looks me up and down and arches a pencil thin eyebrow as if to say 'good luck with that.'

I'm in black jean cut-offs that end around the bum crease and a tight purple racerback tank-top with an inbuilt bra. I know I'm showing a lot of tanned skin with only a nod to boob support. My sexy DIY activewear isn't ideal for running, but Eileen doesn't need to know I've got another purpose for it: tempting TJ. Hah, it sounds like the title of an indie erotica novel featuring a guy with ripped abs on the cover.

It's lovely out as I stroll to the Meadows with Maxie in tow. He's seen me tuck the dog treats in my back pocket, so he keeps jumping up at my butt. 'No, Maxie! You'll get a treat shortly,' I tell him sternly. It doesn't have much effect though. Right, time for a run, so he exhausts himself.

A guy about my age wearing shorts and a muscle t-shirt strolls past with a whippet while I'm doing some limbering up exercises. He pauses to let his dog and Maxie sniff noses.

'Cute,' he says, 'What's its name?' He seems friendly and I notice him checking out my legs as I do a quad stretch.

'Max, he's a Cockapoo.'

'You off for a run?'

'Yeah.'

'Well, I'll let you get on with it.'

I take off at a steady jog with Maxie bounding along beside me then look back over my shoulder, and see the guy is still watching. Woah, maybe I've been missing out on a whole other section of the dating market: male dog owners. I can see the potential; a few loops round the park, collect some numbers and get fit in the process. The Meadows is full of them as well. Is this where all the good men have been hiding?

I have a thoroughly awesome time running around the park, getting loads of sunshine and fresh air, as well as smiling and nodding at all the cute male dog owners. Maxie is happy because he gets dog treats every time I'm puffed and have to stop for a breather, which is quite a lot since I'm not that fit. My short shorts get a few disapproving looks from the yummy mummies with strollers, but fuck them. It's a warm day, and there are other women running around with a lot less on than I am.

I'm enjoying myself so much that I almost forget I'm there on a mission. It's half an hour until TJ arrives home and I have to be there when he gets back, so I can say something complimentary, endure his non-response, and then leave with my tail between my legs.

Of course, as I mentioned to Dee, this is going to make things awkward when TJ and I bump into each other at our flat. But she said that she'll spend more time at his after this, so it won't be a problem. I look down at Maxie trotting along beside me and say to him, 'Looks like you might have Dee walking you from now on, mate. I'm going to be persona non grata.' I know that TJ is going to think badly of me for flirting with him. It's likely going to ruin the friendship that we've formed. But my friendship with Dee is more important; she's got my back and I've got hers.

I barely make it back to the flat, hang up Maxie's lead, and put the kettle on when I hear TJ's key turning in the lock. Maxie bounds down the hallway, then there's the usual rough and tumble and doggy talk. Here we go, I think. I lean against the counter and attempt to look casually alluring.

TJ comes into the kitchen frowning, flicking through his mail, with Maxie padding behind him. His face relaxes into a smile when he clocks me. I melt a little when he doesn't hide the fact he's pleased to see me.

'Hey! I thought I heard the kettle. You're still here.'

'Yeah, the outing to the park took longer than expected. I'm making tea if you want some?'

'Yes, please.' He sits down at the table and starts going

through his mail. 'Ugh, why do they post me these things. Do I look like I need beard products?'

He holds up a flyer showing a hipster guy with a huge bushy beard.

I giggle.

'How did you get on with Maxie?' he asks, rubbing him with his foot where he's lying under the table.

'Oh, fine. We went for a run. Made some new doggy friends. I tired him out for you.'

'Good, thanks!'

I plonk down TJ's tea on the table and peer over his shoulder just as he flicks open an Ann Summers lingerie catalogue. Hmm, time to start flirting, since I've got free reign to do so.

'Dee would love that,' I say pointing at a blue lacy bra and knicker set modelled by a well-endowed girl. 'If you're thinking of getting her a present.'

TJ slips the catalogue underneath the beard flyer and pushes them aside.

'I don't think so.'

I sit down and blow on my tea. 'Yeah, it probably wouldn't stay on too long. You'd be better off with something crotchless.'

A pink tinge creeps up TJ's neck and he sips his tea without saying anything. I know I'm making him squirm and I'm loving it.

'I don't mind tagging along if you want to go to Ann Summers. I could try some things on and you can see if you like them,' I suggest. 'I'm about the same bust size as Dee. But she might be larger. What do you think?'

I push my chest out to see if he takes a gander.

TJ doesn't look my way, just takes another sip of tea and tears open a white, official-looking envelope. 'I wouldn't hazard a guess,' he says dryly.

Wow, not even a boob glance. So far he's squeaky clean, I'd be happy with that if I were Dee.

But is what I'm doing enough to encourage him to come onto me if he is a cheater? I'm embarrassing him, not complimenting him. He's sitting down, so I can't say he's got a nice butt. I'll try something general.

'Have you done something different with your hair? It's very Leonardo di Caprio. In fact, you do look a lot like him,' I say in surprise as if I've just realised it.

TJ gives a snort of disbelief. 'I don't think so.'

'Ah well, perhaps not completely, just round the eyes ...' I trail off, not sure where I'm going with that.

'Are you a fan of Leo then?' he asks.

'Oh, yeah. He was great in *The Revenant*. So hot.'

'He got mauled by a bear and spent most of the movie flat on his back trying to heal his wounds. Then he was covered in scars,' says TJ deadpan.

'Well, he was still babelicious.' *Babelicious?*

TJ's mouth quirks into a smile. 'You're funny.'

'Am I?'

'Aye, you are. Asterrr the star girl,' he says softly, our eyes meet and my stomach does a strange little quiver.

'I should go,' I say and gulp down the rest of my tea. Flirting time is over, he's passed the test with flying colours.

'I'll walk you to the door.'

'It's OK.'

'I insist.'

'Fine.'

Maxie heaves a large sigh under the table and I feel like doing that myself. When we get to the door TJ enquires, 'Did you have a jacket or anything?'

I shake my head.

'Well, thanks for taking Maxie out, he's zonked.'

'Hah, me too, I think I'll be in bed early tonight,' I say leaning against the doorframe to pull on my shoes. I straighten up and catch TJ gazing at me with a wistful expression that I know all too well. I can't resist giving it one last shot. 'What about you? When are you off to bed?' I murmur, tilting my head and peeking up at him coyly through my lashes.

TJ's gaze intensifies making me shiver and goosebumps scud along my arms. His eyes search mine like he's testing to see if I'm joking, but I hold my ground staring into their silvery depths. There's a charged pause and I think he's not going to reply, but he says in a low husky voice, 'I thought maybe now. If you're interested ...'

I nod imperceptibly and a smile spreads across his face. TJ tips my chin up with his forefinger and, as his mouth inches towards mine, all I can think is, 'Aster, you're in soooo much trouble.'

Chapter 26

Carefully, I insert my key into the lock and turn it slowly until it clicks. I creep down the hall quieter than a mouse wearing felt booties. I'm hoping I can make it to the stairs, creep up them and get to my room without Dee hearing. A faint strip of yellow glows underneath her door so I know she's in there. But a dodgy floorboard gives an almighty creak and instantly her voice rings out, 'Aster, is that you?' in a plaintive tone.

My shoulders, which have been hunched around my ears, slump in despair. Shit. Time to face the music.

'Yes, it's me.'

'Can you come into my room, please?'

I feel like I've been summoned to the headmistress' office as I open her door. Dee's sitting up in bed with a book. Her blonde hair is in a loose bun and thick-rimmed black reading glasses are perched on her nose. She actually does look like a headmistress come to think of it.

'Well?' she asks, laying her book down. 'What happened?' Her eyes bore into me like hard blue beads and my upper lip breaks out in sweat.

There's no other way to say it. I just have to tell her the truth. I open my mouth, but I can't form the words. So I close it again.

Dee frowns. 'Come on. It can't be that bad. Did he look at your boobs? Was it a hug that went on for longer than usual?'

Oh God. I can't say it. She's going to freak.

'What *was it*? Just tell me!' she sounds panicked.

'I ... we ... um ... he kissed me,' I say in a small voice.

I close my eyes tightly, waiting for the screech of indignation. The sound of bare feet padding across the floor. The sting on my cheek as she slaps me hard and the accusation of 'slut!' ringing in the air.

But the longer I wait, nothing happens. I open one eye tentatively. But the expression on Dee's face isn't annoyed or even distressed. She's just sitting there looking incredulous.

'He *kissed* you?' she asks.

I nod. Then Dee does something even more unexpected— she laughs.

Now I'm incredulous. Why the hell is she laughing?

'Why is TJ kissing me so funny?' I ask, annoyed.

But she just shakes her head and can't reply for chuckling.

Eventually she calms down. 'It's just, well, your face. You looked so *afraid*. Did you think I was going to slap you or something?'

'Er, yeah, I did actually. I'm not sure why you're taking it so well.'

Dee wipes her eyes with the edge of the bedsheet. 'To be honest, knowing your history, I was expecting you to say you'd slept with him. But a kiss. That's nothing.'

'Um, it kind of *is* something.' I decide to let the dig about 'my history' pass for the moment.

She waves away my comment with her hand. 'Well, it makes sense that it would happen. I haven't let him kiss me yet, and you're my flatmate. He was naturally picturing me in his head.'

I stare at her, she's not getting it. 'Dee,' I say in a gentle tone. 'TJ likes me and I like him. Look, I'm wearing his hoodie. He gave it to me because he was worried I'd get cold.'

He wanted me to stay over, but I said no because I felt too guilty about ... everything. His dark-blue hoodie is miles too big for me, but it's snuggly and warm. The collar of it smells like him and I was turning my head and snuffling it all the way home. He was going to drive me, but I said I needed time to think, so I walked—slowly, because I knew I'd have this to face when I got here.

Dee screws up her nose and shrugs. 'So he let you borrow his hoodie. Big deal. That means nothing.'

I'm getting frustrated. Has she heard anything I've just said about us liking each other? She seems to be in denial. I'm not sure what I can say to make it any clearer. I don't want to hurt her, but she appears determined to cling to the fantasy of her and TJ. And that's all it is, a fantasy of her own making. She built the foundation and Isadora got in on the act once she got wind of TJ's inheritance. Together they've constructed a house of cards and have been busily decorating it and filling it with designer furniture. It's about to come tumbling down.

I try again. 'Dee, he's not interested in you that way.'

'What are you talking about? Of course he is!'

'Dee ...'

'I've heard enough, Aster. I'll talk to TJ tomorrow and sort it out. Just go.'

There's nothing for it but to do as she says. I stand outside her door and scream silently into the sleeve of TJs hoodie. Arrrgh, this is so fucked up!

I take off my make-up, have a quick shower and get changed into a clean tank top and boxers. In my room, I lie on my bed and try to clear my head so I can get some sleep. I have a feeling I'm going to need to have my wits about me in the coming days. But I keep getting distracted by thoughts of TJ. By what we did. I told Dee the truth, that we'd kissed. But there was some other stuff that I didn't go into detail about.

As soon as TJ's lips met mine, I lost control of my senses. I don't have much willpower when it comes to resisting male advances at the best of times, but this was on a whole other level: electric, passionate, and all consuming.

Eventually we came up for air and he hugged me saying 'I've wanted to do that for ages.' We stood for a while with our arms around each other, me feeling giddy from the kiss and astonished that it was even happening. But then my libido kicked in and I slipped a hand down to squeeze his butt and he slid a hand up under my top and we kissed again while his hand roamed over my breasts and I ran my fingers through his hair. Somewhere in between our tongues entwining, him toying with my nipples, and Maxie wandering out to see why he wasn't getting his dinner, my brain made an appearance and I swiftly pushed his hand away. 'I shouldn't be doing this.'

TJ stepped back, frowning. 'Sorry, I thought you wanted to.'

'I do, but you and Dee. I should go.'

I turned to unlock the door, my heart pumping wildly, thinking *Oh no, what have I done, Dee is going to freak!*

Then I heard TJ say from behind me. 'Wait, Aster. There is no me and Dee.'

I turned back to face him. 'What?'

He said again, 'There is no me and Dee.'

'That's what I thought you said.'

TJ sighed. 'I think we better have a talk. And I need to feed Maxie. Can you stay a bit longer? I'll make another cup of tea.'

Leaving Maxie to chomp on his dinner, we went through to the lounge with cups of tea and a block of Cadbury Rocky Road from the treat cupboard on TJ's admission, 'we need sugar, lots of it.' By this time, I was feeling exposed in my short shorts and barely-there tank top, particularly after the make out session by the front door. The ruse Dee and I had cooked up felt contrived and ridiculous. So I gladly tucked the faux fur throw around me on the couch and admired the new IKEA cushions for want of something to say.

'Very comfy.'

'They're foam. The others had duck feathers, it was a bitch of a job vacuuming them up when Maxie ripped into the cushions.'

I laughed a little and it broke the tension.

TJ sat on the floor cross-legged with his back against the couch and snapped the chocolate into bits. He offered me a piece.

His neck was right there tempting me to kiss it but I resisted touching him and pulled the throw tighter around me. 'So is this going to be a "I like you, but it's complicated" story?' I said nibbling on my chocolate.

'No, it's a "I like you full stop" story. After London, after the massage, I thought it was pretty obvious. I tried to tell you, but it came out sounding more like fatherly advice.'

'You can do better than those online jerks,' I quoted him in a pompous voice.

'Yeah. I tried to find out unsubtly from Dee if you were seeing someone when she came to my room to apologise for her behaviour, and she told me she thought you were. It was confusing because you hadn't mentioned it the night before.

Anyway, I decided to keep my distance.'

'And why you got her the hot chocolate at the station and not me.' It sounded so petty, when I said it.

'You didn't want one.'

'I never said that.'

TJ took his phone from his pocket and scrolled through his messages with Dee. There, as clear as day, was a message from her: *Can you get me a hot choc pls, Aster doesn't want one x*

Ho, sly fox. 'So you're not interested in her like that?'

'I was flattered she asked me out and I was happy to get to know her. But we don't have anything in common. Besides, her parents ...' TJ shook his head. 'That whole weekend was a real eye opener. I think if she *was* interested in me, she should've kept them away from me for as long as possible. And Teddy. Ay caramba. He'd eat poor Maxie for breakfast.'

'I think your inheritance may be having a part to play,' I said. 'I didn't think Dee cared about that, but I know Isadora does.'

The muscles in TJ's neck stiffened. 'Oh, you know about it. Did she tell you?'

'No, I overheard Isadora talking to her friend in the garden. She mentioned it and made it sound like you and Dee were a done deal. She was practically picking out Dee's wedding dress and a baby cot for good measure.'

TJ groaned. 'I have to nip this in the bud right now. Dee keeps asking me out and I keep accepting, she's hard to say no to. Now I've met Isadora, I see where she gets it from.'

'So where do I fit into all this?'

TJ looked down at his knees. 'You really want to know?'

'Yeah.'

He inhaled and said in a rush. 'You're smart, funny and sexy as hell. And I want you. That's what I should've said when you were lying there in front of me looking like a glistening goddess.'

Yup, that did it.

'Hmm, it looks uncomfortable on the floor. Do you want to join me under here?'

I lifted the edge of the faux fur throw and he tilted his head back and smiled at me. 'I thought you'd never ask.'

Chapter 27

I'm exhausted by the drama of the evening and sleep heavily. The next morning, I wake up feeling a weird mix of happy and apprehensive. Happy, because of TJ, and apprehensive because of Dee. From last night's conversation, I don't think she's going to give up that easily. Or if she's forced to, she's going to make things difficult for me. Perhaps I need to start looking for a new place to live right away.

I'm reluctant to stay in the flat any longer than I have to, so I quickly dress, collect my laptop and handbag, and head up to WeWork. Thank God, I have a neutral zone I can go to, somewhere filled with people who have no idea what's going on in my personal life.

I head out to the terrace to soak up the morning sun with a coffee, but as soon as I sit down my phone flashes with TJ's name. My stomach lurches.

'Morning,' I answer.

'Hi, how're you? Get a good night's sleep?' he teases.

'Hah,' I say, feeling heat bloom in my cheeks. That's a loaded question if there ever was one. 'Yeah, I did, thanks. I think I needed it.'

I hear the sound of footsteps and ambient traffic noise on the line. 'Where are you?'

'Just heading to my car. I was going to walk, but I'm running late so I'll drive in.' A pause. 'So, did you see her last night?'

'Um, yeah, it didn't go so well. She's totally in denial. You're going to have to talk to her.'

TJ grunts. 'Right. I wanted to get the lie of the land before I ring her. I'll do it now before I get to the office.'

'OK. Good luck.'

'Thanks. I'll let you know how it goes.' I hear the electronic beep of his car door clicking open. 'Aster, last night was …' he pauses searching for the right word and fails to come up with anything suitably descriptive.

Incredible, astounding, magical.

'I know, it was … Just, please, talk to her.'

I get a message from him mid-morning:

I rang her, but it went to voicemail and she hasn't rung back. I'll try again at lunch-time.

Then another at lunch:

TJ
Still voicemail. I get the feeling she's not picking up because she can see it's me. Maybe I should do it by message.

Me
That looks cowardly.

TJ
True. OK, I'll keep trying.

I don't hear anything for the rest of the afternoon and by four-thirty I'm completely strung out. I can't concentrate on work, I've hardly eaten anything, and I've drunk so much coffee my head is all over the place. Waiting is torturous. At last, I get a message from TJ.

TJ
It's done. I rang her from my work phone and she picked up.

Me
How did she take it?

TJ
Not well.

Me
Shit.

TJ
Are you at the flat?

Me
No, WeWork.

TJ
You might not have a good reception when you get home. Let me know if you need an escape tonight. x

Me
OK. I'll message you. x

Great, this is going to be fun. I pack up my stuff and walk slowly back to the flat, feeling as if my stomach is filled with lead. The shit's about to hit the fan.

As soon as I let myself in, I hear a commotion upstairs, it seems to be coming from the kitchen. The sound gets louder and louder as I approach, until I enter the room and am bombarded with thrash metal, steam, open wine bottles, clamouring pots and a whole heap of bad attitude. It's like a party going off but without the fun stuff.

Dee is in the middle of it all, wearing her Gordon Ramsay apron over her work uniform. Her hair is a wild frizzy mess, her cheeks are red, and her mouth pinched looking. She seems to be chopping, swigging wine, and stirring all at once.

'Dee!' I call out to her but she doesn't reply.

I lean over the island, press pause on her Spotify, and the nonsensical raging of the Metal Monks thankfully mutes.

'Oh, it's *you*,' she says balefully, giving me an icy glare.

She reaches over and deliberately presses play on her Spotify and turns the Metal Monks up even louder until it's an earsplitting roar.

There's no way I can talk to her when she's like this, so I leave her to it and go and have a long shower during which I shampoo my hair three times, then put on a five-minute conditioning mask for good measure. When I get out, music is still blaring from the kitchen, but the song is now Sinead O'Connor's *Nothing Compares 2 U* and Dee's singing along—badly. Wow, she's really milking it.

I drag a comb through my hair, slicking it back, and put on underwear, a clean t-shirt, and jeans. I head to the kitchen again to find her chopping onions and sniffling. Oh no, it's like Sam all over again, she's on an emotional roller-coaster. Though if she wasn't actually going out with TJ, I'm not sure where all this excess emotion is coming from.

'Dee?'

She doesn't reply, just ignores me and continues caterwauling along with Sinead.

'Dee, look at me.'

She ignores me.

'Maybe if you turn off the ...'

Sinead reaches the part about going to the doctor and this sets Dee off into a fresh bout of angry chopping on the onions since TJ is kind of a doctor. I try again when she's finished.

'Can we talk ...'

'No, we can't!' she screeches, now looking straight at me

and brandishing the knife. 'I have nothing to say to the slut who's *stolen my husband!*'

I recoil from the insult as Sinead croons on despairingly. But something inside me snaps and a red mist descends over my brain. I scream back at her at full bore, 'He's not your bloody husband! And I'm not a slut! Get a fucking grip you ... you selfish, stuck-up *bitch!*'

Dee's mouth hangs open in shock and Sinead starts gearing up into full vocals for the chorus.

But I've had it. I do a quick U-turn and march out of the kitchen. In my room, I swiftly put on runners, grab TJ's hoodie, my wallet, phone, and keys. Then take the stairs two at a time. I'm in such a hurry to leave, I almost plunge down them headfirst. I grip the banister tightly trying to slow down, imagining Dee is up there willing me to break my neck. *Go on, slut, then I can have him.* Damned if I'm going to give her the satisfaction!

Outside the flat I take big gulps of fresh air, my heart pounding fit to burst from caffeine and post-confrontation trauma. That was bad. So bad. Did I expect we'd sit down over a cup of tea and have a nice chat? Realistically, no. But Dee screaming that I'm a slut and threatening me with a knife while Sinead O'Connor provided the background music? That was way down the list of possible scenarios.

Another possibility for her outburst occurs to me. Did TJ tell her? We didn't discuss any details, he just said that he'd sort it out. Maybe I am a slut because we did sleep together.

Right there on the couch. We didn't even make it into the bedroom. It was *incredible, astounding, magical* ...

With a shaking hand I phone him and start walking. Before he even says hi, I blurt 'I'm headed towards Princes Street. Can you meet me?'

'Sure, I'll meet you halfway.'

I stop and do some deep breathing to try and calm down my heart rate which is going through the roof.

'What happened?'

I give a shaky laugh. 'There was screaming ... There was a knife.'

'Jesus! Are you OK?'

'I'm fine, just a bit shaken. I felt like I was in *Single White Female* there for a moment, but I managed to escape with my limbs intact.'

'Thank God.'

'Did ... did you tell her about ... you know?'

'No, but I think she might have guessed because she asked me and I said it was none of her business.'

'It's OK, she would've found out eventually, I guess. You don't have regrets, do you?'

TJ doesn't say anything and I start getting stressed. 'Hello, are you there?'

'Sorry, I was getting Maxie a treat. No way! Definitely no regrets.'

I can breathe normally again. 'OK.' As long as he doesn't

have regrets, I can handle anything.

TJ messages along the way and says he's at The Grosvenor in Shandwick Place, so I steer towards there. By the time I arrive, I'm shattered. He's ordering a beer, but as soon as he sees me, he says to the barman, 'Can I get a whisky too?'

We share a tight hug and he whispers 'Doctor's orders' in my ear.

'Thanks, I think I may need more than one,' I say, and look around for a free table. 'Can we sit down? I need some food.'

'Yeah, go through. I'll just pay for these.'

When we've found a spot and ordered, I slump, staring blankly at the table, feeling emotionally exhausted. I could put my head on my arms and quite happily go to sleep right there in the pub.

'Drink some whisky,' urges TJ. 'It'll help.'

'I don't think anything will help.' But I do as he says, and take a sip. It burns my throat and makes my ears warm.

TJ rubs my hand. 'Was it really bad?'

'Yeah. I've seen her upset before, but not like this. She was practically manic.'

Guilt passes across TJ's features. 'It's my fault. I've spent too much time hanging out with her. It's not like I don't enjoy her company, but there's just no spark there. I thought she felt the same. She never seemed to want anything more. I guess me agreeing to the London trip and being her plus one made her think I did. But then she invited you, so I thought it was more of a group trip. I don't know, it's confusing.'

I hesitate with my reply, not wanting to go into the whole "Meet the Parents" Dealbreaker that was in play for London, and Dee telling me that she'd asked him out. It makes her sound like a crazy person. I take another sip of whisky. Then our platters of fish 'n' chips arrive, so I use eating as an excuse.

Afterwards, TJ goes to get another beer and I check my phone. Nothing from Dee. My gut shifts uneasily. An image flashes into my mind of her standing stock still in the kitchen holding the knife, her mouth hanging open.

'I know it doesn't sound like the smartest thing right now, but I think I should go and check on her.'

TJ nods grimly. 'Aye, makes sense. You're a good friend.'

'I'm not. If I was, I wouldn't have bonked you last night,' I mutter morosely.

He arches an eyebrow. 'Is that all it was? A bonk.'

'Of course not, that came out wrong,' I say hastily. 'You know what I mean. I'm just feeling like a shitty friend.'

TJ laces his fingers through mine. 'It's understandable that you'd feel like that, but you haven't done anything wrong. She's making out we were in a relationship and we weren't. If we were, I didn't know about it. I mean, apart from the odd hug, I haven't even touched her. She's completely overreacting.'

'Didn't you hold hands though?'

'I don't think so.' TJ frowns as if trying to remember.

I look down at our joined hands. 'Not like this?'

'Definitely not like this.'

I feel a smidgeon better.

'Are you going to stay there tonight?' he asks. 'I don't want you getting skewered in your sleep.'

I give a little laugh and finish off my whisky. 'I don't think it will come to that. She's probably calmed down by now.'

'You're welcome to stay at mine if you change your mind.' He says it nonchalantly, but there's an underlying need in his voice and I know what he really wants.

'I can't,' I say softly. 'I want to. But I can't. Not until things calm down. Besides, my laptop's at the flat and I've got work I need to do tomorrow.'

'Well, it was worth a shot,' he says briskly, avoiding my eyes and downing the last of his beer. 'Yeah, I need to get back soon too.'

'Thanks for this, for meeting me. It's helped.'

'Least I can do since I got you into this mess.'

'Oh, I think we both got into it together.'

He stares into my eyes. 'No regrets though, right?'

I shake my head. 'Nope, no regrets.'

Chapter 28

I catch a cab back to the flat around nine and, like last night, try not to make a sound when I'm opening the door. But it's all dark and quiet on the Western front. Only when I'm creeping quietly up the stairs do I hear it. A muffled sob coming from Dee's room. Then another. Oh no.

Padding back down, I listen at her door. There are more sobs. My heart breaks a little. I can never not go to her when she's crying.

'Dee?' I push open the door. It's dark and stuffy. I can barely make out her faint outline curled up into a ball on the bed. I shuffle over to her bed and my foot kicks something that makes a metallic twanging noise. My nostrils flare when the smell of vomit hits. But at least she had the foresight to use a bowl. Silently, I pick up the bowl and go into her en suite, tip the contents down the loo without looking, flush, then rinse it out in the sink, trying not gag.

When I go back to the bed, the sobbing seems to have stopped. I sit on the side of her bed gingerly and put my hand on her shoulder. She doesn't pull away and, after a while, I feel her forehead. She's hot and sweaty like she's been lying here for hours.

'Can I switch on the bedside light?' I ask.

She nods and flinches from the light, hiding her face with her hands. I notice then she's still in her work clothes, as well as the Gordon Ramsay apron. She removes her hands from her face. It's blotchy and puffy; her eyes swollen slits. She looks drugged. But it's just from crying. Also, I don't think much of the wine ended up in the cooking. The knife is nowhere in sight, thankfully. I feel glad I didn't stay at TJ's, seeing the state she's in.

'Come on, let's get you changed.'

I find a clean t-shirt in one of her drawers and help her sit up. Her limbs are floppy and she doesn't seem able to cooperate, it's like trying to undress a life-size porcelain doll. Somehow, I manage to get a t-shirt on her and tuck her in under the duvet.

She still hasn't said anything. I sit there and hold her hand, trying to be silently supportive.

I'm in a reverie and almost nodding off when Dee says, 'Thanks.'

Her voice startles me but it's a relief that she sounds normal.

'That's OK. Do you want some water?'

'Yes, please.'

I hand over her water bottle from the bedside table and she sits up and almost drinks the entire thing. Then flops back down on the bed again with an anguished gasp. 'I feel sick.'

I pick up the bowl and bring it next to her but she pushes it away blindly. 'No, no.'

'Maybe sit up. Just in case'

She sits up groggily leaning forward and I rub her back. God, how much did she drink? I'm considering calling 999 when she gives a deep sigh. 'I feel a bit better.'

'I'll get you some more water.'

When I return, she sips it slowly.

'Thanks,' she says again.

Her colour is better and she looks more awake. She gathers her thick hair into a topknot with an elastic from her wrist. I hand her a washcloth I've rinsed out in cold water, so she can wipe her face.

'How much did you drink?'

'I'm not sure. I would've slept it off.'

'I guess,' I say.

'I didn't think you'd be home tonight,' she says dully, leaning back on the pillow.

There's a barb in there, but I don't react to it and just say, 'I was worried about you.'

'Were you with TJ?'

There's no point in lying. 'Yes, we were at a pub. I was upset and he met me there.'

She grunts. 'Nice that you had someone to comfort you.'

'Dee, you can't make me feel any worse. I already feel like shit.'

She folds her arms in headmistress mode. 'You knew I liked him. Yet you went ahead and shagged him. I guess that's no surprise.'

I hang my head. Ouch. 'I'm sorry. I know you liked him. But I think you're overreacting a little.'

'I don't think so. He was the first nice guy I've been out with since Sam,' she says sharply. 'We've spent time together and get on well. I introduced him to my parents. Doesn't that count for something?'

'And there's his inheritance ... I heard Isadora on the phone,' I say hesitantly.

Dee gives a dismissive grunt. 'Oh yes, Mummy thought a lot more highly of TJ when I told her about that.'

Yup, I think.

'But it's not about that for me, that was to keep them off my back,' Dee continues. 'I liked him despite it.'

Her voice is getting that high pitched squeaky tone that means she's going to cry again. I grab her hand. 'There are other guys out there. He's not the only nice one in Edinburgh.'

'Are you serious? You've seen what's online,' she scoffs. 'I keep getting lewd messages from guys obsessed with women in yoga pants. They're so awful that I can't even be bothered sending them the screening test. I don't want to go out with any of them.'

'But you broke out of that. You did so well with meeting TJ, you can do it again.'

'Yeah, I did all the groundwork, and you ruined it. I found him first.'

'He's not a toy. We shouldn't be fighting over him.'

'So you'll stop seeing him then?' she challenges.

I let out a breath. 'I really like him though.'

'Well, so do I.'

'But he likes me.'

'Maybe he's just been ... waylaid by you.'

Waylaid?

'What did he actually say on the phone?' I ask.

'That he was attracted to you.'

'And what did you say?'

'I asked him if you'd slept together and he said it was none of my business. That's when I knew you had. I told him he shouldn't get his hopes up with you. You know you're the queen of one-night stands, Aster. I knew it was a risk sending you to tempt him and that I'd get hurt. But, in retrospect, the fact that you've slept with him is a good thing. Now it's out of the way, I'm pretty sure if I wait a couple of weeks, he'll come crawling back to me. Once you've got him out of your system.'

What the hell? I drop her hand like a hot stone. I haven't given Dee enough credit. She's playing the long game with TJ. It's like Isadora trying to win Michael all over again.

I'm not sure if Dee told him any details about my dating history, but I'm relieved to see a message from TJ when I go upstairs to my room.

Hi, I'm off to bed. Hope Dee's OK and you're still in one piece. X

That's nice of him to be worried about her. Little does he know he's in danger of being recruited into the Crowley-Smythe family tree whether he likes it or not! I decide to keep a lid on that for the moment.

Hey, she had too much to drink, and is sleeping it off. No severed limbs. Miss you. Xx

I get an instant reply.

Miss you too. Any chance of meeting up tomorrow night?

I'm torn. I start typing, trying to get across that I want him but it's not the right time and hope that he'll understand:

I want to but Dee ... [delete]
Maybe we shouldn't ... [delete]
Perhaps let's wait ... [delete]

Fuck it. I'm not going to stand aside submissively and let her get TJ by default. I need to fight for him:

Yes, definitely xx

The kitchen looks like a bomb site when I go in there late next morning. There's mess everywhere. Empty wine bottles lying on their sides, half a loaf of bread with the middle gouged out of it (was that her dinner?), a saucepan with a greenish-brown sludge in the bottom, possibly lentils and kale (the jury's still out on that one), spice canisters that have rolled onto the floor spilling their contents.

And sitting at the kitchen table with a cup of coffee and calmly reading is a woman. I stare at her uncomprehendingly until the realisation hits me. It's Rosie. She's come home this morning and walked into all this.

She glances at me with a bemused smile. 'Hi. Did you guys have a party last night? Pity I missed it.'

'Yeah, a get together with some friends,' I say cagily.

'Sounds fun.' She surveys me with a critical eye, looking perfectly groomed as usual. Her brown bob even has a curling-tong wave through it. I feel like an untidy tramp in comparison. 'You look a bit rough,' she remarks.

'Yeah.' *Thanks for pointing out the obvious, Rosie.*

'Cool, well, I've got some errands to run in town but we should catch up properly soon, maybe have a flat dinner one night or something? I've got a few weeks off, so I should be around a bit more. Maybe we can have another party.' She eyes the burnt orange dust trail of paprika on the floor.

'That sounds great.' I try to inject enthusiasm into my tone. 'I'm out tonight, but Dee should be around.'

'Great, I'll chat to her about the rent then.'

'Rent?'

'Yes, I got an email from her last night. She's putting up the rent. It's quite a big increase which was rather a surprise.'

It's news to me too, but I go along with it.

'Ah, yes, the rent, hah! Yeah, that's a bummer.'

She nods and gives me a quick hug then says bye and leaves, not bothering to clear away her coffee cup sitting on the table. Grrr, am I a maid now? And what about the kitchen? Do I leave it for Dee or clean it up? I'm itching just to leave it, bugger her.

But I end up tidying because I can't bear to look at the mess. Typical, Rosie is away for weeks then she turns up in the middle of a shit show. I wonder if I should warn her that Dee's under the weather and won't be up for talking about much of anything, let alone rent. What the hell is that about?

At WeWork, I check my emails and sure enough there's one from Dee sent to Rosie and me at 9.40pm last night, about ten minutes after I left to go up to my room:

Hi guys,

Due to mortgage interest rates skyrocketing, plus the increasing rents in the area, my parents have decided to put the rent up. I'll let you know the exact figure shortly, but it looks like it will be an extra eighty pounds a month. Sorry for the inconvenience and hope you understand.

Edie

I inhale sharply. Another eighty pounds a month! Shit. Dee's severely pissed off about TJ and twisting the knife to make life difficult for me. And she's dragging Rosie into it too!

Chapter 29

Still reeling from the rent increase email, I receive another nasty surprise during the morning when one of my regular clients drops me without warning. I'm getting panicked that Dee's been contacting people behind my back and telling them I'm a slut and they shouldn't work with me. I know it's just paranoia, but it's starting to feel like that.

The only high point of the day is a message from TJ saying he's looking forward to seeing me tonight. It's a sweetener taking the edge off the bitter taste in my mouth. And the more I think about Dee's email, the more it irritates me.

On impulse, I log into Trello and bring up the dating board. I have quite a long list of cards in "Aster-Rejects" and a couple in "Aster-Potentials". Dee has only one card "TJ-physio" under "Edie-Seeing". I delete my "Potentials" and shift TJ's card over to my "Seeing" column.

If she wants to play dirty, then I'm happy to oblige.

I spend the rest of the afternoon job hunting and editing an indie author's debut dystopian novel. It's about aliens landing on earth and setting up social media accounts to troll people and make them commit suicide as part of a master plan to take over the world. For a first novel, I'm quietly impressed, though he's been overzealous with the semicolons and I'm patiently weeding them out.

I'm in the ladies' doing a "natural but naughty" make-up look when I get an email notification telling me that Edie has moved the "TJ-physio" card back under her name. Annoyance jerks through me. Seriously? I log in on my phone and put him back under mine. Five minutes later, another notification. She's moved him back again.

This goes on, backwards and forwards, until I reach TJ's flat, where, on my latest move, I can't resist including a comment:

Having a date with him now.

Hah, that'll teach her. But moments later, she moves him back and comments:

Say hi from me.

I'm chewing on this latest development when TJ opens the door with a 'Hey'. I pocket my phone and give him a hug which turns into a smooching session on the front doorstep, with Maxie jumping up at us wanting attention. When he starts barking, we part lips breathlessly and smile at each other. 'Nice to see you too,' I say, giving TJ another quick peck and bending down to rub Maxie's ears. 'Hello. You're a noisy boy tonight.'

'Come in, I'm sorting out dinner, ours and his.'

'Ooh, what's on the menu? I'm starving.'

'It's a surprise. Perhaps not a good one. My cooking skills need some practice.' He laughs and looks bashful which makes me want to kiss him again.

But I just say 'Smells good whatever it is.'

When I'm following him down the hallway to the kitchen, I take out my phone and move his card back to mine and quickly type:

Sorry too busy kissing him to relay messages.

Sorry not sorry, hah!

I don't hear back and imagine that's sent Dee straight to the nearest bottle shop and then to her room for another bout of crying. I sit quietly at the table watching TJ cook and feeling guilty that I've caused her pain. My phone buzzes. Expecting to see a barrage of insults, I peer at her message and do a double take. She's moved him back to her column and commented:

I hope he used tongue.

A loud snort escapes before I can stop it. TJ turns with a

querying look and a half smile. 'Seen something funny?'

'Um, yeah, a Reddit post.'

'Can you send it to me? If you think it's funny, I'm sure I will.'

'Ah, sure.' That's nice of him to say but yikes, now I have to find something that will make him crack up. No pressure.

I do a quick search for "funny dog videos reddit" and send him one of a dog chasing its tail and falling into a swimming pool. He watches it while he's stirring and chuckles.

Phew. Maxie hooks his head onto my lap and stares at me with his soulful brown eyes. *Yes, I know, I fibbed to your owner.*

TJ puts two gleaming white plates on the table and piles on what looks like beef goulash, a side of rice, and a whole heap of beansprouts on top. It looks ... interesting. 'It's Hungarian,' he explains when he sees me staring. 'Our receptionist gave me the recipe the other day when I said I wanted to try something international to, er, impress someone.'

I assume the someone is me, and hope it tastes a whole lot better than it looks. 'You're brave taking on a Hungarian recipe for a first date.'

'Oh, is this a first date?' he teases.

'Well, I assumed, since you're in your first date garb.' He's wearing the suit pants and shirt he wore to the Scrabble evening, with an apron over the top.

'That was an interesting evening,' he says, putting salt and pepper on the table. 'You were quite distracting in that pineapple t-shirt.'

'Really?' I'm itching to message Dee *that* piece of info.

He kisses the top of my head as he goes past and warmth spreads over me. 'Yes. Really. Now eat and tell me you like it even if you don't.'

I take a bite. 'Yum!' It tastes OK surprisingly, but could use some salt. I sneakily add a decent pinch while he's at the counter putting the pan in the sink.

When he sits down, I say, casually, 'So you were checking me out at the Scrabble thing?'

He laughs. 'I knew that would get a reaction.'

'I'm just curious. You seemed ...' I want to say uptight, but I know it will sound rude, so I settle for '... disinterested.'

'I was Dee's date. What was I supposed to do? Stare at you with my tongue hanging out?'

Well, she *was* snogging my date in the kitchen ... but TJ ogling me on the sly, I like hearing that.

'I wouldn't have noticed if you were. I was too annoyed that you beat me,' I say.

'Aye, that was extremely satisfying. I wouldn't mind having another game just to piss you off again.'

I snort. 'Whatever. You just got lucky with your letters.'

TJ's mouth has a hint of a smirk and his eyes blaze into mine, there's no denying the heat between us. It's giving me such carnal thoughts, I can hardly eat. But it would be an insult to the chef not to, so I drag my attention back to the food. Besides, I have a feeling I'm going to need my strength tonight.

During dinner TJ enquires about Dee and I repeat what I said in the message, that she drank too much, and add that she was upset as can be expected. But he doesn't ask too many questions and I get the feeling he doesn't want a rehash. Neither do I, since I'm already doing battle with her on my phone.

Afterwards, TJ suggests we have chocolate for dessert in front of the TV and I agree eagerly. Oh ho, I think, that's an excuse for giving the couch another workout. But he does seem to want to watch something, so I rein in my raging desire with difficulty. A quick splash of water on my face in the bathroom helps. I consider having a cold shower, but that might look weird. Instead, I move his card back to my column and comment:

We're snuggling on the couch with Netflix and chocolate.

Ouch, that's Dee's favourite pastime, and the fact I'm snuggling with TJ has got to get her where it hurts. I'd be climbing the walls right now if I were her.

In the lounge TJ's found something to watch. I laugh when I see what it is. 'Oh no! Not *Outlander*!'

'Well, you said I should watch it.'

I settle myself next to him, chuckling, and he puts his arm around me.

'Salted caramel or mint?'

'Mint, please.'

TJ traces my lips with a corner of chocolate, then pops it in my mouth and follows it up with a lingering kiss, so we both get to taste the sweet minty goodness. Mmm I'm loving this evening so far.

We're halfway through the first episode of *Outlander* when my phone buzzes. I ignore it, but not knowing what Dee's said gnaws away at me, until it gets too much.

'I have to use the loo.'

'Again? OK, I'll pause it.'

In the bathroom I check my phone. What the? She's moved his card back and commented with:

Goodie, we can do that on our date in two weeks' time.

I shake my head in disbelief. Aaargh, give up and let me have him, woman! I can't deal with her right now. I want to enjoy being with TJ. I flush and wash my hands in case he's listening, then go back out. He smiles. 'All good?'

'Yup. You want to keep watching?'

'Yeah, I'm getting invested now.'

'Oh.'

God, what have I started? Now he's hooked and there are

six bloody seasons! We continue watching until there's an intimate scene with Claire and Frank and I feel him shift next to me. Next thing his hand is on my upper thigh. I don't say anything but move closer to him. His hand creeps towards my crotch and I hold my breath. Two fingers slip down and start rubbing me. Wordlessly, I unzip my jeans, unfurl my legs, and his hand dips inside my knickers. When he discovers my wetness, he sighs in approval and his fingers explore thoroughly. I bite my lip, trying to stifle my groans but a few escape.

'Do you like that?' he murmurs, flicking lightly with the tip of his finger.

'Fuck yes.' I push my jeans and knickers down round my thighs to give him better access.

'That's a good view,' he says huskily.

He massages me with the heel of his hand, then his fingers again, long strokes and short flicks until I'm drenched and writhing. He keeps the tension right on a certain point and doesn't let up, going round and round. My stomach and thigh muscles tense as pleasure builds (oh God, right there, keep doing it right there) then it peaks and flows over me like a fast-moving stream, and I'm carried along helplessly, shuddering and quaking, until I have to gently push his hand away.

I lie there breathing heavily for a moment, then weakly pull my jeans and knickers back up.

TJ doesn't say anything. He breaks off a piece of salted caramel and hands it to me. We munch on chocolate watching the TV, but I feel like a cartoon character with stars circling over my head. *That was freaking awesome.*

'So do you want to go to the bedroom or are you one and done?' he says at last.

I grin up at him. 'I'm just getting started.'

TJ says he'll sort out Maxie in the kitchen so he doesn't disturb us and I scamper off to the bathroom again; sit on the toilet lid and take out my phone. Oh, Dee, you've had it now. I move TJ's card once more and type with relish:

He gave me a fantastic orgasm. I came so hard.

Take that! My nerve endings are still tingling as a reminder. Feeling pretty victorious, I splash some water on my face and almost give myself a high five in the mirror. Then my phone buzzes. What? There is nothing, nothing, she would have to say to that! I check and see she's moved him back again and commented:

Excellent. I look forward to my turn very soon.

She's so calm about it, it's unnerving. Like she knows something I don't. But TJ and I are solid, so whatever little mind games she's playing, they aren't going to work! Still, it's infuriating and ruining my post-orgasmic glow. I drag him back into my column and type determinedly.

Going to fuck him now. Nighty night!

I use the toilet, do a refresh ready for round two with some damp toilet paper and wash my hands a couple of times, but there's no reply. Good, that's done the trick and made her think twice before messing with me.

Chapter 30

TJ's in bed with the duvet draped across his hips and his hands laced behind his head. The bedside light illuminates his bare chest and the intensity in his eyes takes my breath away. Slowly I peel off my t-shirt, jeans, and underwear with his gaze scorching me, then dump everything onto his pile of clothing beside the bed. Lifting the edge of the duvet, I slide under and he takes me in his arms, our warm flesh melding. I'm primed for some naked action since our initial encounter was a mad fully-clothed scramble of ripping down zippers, tearing open a condom, and frantic coupling. It was hot, but not sensuous skin-on-skin like this is going to be. I'm wired and ready to go all night. Though, whether I'm wanting to impress TJ or trying to prove something to Dee, is another question entirely.

Twenty minutes later, I'm undulating on top of him enthusiastically in the cowgirl position while he strokes my thigh with one hand and squeezes a jiggling breast with the other. But my eyes keep drifting to my phone. I can see it in the pocket of my jeans beside the bed. Has Dee responded? What if I've pushed her over the edge with my last comment? I imagine her curled up in a corner, grasping a bottle of vodka and crying uncontrollably.

I try to put it out of my mind and concentrate on what I'm doing. So far I'm two orgasms down, and TJ hasn't even had one. I give him the Aster special and lean forward, clenching him tightly and slow the pace, rocking slowly up and down. TJ starts softly moaning, 'Oh yeah, oh yeah' and he comes, causing another delicious orgasm to shatter over me. Three in one night! So far TJ is nailing the must-haves for my ideal man: horniness, cunnilingus and stamina.

You were right, Dee, I need a man who can satisfy me mentally and physically ...

But when we're lying together, sweat cooling our tangled limbs, and taking a breather, TJ comments 'You're really good at this,' which puts me on guard.

'So? It's not a crime,' I say defensively.

'I wasn't insinuating anything. I love that you're in touch with your sexuality. It's very alluring.'

'Is it?'

He kisses my temple and says softly, 'Yeah, it is.'

I let out a silent breath.

But then he adds, 'Have you had many boyfriends?'

'Oh, er, a few. No one special.'

'Because of what happened at school?'

'Maybe. I don't know. I haven't had much luck with men.'

'I can't imagine why.'

I assume he's trying to understand what Dee said in London, why I've never had a proper boyfriend. *Yikes*. I need to get him off the topic of my love life, so I'm not backed into a corner. I'm not ready to discuss my dating habits just yet. 'What about you?' I ask.

'No, no boyfriends,' he teases.

'Haha.'

'Just a couple of girlfriends in my twenties that lasted a year or so, then one long term relationship for six years.'

'Beth,' I say automatically without thinking. I feel his body tense beside me.

'How do you know about her? I haven't even told Dee her name.'

Shit.

'I may have seen the CD on the bookshelf. I assumed she was your ex.'

There's a loaded pause. 'And you just happened to buy a CD player ...' he says.

I sigh. 'OK fine. I bought the CD player for the sole purpose of listening to it.'

TJ doesn't say anything, but I feel his arm muscle twitch.

'Are you mad?'

He shrugs. 'I assumed you had when I saw it.'

I groan and bury my face in his chest. 'I'm sorry. I'm a terrible, nosey house sitter. If it's any consolation, it wrecked me.'

'Wrecked you how?'

'It made me bawl my eyes out. I guess I connected to the whole unrequited love thing. That you gave it to her and she didn't want it. It must've been a kick in the guts.'

'I didn't though,' TJ says.

'Huh?'

'I never gave it to her. I was too chicken.'

'Oh.' That puts a different spin on things. I'm not as hating on Beth now.

He rubs my arm slowly. 'It was supposed to be this grand gesture to try and win her back, but I decided to just let it go. What was the point? I'd be setting myself up to fail. She didn't want me.'

'Oh, TJ.' I can feel myself starting to get emotional. Bloody Bryan Adams.

'It's fine. It's taken me a while to get over it but I have.'

'What happened? If you don't mind me asking.'

'My dad was ill. For a long time. Cancer. It put a strain on mine and Beth's relationship because I was taking him to chemo and helping my mother out with looking after him. Plus, trying to hold down a full-time job. Beth spent a lot of nights here alone with Maxie. Then Dad's condition worsened and he went into a hospice for end-of-life care. Beth was never that close with my family; I think she visited him once the whole time he was ill. She said she wasn't good with death,' TJ says flatly.

'Maybe it made her evaluate her own life. I came home one night and she said that was it. She'd had enough and wanted to travel around Asia, so she packed her bags and left. Two days later my dad passed. So it was a double whammy.'

Geez Beth! I kinda get you but ... kinda hating on you again.

I don't know what to say except, 'I'm sorry. That must've been incredibly difficult.'

'Yeah, so that's why I haven't been on the dating scene. I had a look at a few sites, but it didn't do much for me. It seemed like a meat market. Besides, I don't know who these women are or how many men they've been through. I could be one of fifty.'

I gulp nervously.

'When Dee asked me out, it was easy and natural. None of that online stuff. Maybe I'm old fashioned in that respect.'

'You do know that I've been online dating?'

'Yeah. How's that going for you?'

'I'm thinking of giving it up.'

'Oh, why would you do that?' He rolls over and tightens his arms around me, and I kiss his neck.

'No reason. But I may have met someone I quite like hanging out with. And he's pretty hot too.'

'Hmm, would the fact that he's made you come three times in a row have anything to do with it?'

'No. But if we're counting, I'd be up for a fourth. You're pretty amazing.'

'Am I now?' TJ grins and kisses my lips lightly, but responds with more urgency when I eagerly slide my tongue into his mouth. Mmm, he has a way of kissing that gets me excited and slick beyond measure. By my urgent rubbing against his thigh, I'm sure he can feel I'm more than ready but he makes me wait for it. Kissing leisurely down to my breasts, he takes his time on each one, but his nipple sucking is so expert I almost come without him doing anything else. He descends lower, tracing a line down my belly, his tongue like a hot guided missile. When he finally reaches his target and starts swirling, my desire becomes supernova, and I hastily guide him inside me for a mutual explosion that leaves me gasping. Jesus, sex with TJ is off the charts! He's better than anyone I've ever had. It's beginning to scare me.

The next morning we're both feeling the worse for wear, TJ more than me. I tell him to stay put and relax, while I feed and water Maxie. Then I make a mound of toast, liberally spread it with Whole Earth organic peanut butter and pour a couple of cups of strong coffee.

We have breakfast in bed; me crossed-legged in my t-shirt and knickers, and him still naked under the duvet. In the light of day, some of the things we did last night keep flashing before my eyes, and I feel almost shy around him which is weird for me. But TJ doesn't seem to care and soon his lighthearted teasing and affectionate cuddling make me forget about any awkwardness. I realise I enjoy that part of being with him immensely. Just as much as the sex, which was pretty damn hot, so it's a revelation of sorts.

I could get used to this ...

Maxie comes in looking for attention, jumps on the bed and tries to eat our toast to much uproar. I'm so immersed in the happy family dream that I almost forget I've got a big problem waiting for me back at the flat.

When TJ goes to have a shower, I check my phone, dreading what I'm going to see. To my relief, there's been no movement on the "TJ-physio" card overnight, and no further comments. Either she's given up the fight or drunk herself into a stupor.

TJ comes back in with a white bath towel slung loosely around his hips whilst drying his hair with a smaller one. He sees me whispering in Maxie's ear and narrows his eyes suspiciously.

'What are you two up to?'

'Nothing,' I say innocently. When his back is turned to rummage in his dresser drawer, I whisper 'Go get it!' Maxie leaps off the bed in a single bound, grips the towel in his teeth, and scampers off down the hall with it, leaving TJ bare-butt naked. 'Hey, come back here!'

I crack up. 'He's so smart!'

'You're a bad influence on him.'

He strides over and wrestles me back on the bed, holding my arms above my head with one hand and tickling me with the other, until I'm screeching. He's surprisingly strong, but I manage to twist out of his hold and get in a few good whacks on his butt.

'I have to go.' He's lying on top of me breathing heavily and I can feel a distinct hardening between my legs.

I wiggle my hips. 'Are you sure?'

'Yeah, not all of us are freelancers.'

'Pity. I can make it worth your while.' I whisper in his ear exactly what I'd like to do to him.

He groans. 'Temptress.'

'Yup.'

'Maybe I can be late this morning.'

After TJ manages to extract himself from my arms and get dressed, he's running extremely late and has had to ring the receptionist to say he had car trouble.

'This was fun,' he says to me at the front door. 'More than fun. It was the best night and morning-after I've ever had.'

I'm feeling pretty much the same, and I grab him in a hug. 'Me too.' He kisses me tenderly, caressing the back of my neck and my heart starts fluttering madly. 'I've really got to go,' he murmurs, resting his forehead against mine. 'But I don't want to.'

'I wish you didn't have to go either.'

'Stay for as long as you want. Just give Maxie a chew toy and he'll leave you alone.'

'I might take him for a walk. Then I'll head off.'

'OK. If you don't mind, that would be great, thanks. I'll

message you later.'

He gives me one last lingering kiss on the lips, and races to his car. I stand on the front door watching him go with a sudden ache in my chest. I'm reluctant to analyse it too deeply. All I know is I miss him like hell and it's barely been two minutes since he left.

Chapter 31

It's late afternoon, I'm still at WeWork, but I know I can't avoid Dee any longer. Besides, I need to go home, change my clothes and generally sort my shit out.

I pack up my laptop and make my way back to the flat dragging my heels. I used to look forward to coming home, to hanging out in the kitchen while Dee cooked some cordon bleu concoction, talking about guys, having a drink and a laugh. Part of me can't believe I'm going through this with her. Surely we can work it out. *My best friend Dee ...*

When I walk up the steps to the front door, I see a crisp white envelope affixed to the front door with Scotch tape and "Aster" written on it in Dee's handwriting. What's this? I draw out a sheet of note paper with a Liberty Hotel header and stand there reading it. No fucking way. I insert my key in the lock and turn it in all directions but nothing. In disbelief, I read the note again, but Dee's neat, flowing script is brusque and clear:

Aster, I can no longer tolerate us living together. You can make arrangements to pick up your things with Rosie. Your key won't work, I've changed the locks.
Edie

Fuck, Dee has evicted me. I have nothing but the clothes on my back, my handbag, my phone, and my laptop. I don't even have my chargers!

With my chest tightening in panic, I press the buzzer multiple times and bang on the door but no one answers. I try ringing her, but it goes straight to voicemail.

Dee, I can't believe you've gone to this extreme. Locking me out of the flat? Without any notice? This is crazy. Please ring or message me asap!

Then I try Rosie, who picks up on the third ring.

'Rosie? It's Aster. Are you near the flat?' My voice sounds distraught to my own ears.

There's a pause then, 'No, I'm not and I can't let you in until tomorrow. I'm in Stirling visiting a friend.'

'Oh. So you know about Dee evicting me without notice?'

Another pause. 'Yes, I know about it.'

'Whatever she's told you, it's bullshit. I can explain.'

'She said you might say that.'

My chest tightens further.

'Is she at work? Or is she in there hiding from me?'

'Stay away from her,' says Rosie sharply. 'You've done enough damage.'

'What exactly has she said?'

Rosie sighs and says, 'You've fucked up big time, Aster.

I'll see you tomorrow at ten, you can collect your things then.'

Then she hangs up on me.

There's nothing for it but to walk away from the flat in a daze. The lack of sleep from last night isn't helping. I'm not sure where else to go, so I head back to WeWork in shock.

When I get there, I grab a coffee, sit on a couch, and attempt to get my head around what's going on. But I'm too upset to think straight. My phone is running dangerously low, so I turn it off to preserve the battery in case Dee gets in touch. But after talking to Rosie, I'm not too hopeful about that.

TJ messaged earlier and we had a nice exchange of 'miss you, me too, thinking about you, wish I could see you' etcetera, so at least he's not waiting on a message from me. The last thing I want to do is to turn up on his doorstep like a damsel in distress. Not cool when we've had such a full-on night. I wanted to let it breathe a little. It's too soon and too much to ask of him to let me stay if Dee has kicked me out, which is what the situation looks like. Shock is turning into cold realisation at my predicament. We don't have a contract, it was a verbal arrangement, and it's her flat, so I don't have a leg to stand on. Dammit, I had a feeling something was brewing, I should've tried to find another flat sooner.

I gulp more coffee. It tastes bitter, but it does the job of perking up my brain cells. My main priority is to gain access to the flat so I can get my chargers, otherwise I'm stuffed for work. I remember TJ said he called Dee from his work phone, so maybe I can get him to do that. But that would mean involving him.

Perhaps I can send her a strongly worded email to get her to let me into the flat tonight. I fire up my laptop. But when I go into my Gmail I see that Dee has sent me a message with the subject line "Aster". It has the same feeling about it as the envelope on the front door. Maybe it's the email version, or maybe it's something else.

I'm not sure I want to open it, but I force myself to in case it's in reply to the message I left her. But the email hasn't been addressed to me, it's addressed to TJ, and I'm BCC'd in. There's one line of text and two attachments. With mounting dread, I read what she's written to him:

I thought you might want to see this. Just looking out for you as a friend.

Oh God. I can't bring myself to look at the attachments. I know they're going to be bad whatever they are. I shut my laptop with a bang and sit there with my heart galloping. What has she sent him? I know I have to look at them otherwise I'm going to be ignorant. Which isn't a good position to be in if she's dragging my name through the mud.

Taking a deep breath, I open my laptop and look at the

email again. TJ hasn't replied which is a good thing. Unless he's replied to her and I haven't been party to the conversation. Now or never. The first one is a screenshot of the Trello board showing my two columns. The "Rejects" column with all the cards of the guys I've dated. And the "Seeing" column with the "TJ-physio" card. OK, there are a fair few in the "Rejects" column, but I'm not sure it makes any particular point. It suggests that I haven't found Mr Right yet. Surely TJ's not going to be bothered about that? It matches with what I told him last night—that I haven't had much luck with men.

Feeling more confident, I click on the second attachment. Again it's a screenshot, I zoom in to see what it is, and balk. It's my comment exchange with Dee from last night but only my side of it. Her side has been conveniently left out.

Sorry too busy kissing him to relay messages.
We're snuggling on the couch with Netflix & chocolate.
He gave me a fantastic orgasm. I came so hard.
Going to fuck him now. Nighty night!

I groan inwardly. The two attachments collectively make me look like I'm a cheap hooker working my way through the available men of Edinburgh, including TJ. No wonder she was so cool and calm about what I was commenting, she was setting me up. I feel like a fly that's been netted by a black widow spider.

I'm going to need to do some major damage control with TJ if I want to keep seeing him. I flick on my phone to see if he's messaged me. He hasn't. Nothing from Dee either. My battery is down to five percent. Do I risk ringing him now and it dying on me while I'm trying to explain myself? I don't even know what I'm going to say. The truth, I guess. *'I've dated a lot of men. None of them meant anything until I met you, now I only have eyes for you TJ.'*

It sounds a little unbelievable.

In the end, I do nothing. I switch my phone off, then on again so many times that eventually it dies, letting me off the hook. I know I should get dinner, check into a cheap hotel for the night, so I can have a shower and a decent night's sleep. But I feel like a skittle knocked sideways by a bowling ball, I can't seem to make any practical decisions. All I can focus on is: Rosie. Ten o'clock. Tomorrow morning.

I have a bag of peanuts in my backpack and nibble on them, but I'm not feeling that hungry. The sun goes down and I top up my coffee. I pace around the office space, hyped up on caffeine, and spend half an hour trying to dislodge a bit of nut stuck in my tooth. I lie down on the couch, think about TJ, and try to hold onto happiness. But somewhere in the middle of the night, it sprints away from me.

'Aster, wake up.' A hand on my shoulder and a voice in my ear makes my eyes fly open, and I sit up looking around groggily. Where the hell am I? Stacey is crouched in front of me, her forehead wrinkled in concern. I groan inwardly as the events of yesterday start coming back with stomach churning clarity.

'Are you OK? Why are you sleeping here on the couch?' she asks gently. 'Did you have a late one?'

I shake my head, unable to speak.

'Have you had trouble at home?'

Her voice is kind and it makes my eyes prick with tears. I nod and swipe at my eyes with the back of my hand.

'Here, have some water.' She hands me her reusable water bottle, and I take a deep swig then another. All the caffeine I drank last night must've shrivelled my kidneys.

'I had a bad fight with my flatmate,' I say at last, knowing she deserves an explanation. 'I'm temporarily homeless. She owns the flat, well, her parents do, and she's kicked me out and changed the locks.'

'God,' says Stacey, raising her eyebrows. I can see she's taken aback by my admission. 'That's rough. Can you talk it out with her?'

'I want to, but she's ignoring my calls and messages. Well, I think she is, my phone died last night, so I haven't been able to check it.'

Stacey looks at me considering, and I can almost hear her brain whirring.

'Do you want to stay at mine? I haven't got a spare room

but I can offer a pull-out couch in the lounge.'

I'm not a religious person, but at that moment it feels like God has stepped in and said 'Right, you need some help. Here it is. And don't say I never do anything for you.'

My laptop is still half charged, so I do some work for a couple of hours. I tell Stacey about the appointment with Rosie and she says we can head to her flat in Fountainbridge afterwards. She doesn't ask any questions, which I'm grateful for.

Yesterday morning with TJ feels like a dream. Was I really laughing and joking with him and eating peanut butter on toast? Did we make such exquisite love that I felt, in the words of Bryan Adams, like I'd died and gone to heaven?

And that's why the whole thing was doomed to failure in the first place, I tell myself in the bathroom mirror, looking at my puffy red-rimmed eyes and matted hair, with disgust. *You were stupid to think a guy like TJ would ever fall in love with you. You're a slag. You'd be better off settling for someone like Richard. You could have all the soulless sex you want and he wouldn't judge you for your past because he's just as bad.*

Rosie buzzes me into the flat on the dot of ten and says 'Come to the lounge' in a voice as hard as nails. From her tone, I'm surprised Dee hasn't hired armed guards to escort me in case I try to steal anything. Dee's bedroom door is shut and I assume she's at the hotel, making Rosie do her dirty work for her.

It feels odd being inside the flat. Familiar, because it's where I've spent the last two years of my life, but at the same time like I'm a stranger intruding on Dee's space.

Rosie is standing in front of the window with her feet planted firmly and her arms clenched by her sides, as if expecting me to put up a fight. 'I'll keep it short,' she says. 'You've got half an hour to pack and get out.'

'Whatever she's told you, it's a lie,' I say, refusing to be intimidated.

Rosie sucks in her cheeks as if to say how dare I even speak to her. She folds her arms and looks down her nose. 'All I know is that you stole Dee's boyfriend and then taunted her with it. She showed me the messages you sent last night, I was disgusted. She was a mess.'

'Crying and drunk?'

'Yes!'

'I thought she might be,' I say dryly.

'You don't even *care*!' she exclaims. 'Dee has been a good friend to you. Who do you think you are?'

Her eyes are skewers.

'You haven't been here, Rosie,' I say patiently. 'You've walked in on the tail end of a drama that's been going on for weeks. Don't jump to conclusions, Dee's feeding you bullshit.'

'I *saw* the messages. With my *own eyes*!'

'You saw what Dee wanted you to see. She's painting me

as the villain. But I didn't steal TJ, he was never in a relationship with her.'

'You're full of it. Just get out,' she spits.

'Whatever.' I can't be bothered arguing with her. I need sleep and food.

I leave her glowering in the lounge and head upstairs to my bedroom. I'm too drained to feel much of anything. All I focus on is getting my chargers, packing, and leaving the flat as soon as possible.

My backpack and wheelie suitcase are soon filled with clothes and underwear, the Kindle and the CD player placed on top. I don't have a whole heap of stuff, even though I've been living here for two years. The furniture and bedding came with the flat and I'm not a huge shopper. My main purchases were books, but since I got the Kindle, I haven't even been buying those. I've given most of them to Dee.

There's nothing in the kitchen that's mine, it's all Dee's, so I don't bother going in. I'm half expecting Rosie to be at the bottom of the stairs in a military stance, but she's not there nor in the lounge when I check. My eyes fall on the bottom shelf of the bookcase. Should I filch the Scrabble since I bought it? But I know, years from now, even if I'm in another apartment with new flatmates or I've bought my own place, it will remind me of Dee.

Nostalgia is a real bitch but I refuse to let her overwhelm me.

I have some difficulty manoeuvring out the front door and down the steps with my bags, but once the door is shut and locked behind me, there's nothing more I can do. So that's it, two years of my life over, bam, just like that. *Oh well, onwards and upwards*, I think, trying to stay positive. At least I'm not sleeping in the gutter.

By the time we reach Stacey's Fountainbridge flat, my stiff upper lip is starting to wobble, but I manage to keep it together so I don't collapse into a bawling mess in front of her.

'Is it OK?' she asks, as we look at the pull-out sofa bed we've made up with a pillow, sheets, and a duvet. Her flat is tiny, the lounge barely large enough to fit a two-seater couch, a twenty-six-inch TV, and a small armchair. Along with my backpack and wheelie, there's not a hell of a lot of space to walk around in. But I'm not at WeWork or at a hotel eating into my savings, so I'm grateful she's letting me crash.

'It's fine,' I reassure her quickly. 'I'll start flat hunting today so I shouldn't be here for too long. Direct me to the nearest power point and I'll charge up.'

As soon as I plug in my phone and it starts charging, I ring TJ. I have a feeling it's going to be a hard conversation. The fact that he hasn't messaged me at all since our last exchange is telling.

He doesn't pick up and it goes to voicemail, which I've

been praying it does because I'm a cowardly custard. I leave a message asking him to call me back, managing to keep my tone even, until the last word, 'please', which wavers slightly.

Then the waiting begins. I can distract myself to some degree by finishing off the indie author's editing. He's been sending me 'are you nearly finished?' emails because he wants to publish shortly and I'm a day over the deadline. I'm reading through the last page and feeling depressed—spoiler alert: it's not a happy ending, the aliens make everyone kill themselves—when "TJ" flashes on my phone. An iron fist gently squeezes my guts. *Breathe, it may not be that bad, at least he's ringing you.*

'Hi!' I answer cheerfully. 'How's things?'

'Hi,' he replies and I hear it. Wariness.

'I was just calling to check in. I miss you. Have you had a busy day so far?' I'm about to launch into some meaningless chitter chatter but he interjects.

'I'm on my lunch break, so I can't talk long, but I got an email from Dee yesterday. It was weird. I thought it was spam.'

My heart leaps. Maybe he didn't click on the attachments.

'But the email address seemed legit. So, I clicked on the attachments.'

'Oh.' My heart sinks.

'Are you involved in a dating experiment? There was a screenshot showing a whole heap of guys under "Aster-

Rejects",' he says, sounding unsure.

Maybe once he understands the intent, he'll be fine.

'It's not a dating experiment, it's more for dating protection,' I explain. 'We've been using a screening questionnaire. Guys have to answer six questions suitably before we agree to go on a first date.'

'Right ...' he says slowly. I decide not to mention the tweaking of the profile and the photo, best keep it simple.

'It was Dee's idea to use a project management tool. So I created a board on Trello to, er, manage them ...' I trail off.

'Manage them?' he echoes. 'How many guys constitutes needing Trello?'

'Erm, at a guess, maybe fifty.' I cringe at the amount, but I have to be honest. There's been a slew of new sign-ups recently since the weather's getting warmer and men are venturing out of their caves.

'But even with the questionnaire, it's a struggle to find anyone decent. Dee gave up when she met you. I kept slogging away since I thought you were with her.' I know I'm saying too much. *Shut up, Aster.*

'How many of those guys did you sleep with?'

My heart starts pounding. Here we go. I give a nervous laugh. 'I'm not sure why you'd want to know that.'

'I saw my name under "Aster-Seeing" and it's me you're talking about in the second attachment because of the Netflix and chocolate reference—so yes, I want to know.'

My mouth is as dry as sandpaper and I wet my lips nervously.

'TJ, you shouldn't ask me this.'

'How many?' His voice is steely.

I don't want to tell him. He's not going to like the answer. But I make myself say, 'A few.'

I was trying to be a good girl and keep to the "no sex until they're worthy" rule. But I wasn't always successful. I'm regretting that now.

'How many is "a few"—two or three?' he asks.

'Um, more like a dozen,' I say somewhat defiantly. It's his fault, he kickstarted my libido and it had nowhere to go. And some of the guys that passed the screening were cute. Terrible conversationalists and boring as shit, but cute.

I hear TJ suck in his breath and, for a moment, I think he's going to hang up on me but he says, 'Noah was on that list of rejects. Did you sleep with him?'

'No.' I breathe a sigh of relief, thank God, I didn't.

'Did you do anything else with him?' Damn.

'Um, kissing and a small hand job,' I admit reluctantly. It was after the hiking date. I went round to his place for dinner, and it *was* a small hand job because he wasn't very big. And he ended up asking questions about Dee for most of the night. So I don't think it counts as a hook-up. But I don't mention that because TJ is worryingly silent on the other end of the line.

'TJ those guys meant nothing,' I venture, taking his silence for hurt. 'Everything's changed because of you. I don't ever want to go on another online date. That's massive. Do you know what I'm saying?'

'Not really.'

'You're different. Being with you is different. It's more than just sex, I want to be with you.' As I'm talking, I can feel him pulling away. 'Please don't shut me out.'

'I feel used,' he says tightly, 'Those messages, you sent them to Dee last night. What was that about?'

'She was goading me! You didn't see what she was sending in retaliation. I got home last night to find she'd kicked me out of the flat and changed the locks. You're not going to take her side, surely?'

'I'm not taking anyone's side, but after that email I'm seeing things a lot more clearly. I thought you and I were on the same page, but now I know I'm just one in a long line of men.'

'No, you're not! We are on the same page!' I cry in frustration.

'I don't think so,' he says brusquely, and my heart cracks at his tone. I knew this was going to happen, so why am I surprised?

'So that's it then,' I reply bitterly. 'You've decided I'm good-for-nothing slut.'

'Don't put words into my mouth.'

'Why not? It's what you're thinking.'

'No, what I'm thinking is that we're different people and this, whatever it is, isn't going to work.'

He sounds so firm and decided on the matter, that I can't think of a single thing that will persuade him otherwise. I stay silent as he says politely that his lunch break is over and that he hopes I find the right guy online and hangs up.

That all went rather well considering, I think; then abruptly burst into tears.

Chapter 33

Two weeks slip by and I don't hear anything from TJ. I'm not expecting to, after our conversation, but Hope, like her sister Nostalgia, is also a bitch. I keep picturing TJ watching *Outlander* on the couch with Maxie and yearning for me. But then again, I have a vivid imagination.

I'm still at Stacey's and dependent on her goodwill because I haven't been able to find another flat. I don't have a reference from Dee and it's proving to be a sticking point with landlords when I say I can't get one. It's obvious some kind of shit has gone down and they don't want to take a risk on me. I'm considering doing house sitting again, or leaving the UK altogether and exiling myself to a remote island.

Life is rather depressing, so when Stacey suggests going out for the girls' night with Fleur again, I'm up for it. She's still keen on the idea of going to a lesbian bar to avoid getting hit on by men; Fleur isn't bothered either way, and at the moment, all I want is to have a drink and hang out with people who won't judge me.

From the outside, the place we go to in Lothian Road doesn't look any different to a normal bar. But when we get inside, the difference becomes clear, there's an overabundance of women.

'Have you been to one of these places before?' I shout to Stacey above the music.

She shakes her head. 'Never. I figure it's a safe space though.'

But as soon as we come in the door a number of hair-sprayed heads turn our way and I can feel mascaraed eyes roving over my body. Stacey and I had a few strong gins before we went out and were experimenting with her clothes for a laugh, some of them are a bit risqué and kind of punk. She's wearing a ripped dress barely held together with safety pins, fishnet stockings and stilettos. I'm in a skimpy magenta crop top, revealing an expanse of midriff, black hot pants, and doc martens. I also finally had a haircut the other day and the tomboy style is giving off a distinct butch vibe. Fleur cracked up when she saw us and said we looked like we were on the pull. What was I thinking dressing up like this? It's not a safe space, I'm probably going to get hit on.

I tell the others to find somewhere to sit and I'll buy the first round. The bar is two people deep and I'm minding my own business, trying not to bump elbows with anyone so I don't have to start a conversation, when a familiar voice drawls in my right ear, 'Hello, Aster.'

I turn slowly and come face to chin with the last person I'd expect to see in a lesbian bar: Richard McAllister. He's wearing a black shirt and jeans and is sipping from a beer bottle.

'Richard,' I say, unable to stop a faint horror creeping into my tone. 'What the fuck are you doing here?'

He shrugs. 'Having a drink, meeting some people.'

I catch a whiff of his aftershave as someone jostles him closer to me; still Sauvage. 'You do realise this is a lesbian bar?'

'Of course. I like a challenge.'

'You're hanging out here because you think you can turn one of them?'

'It's happened before,' he says defensively. 'Remember the ex-girlfriend of my flatmate?'

'How could I forget,' I say dryly.

'In fact, I think I'm onto a good thing. Maybe two good things.' He gestures to the side where a pretty girl in a slinky silver dress and dangly earrings is talking to her less attractive friend. They're both sneaking glances at Richard.

'Looks that way,' I say. Wow, he never changes. 'Are you getting them drinks?'

He nods. 'Yeah. So, how's the online dating going? Are you playing for the other team now?'

'No, just here with a couple of friends, they're trying to avoid men hitting on them. If I'd known you'd be here, I would've suggested going somewhere else.'

'Haha, very funny.' He gives me an appraising glance. 'You're looking good.'

I roll my eyes. 'Don't start hitting on me, you've already

got two lined up.'

'Why stretch for the top branches when I've got low hanging fruit right next to me?'

'Whatever,' I scoff. 'I'm not that easy.'

He leans forward and murmurs in my ear, 'Oh, we both know that you are, Asterrr,' and I shiver.

The bar crowd has thinned, and is only one deep now. I'm growing impatient to order and get the drinks, so I don't have to talk to Richard for much longer. If he starts setting his sights on me, then I'm going to have to summon my non-existent willpower, and I don't have Dee as my back up.

But then Richard comments idly, 'Don't worry, I won't hit on you. I promised her I wouldn't.'

'Promised who?'

Richard smirks. 'That flatmate of yours, Edie, at the Liberty Hotel. She kept her end of the bargain, so I'm keeping mine.'

I'm confused. 'What bargain?'

'She said that you deserved a nice guy and I should stay away from you. I had no intention of doing anything of the sort. But she said she'd make it worth my while if I promised I would.'

I swallow hard. Oh no, Dee, you didn't.

'I thought it was a strange thing to do for a flatmate, but hey,' he shrugs, 'if a woman's offering to suck me off in a posh hotel room, I'm not going to turn it down.'

The bar with its brightly coloured bottles, swims before my eyes then rights itself again.

Richard is still talking. 'Didn't take long either, she was pretty good. Not the best I've had, but still in the top five.'

Oh my God, Dee. My stomach heaves and I taste bile. I have to get away from him before he gives me any more details. As I blindly I push my way through the crowd of women that's formed behind us, I hear Richard yelling after me, 'Hey, is she on Soul Connexon?'

When I get back to Stacey and Fleur, they're sitting on low leather couches, flanked by a couple of women, lesbians I assume. All four of them seem to be getting on like a house on fire judging by the cackles of laughter, gesturing and general merriment.

'Aster! There you are,' Stacey says looking up but then sees I'm empty handed and purses her lips. 'Where are the drinks?'

'I'm sorry, I have to go,' I mumble. 'I'm not feeling well. Bad period cramps.'

Stacey's fleeting annoyance turns to sympathy and Fleur looks round curiously.

'Can I have the key?'

'Sure.' Stacey rummages in her purse and produces the house key (another reason why I need to find a flat, there's only one key!).

'Thanks. Here, drinks are on me.' I give her twenty

pounds. 'The bar's not too busy, just avoid a tall, good-looking, blond guy. He's on the pull and he's a snake.'

I don't want to wake up tomorrow and discover Richard cooking toast in the kitchen, grinning like the Cheshire cat.

'Greer can go up to the bar then,' says Stacey grinning, 'She's immune to the charms of men.'

I glance at Greer who's been checking me out curiously. She has long shiny chestnut hair, killer cheekbones, and is wearing a low-cut red dress showing a fair amount of creamy cleavage; your typical lipstick lesbian. Richard would pounce on her.

'Even she won't be safe,' I say sharply. 'Be on your guard.'

'Gosh, OK, we will,' Stacey says with an unconcerned laugh. 'Hope you feel better soon. There's some Ibuprofen in the medicine cabinet if you need it and, oh, can you let me in later?'

'Yes, just buzz, I'll keep my phone on too.'

As I leave the bar, I know my warning about Richard came across as overly dramatic, but Stacey doesn't know him like I do. What was Dee thinking?! She'd be fired on the spot if anyone found out. Richard must've talked her into it somehow. He's a sex fiend, an incubus—TJ's word describes him perfectly. But if I'm as bad, does that make me a succubus that preys on men? Does TJ see me that way? The fact he hasn't called means he probably does. How the hell am I ever going to convince him that I was telling the truth. That everything's different now. That he's my Mr Right?

The next morning, I congratulate myself on successfully evading Richard's clutches. Not only that, I warned other women about him as well. My feeling of victory is short-lived, however. On the way to the kitchen to make a cup of coffee, I notice that Stacey's bedroom door is wide open. And her bed hasn't been slept in. Damn, did she fall victim to him?

I check my phone as I remember I was meant to let her in. No messages. Did she buzz and I didn't hear her? Perhaps she decided to spend the night at Fleur's, but she lives in Portobello so it doesn't make sense for her to do that. The only other explanation would be ... Woah, maybe I'll keep a lid on that conjecture until I have more proof. I send her a message saying I'll work from home this morning and can let her in.

Stacey buzzes around lunchtime and comes in wearing baggy jeans and a black Portishead t-shirt. There's a Tesco bag screwed up in her fist. With her smudged eyeliner and pale face, she looks a little fragile.

'Good morning,' I say, eyeing her. 'I was going to make some coffee. Do you want one?'

'Yes, please.' She sits down at the small breakfast nook in the corner, puts her head on her arms and lets out a groan.

By now I'm dying of curiosity. 'So how was the rest of the night?'

'There were quite a few cocktails. I lost count. And

dancing. So much dancing. Possibly some puking in the loos.'

'Oh no! So where did you spend the night, dare I ask?'

She doesn't reply for a bit, then I hear a muffled, 'Maybe best not to ask.'

'Male or female?'

She lifts her head and opens one eye to squint at me. 'What do you think?'

Ooh hoo, she didn't!

'I'm assuming since we were at a lesbian bar the odds are in favour of it being female. And that it was Greer.'

She nods, looking a bit green around the gills. 'You assume correctly.'

I hand her a coffee and lean against the counter sipping mine.

'Is that gear hers?'

'Yeah, I spent some time talking on the great white telephone in her apartment and my dress needs a wash.' She kicks the Waitrose bag towards the washing machine.

Maybe that's all it was, nothing more. Holding her hair back and offering a place to crash. 'Did she look after you? That was nice of her.'

'Yes, it was; she is, ah, nice,' Stacey says. She winds a loose thread from the t-shirt round her finger and blushes scarlet. So obviously something did go on. I'm in murky waters here, so I'm not sure if I should say anything, in case she feels weird about the whole thing.

'All that matters is that you had a fun evening,' I say hesitantly. 'And if ... stuff ... happened, you could just chalk it up to experience,' I add.

'Only one problem with that,' she says, arching her back and wincing as it clicks into place. 'I kind of like her.'

'Oh, well, that's OK too,' I say quickly. Phew, it's a minefield. However bad my problems with men are, at least I'm not considering playing for the other team. That's a whole new ballgame!

Chapter 34

After finishing her coffee, Stacey goes off to have a shower, and says she might have a nap afterwards. I collect my laptop and set up in the kitchen, determined to find a flat as soon as possible. Stacey may want privacy to explore her blossoming relationship with Greer and won't want me in the lounge hearing everything through the paper-thin walls. Besides, I'm feeling claustrophobic because I'm used to my spacious double bedroom with its queen-sized bed and inspiring view of Calton Hill out the window. I told myself I wouldn't miss the flat but I do. I had it good. The location was amazing, the WeWork was up the road and, most importantly, I had a ball living there. I had a ball with Dee. I wasn't ready for it to end.

By mid-afternoon, I've lined up a few flat viewings for next week so I'm feeling more hopeful. Perhaps I can get Stacey to give me a reference and skew the timeline to six months rather than two weeks. I'm about to close my laptop and go for a walk when I get an email notification from Trello:

Edie moved the card "Richard-RBS" to "Edie-Potentials".

I stare at it blankly until I manage to register what I'm reading.

Oh no. No, no, no! Richard must've contacted her through Soul Connexon. That slimy weasel! Maybe he didn't have any luck turning the lesbians, and talking to me last night made him think about Dee again and feel horny. But why is she agreeing to go on a date with him, especially after their history? I force myself to close my laptop. It's none of my business who she sees or what she does.

But the more I think about what happened at the hotel, the more agitated I get. My mind keeps picking at it like a sore that's scabbed over. It's fucked up. But is it? What if she knew exactly how to get him off my back? *If she hadn't, Richard would've snared me. He wouldn't have left me alone. He'd be a permanent fixture in my life.*

As afternoon turns to evening, knowing Dee's going on a date with Richard becomes unbearable. Finally, I pull on my shoes. I have to do something.

The next bus to Royal Mile is a twenty-minute wait so I ditch that idea and set off at a fast trot. The walks with Maxie have upped my fitness level, but I'm still puffing by the time I reach Grassmarket and have to stop for a breather. I'm not sure what I'm going to do. Barge into The Devil's Advocate like Gandalf shouting 'You shall not pass!' as if Richard's the Balrog? There's also a good chance Dee won't listen to me. But I'll have to cross that bridge when I come to it.

Advocate's Close is empty and spookily lit by the dull glow of a single lamp across from the bar. I have to force myself to go down there. At the entrance, there are two ghosts making awkward small talk. 'Scared of the bogeyman?' says ghost Richard with a leer. 'Want me to walk you to the end?'

'Yes, thanks,' says ghost Aster, like a fool.

They glide off down the stairs and I watch them go. That right there, I think. That was my mistake. I should've gone the long way round. The kiss in the close fired him up and made him latch onto me. It's my fault Dee is now in his clutches.

I hurry down the last few steps and into the bar. It looks the same as it did when I met him for my date. Low lighting, a scattering of couples. The barman is talking to a guy sitting on one of the stools. However, it's not Richard and there's no sign of Dee. I check my phone. It's around the same time I met him. Their date could've been earlier or maybe it's planned for later. It could be a different day. But I know him, he'll strike while the iron's hot.

I watch the barman pour a measure of vodka into a cocktail shaker and say something to the guy. I could ask him if they were here. If not, I'll get a drink and hang out at one of the tables. *Smart girl, now you're thinking.*

The guy at the bar pays and takes his drinks to a nearby table, where a girl is sitting scrolling on her phone. I replace him on the stool.

'Hi,' says the barman pleasantly. 'What can I get you?'

'An orange juice please, no ice.'

'Right. Is that all?'

'Um, I'm supposed to be meeting someone,' I say, and make a show of looking around. 'I'm horribly late though. Have you seen him? Quite tall, blond hair, wearing a suit.'

The barman screws up his nose like he's smelt something nasty. 'His name's not Richard, is it?'

'Yes!' I say, 'That's him.'

'Aye, I know him.'

'Was he here?'

'Aye, you just missed him, like literally. But he was with someone else.'

'Was she blonde? Petite?'

He nods. 'I'd do yourself a favour and give him a wide berth.'

Shit. I have to go. I chuck a five-pound note at him and dash out the door.

Outside, I hesitate looking down the steps at the dark close. The bogeyman has already been and gone, I remind myself. He's on his way to the flat with Dee. Navigating the close as fast as I can, I come out onto Cockburn Street. Glancing around wildly, I catch sight of a figure, three doors up, about to slither into a building: Richard.

I sprint up the hill and reach the door just as it's about to slam shut. Jamming my foot in the space, I stand there breathing heavily. 'Got you, you smarmy bastard,' I mutter to myself. A man walks past with his dog and looks at me suspiciously. 'Alright there, love?' he asks.

'Yes, just making sure I have my key before I go out.' I rummage in my handbag and produce my old flat key to show him, the one that doesn't work.

He nods and walks on. His dog, a wiry black terrier, trots behind him and pauses to sniff at my shoes—I suppose it does look like I'm up to no good.

Inside the entranceway, the stairwell is dark and quiet. There's a small square window letting in a faint yellow glow from the street lamp outside. There's only one flight of stairs and when I get to the top, I'm faced with three doors. Which one is his? A giggle floats out from the middle door. It's Dee, I'd recognise her laugh anywhere. I inhale, breathe out slowly, psyching myself up, then bang hard on the door with my fist.

The door swings open to reveal Richard with a half-grin on his face, holding an ice-cream scoop. 'Hi, Richard.'

He looks at me in bewilderment. 'Aster. Wha ...?'

'I'm looking for Dee,' I interrupt in a don't-mess-with-me tone, then barge into the apartment before he has a chance to shut the door in my face.

Richard has no choice but to step back and let me through.

'Be my guest,' he says sarcastically, holding up his hands. The overpowering odour of Sauvage envelops me as I pass by him. God, does he bathe in it?

I survey the room. It isn't a sex dungeon as I was expecting but a normal apartment; open plan, with a lounge, kitchen, and bedroom rolled into one large space. Then I realise, it's not that normal because there's no furniture whatsoever apart from a super king-sized bed in the middle of the room, placed like a show piece. It's made up with a black silk duvet and half a dozen matching pillows. *So this is where the action happens*, I think. Where the demon gets his kicks. Richard doesn't relax and watch TV like normal people. The bed is his one and only form of entertainment.

And tonight's main feature is sitting on the edge of the bed in her work uniform. Dee's been unbuttoning her blouse, but she stops when I appear.

'Aster!' she exclaims, looking almost pleased to see me.

I can tell by her voice that she's had a bit to drink. The way Dee's been drinking lately, I'd say Richard had to buy her a few to get her to this state. But she's sober enough to remember what's happened between us. Her look of surprise changes into a frown. 'What are you doing here?' she asks frostily.

'Good question.' Richard leans against the kitchen counter and stares at me stonily. 'I don't remember inviting you to our little tête-à-tête.'

'I got a notification from Trello when you moved his card,' I say to Dee, ignoring him. 'I figured he'd do the usual routine. I was right. Come on, we're going.'

She looks at me hesitantly, then at Richard who smirks. He bends down and gets a tub of Ben & Jerry's out of the freezer.

'I don't think so,' he drawls. 'Edie and I are going to play the Caramel Chew game. Then we're going to fuck. If you don't want to witness that, I suggest you leave. But you're welcome to watch or join in. Two at once, my lucky night.'

Ugh, he's foul. How did I ever think he was sexy?

'Dee, you're better than this,' I tell her. 'You can do better than him.'

'I don't think I can,' she says. 'And why not him since I'm back to square one?'

Richard takes the top off the ice cream, digs in the scoop, then looks round at Dee. 'Are you going to get undressed?'

Dee nods and starts unbuttoning her blouse again.

'Dee,' I say urgently, 'Listen to me, you don't want to go down this road. I've been on it. It's meaningless. Besides, he's a sex demon.'

'Steady on,' says Richard, pausing in his gouging of the ice cream and frowning at me. 'Sex demon's going a bit far. I prefer to think of myself as a pleasurer of women.'

'Shut up, Richard.'

Dee takes off her blouse. 'Please go, Aster,' she says tiredly. 'I don't want you to see this.'

'Bra off,' commands Richard. 'This is nearly ready.'

He's digging out all the chocolate caramel chunks and placing them in a bowl.

Obediently, Dee unhooks her bra and places it on the bed beside her. Richard runs a swift glance over her creamy globes with their rosy nipples. He licks his lips. 'Assume the position,' he says, and she lies back on the bed.

I'm getting desperate. 'Kiki Dee!' I shout.

Her parents' nickname makes her sit up abruptly and look at me in exasperation. 'What?'

'I'm in love with TJ, but I've lost him,' I blurt before I can stop myself. 'He dumped me after you sent him that email.'

She looks at me impassively. 'I thought you were seeing him since he's still on the board.'

'That's wishful thinking on my part. I haven't spoken to him for two weeks.'

'Well, you'll get over it. Just move on to someone else like I have.' She glances at Richard who's still digging into the ice cream.

'I can't. I don't want to move on.' My lip quivers.

'Too bad. It serves you right for stealing him.'

My eyes start watering and I must look distressed because something changes in her face, the hardness seems to soften into curiosity. 'Is it love-love? Like real proper love?' she asks hesitantly.

I nod. 'I love him so much. It hurts like crazy.'

I've been sobbing away at night under the bed covers like

a mad woman, jamming my fist in my mouth, so Stacey won't hear me. Grief is the third bitch sister, and I'm having trouble shaking her off.

All the stress and angst I've been feeling about TJ's rejection comes to the surface. I haven't been able to talk to anyone about him until now. I sink to my knees in front of her, as if I'm praying to a topless Virgin Mary. 'I've never felt like this, Dee. It's the real deal.'

'You really love him?' she asks again, like she can't believe it of me, Aster, the queen of one-night stands.

'I do,' I moan, 'But he hates me now. It's ruined.'

'True love doesn't exist,' pipes up Richard who's been listening to all this. 'It's a figment of your imagination.'

We both ignore him.

Dee is gazing at me. 'I guess I'm to blame.'

'Can you help me?' I beg. 'Please. You're the only one who can fix it.'

She grimaces, like I've asked her to unblock a toilet with her hand because there's no plunger. Then she sighs. 'OK, but you better not be lying.'

The sense of relief I feel is momentous. Thank God, she's back. 'I'm not lying,' I say. She nods and puts on her bra, then her blouse, and starts buttoning it.

Richard's eyes bulge toad-like out of his head. 'Hey, what are you doing?'

'Sorry, Dick,' Dee says 'I've changed my mind. My friend

needs help and that's more important than your ridiculous sex games. Toodle-oo.'

The last image I have of Richard is him standing there scowling, with an ice-cream scoop, a hard-on, and a melted pile of caramel chocolate.

Chapter 35

'It's not going to work,' I say, my insides lurching around like a buoy on the ocean.

'Oh, ye of little faith. It'll work. Trust me.'

I give Dee a scathing glance. 'Trust you. How do I know you're not going in there to throw me under the bus?'

She places her hand over her heart in mock agony. 'Aster, you wound me. Surely, we're past all that. Calm down and eat your lemon cake.'

I do as I'm told and take a forkful of cake. But it feels like a lump of lead when I swallow. We're seated in a café across the road from TJ's work and my nervousness about what Dee is going to do is barely containable.

After the showdown at Richard's place, Dee and I patched things up. When I say "patched things up", I mean we had a three-hour long session in the lounge of her flat, with Rosie involved too. Dee broke down and confessed she'd been insanely jealous of TJ liking me and had "over-emphasised" their relationship in an attempt to sabotage me.

'I knew he was into you when we were on the hike,' she said. 'He couldn't take his eyes off you. It was driving me mental. I guess I wanted him to look at me like that. I was sick of you getting all the good guys.'

'I'd hardly call Richard a good guy. He told me what happened at the hotel. Dee, how could you!'

She shrugged. 'I pushed you into going on a date with him, and I saw how difficult he was making things for you. It was my fault you were in that situation.'

I shook my head. 'But doing that?'

'I cleaned my teeth twice afterwards.'

'Eurgh. Well, thank you, I guess. It did work, but I'm not sure I could've made the same sacrifice.'

'You tracked us down and stopped me from sleeping with him, that definitely counts!'

'But I'm just like him though! I can't get on my moral high horse when I'm the "queen of one-night stands" as you put it.'

'I just said that to annoy you. Of course, you're not like him. He sleeps with women with no intention of finding a partner. You've been looking for Mr Right. Trying before you buy.'

And so it went on. An hour into the session Rosie left as she had no idea what the hell had been going on or who we were talking about. She went off, muttering something about needing to pack for her next trip.

We were having such a great time bonding and reminiscing about how badly behaved we'd been, that we ordered Chinese takeaways and Dee even opened a bottle of wine. We settled back on the couch with our feet on the coffee table.

'Just one glass. I've been drinking so much lately, I think I'm turning into an alcoholic.'

'Maybe addictive personalities run in the family,' I told her. 'I saw Isadora smoking weed in the garden.'

Dee gasped. 'I never knew Mummy did that!'

'From the way she was burying it in a hidey hole, I'd say she's pretty practised at keeping it a secret.'

'What a hypocrite, she's always going on at me about the dangers of drugs,' Dee said disdainfully.

'Do they still think TJ is your potential husband?'

'No, I said that it didn't work out. Daddy wasn't bothered, I think he's still sore over TJ beating him at chess. But Mummy was upset, she'd told all her friends there was going to be a wedding in June.'

I cracked up. 'Imagine how happy she'll be when you finally do get hitched.'

Dee let out a despondent groan. 'If *that* ever happens. At least you've got TJ.'

'I haven't got him! I haven't spoken to him for two weeks! He hates me, remember?'

'Oh, yeah. Sorry.' She rested her head on my shoulder and patted my hand. 'Don't worry about that. I'll sort it.'

I rested my head on hers. 'Is it weird that I hated you, but missed you at the same time?'

She chuckled. 'I missed-you-hated-you too. But I have gotten used to you not being here, so I can play Taylor Swift at full volume, it's been great.'

I shuddered. 'Glad I missed that. Which reminds me, I've got some flat interviews shortly, can you give me a reference?'

'Oh. Why don't you move back in? If you want to, that is.'

'Hmm, maybe some distance is necessary in light of everything that's happened. But I'll still come round and hang out.'

'You'd better. I'll need one friend since I'm going to die a sad, lonely old woman. Maybe I should look at getting a cat after all.'

'Well, you could. But if you're interested in male company, Noah wouldn't shut up about you when I was at his place.'

'Oh?' She perked up at that.

'Yes, but just to warn you, he's got a teensy tiny dick, so don't act surprised when you see it.'

Dee started laughing so hard she almost fell off the couch.

'It's time,' she says now, getting up from the table and adjusting her turquoise windbreaker over her lycra leggings, so it covers her bum. Apparently TJ will take her more seriously if she's wearing activewear.

I take a deep breath. 'Tell him that ...'

'I know what to say,' she interrupts calmly. 'Just sit here and chill. Listen to Spotify or something.'

Easier said than done when I'm balanced on a knife edge. TJ could be receptive or he could shoot me down in flames, I have no idea which one it will be.

I watch out the window as Dee crosses the road. When she reaches Vital Physiotherapy, she looks back at me, gives a thumbs up, and goes in.

She's made an appointment under another name, Evelyn Smith, so TJ won't realise it's her. It's sneaky, but she was worried that if she used her own name, he'd transfer her onto another physio at the practice; there are apparently five of them working there.

The appointment is for twenty minutes, so I figure if she comes back after two, then he's not interested. If she comes back after the full twenty, then I'm in with a chance.

After ten minutes, she's not back yet and I've finished my lemon cake, drunk my tea, and listened to two songs on Spotify. At fifteen minutes, I've started gnawing on a hangnail. Twenty minutes comes and goes. That's good news surely? When twenty-five minutes have clocked over and my nerves can't take it anymore, I spy Dee at the reception area. She seems to be chatting with the receptionist and paying her. Then she walks out and crosses the road.

As soon as she enters the café, I round on her. 'What took you so bloody long? I was dying here!'

Dee gives me a sympathetic look. 'Sorry, I know it took ages. Hang on, I'll get some water. Then I'll debrief.'

I notice then that her face is flushed and she's out of breath. What does that mean? Dee buys a bottle of water, sits down at the table opposite me, and starts gulping it. It feels like it takes forever before she wipes her hand across her mouth. 'That's better.'

'Well? What happened!'

She smiles smugly. 'I think he got the message.'

'Start from the beginning.'

'So, I went over there and sat in the waiting room. He was with another patient, running five minutes late ...'

'OK, you can speed it up a bit,' I say impatiently.

'Geez, make up your mind. Anyway, so he came out with his pleasant physio face on, but then he saw me and his expression got all angry looking. "You," he growled and I smiled beguilingly and said "Yes, it's me".'

'That doesn't bode well,' I say worriedly.

'It gets better. He said "Do you even have tennis elbow, *Evelyn*?" and I said "Possibly, I'd like you to take a look at it." He rolled his eyes and said, "Fine, come through".'

'Well, at least you got into the examination room.'

'Yes, that was the main goal.'

'What then?'

'I told him that I was there under false pretences and that I wanted to apologise and to explain everything. He started protesting and I said, "Just shut up, TJ, and listen to what I have to say". Then I gave him the speech.'

'How did that go down?'

'Pretty well, I think. I may have improvised a little, but I got it all out.'

'Improvised?'

'I said you were pining for him and off your food. I thought that was the pièce de resistance, since he must know by now that you've got the appetite of a horse.'

'What?' I shriek. 'That wasn't in the script!'

'Don't worry, he didn't scream at me to leave.'

I let out a breath. 'What *did* he do?'

'He looked ... thoughtful.'

'Thoughtful?'

'Yeah. Then he said that since I was there that I might as well do some exercises to strengthen my ankle. So he made me do a whole lot of jumping jacks, then I had to hop around the room on one foot. Bastard.'

I smother a giggle. That sounds so like TJ. God, I miss him even more now.

'So how did it end?'

'He told me to pay at reception, then turned to his computer and started writing up some notes. God knows what he was typing.'

'That's it?'

'Pretty much.'

'Wow, OK.'

'What were you expecting him to do?'

'I don't know.'

But I do know. I look at my phone. If this was a rom-com, a message saying 'Aster, I miss you too. I haven't been able to eat for weeks would appear right about now. Annnyyy second now …

'Come on, let's get out of here. This is his local, he might pop over to get some afternoon tea.' She stands up and slings her handbag over her shoulder.

But I don't move.

'Dee?'

'Hmm?'

'How did he look?'

'He looked like TJ.'

'But did he look thinner, like he hadn't been eating, or miserable around the eyes?'

'Ah, his hair was possibly a little dishevelled, like he'd been running his hand through it in a crazed "I can't get her out of my mind" type of way. I don't know! He didn't have "I love Aster" written in magic marker on his forehead. We've done everything we can do. You'll have to wait for him to process it.'

'How long will that take?'

'I have no idea. Do you want me to go back over there and ask him?'

'No!' I say hurriedly, collecting my phone and jacket. Knowing Dee, she would too.

Chapter 36

Over the next few days, I meet the fourth bitch sister: Waiting. She's the worst of all. I become so irritable and nervy waiting for TJ to message me, that Stacey snaps. One morning after a particularly grumpy reply to one of her questions, she says pointedly, 'I love having you here, Aster, but I'm going to need my lounge back soon. Any luck with flats so far?'

'Er, not yet, I've got a viewing tomorrow though,' I say, surprised at her tone, and thinking, *shit I better pull my head in, otherwise I'm going to get kicked out.* I message Dee to remind her about the reference and she says she'll send it to me this afternoon. I head off to WeWork to get out of Stacey's hair and do some positive affirmations on the way: "I will find a new flat" and "I will get my shambles of a life together".

Perhaps it works, because there's a bit of good news waiting for me when I arrive. A friend of a client, Mia Hamilton, has emailed saying she urgently needs an editor, and that she's heard good things about me.

'It's a feminist blog,' Mia explains when I ring her to find out more. 'It's not about hating men, it's more about empowering women, especially the younger generation. I've started doing a podcast and I need someone who can polish up my transcripts and turn them into articles for the blog.'

'What topics do you talk about?'

'Oh, all sorts of things; the female body, the beauty myth, sex, love, domestic violence, gender inequality in the workplace, online dating, you name it. If you've got any ideas for the podcast, I'd be happy to hear about them as well.'

'I can certainly help you out,' I say, a smile spreading across my face. 'In fact, I've got some titles all ready to go.'

'Oh great!' exclaims Mia enthusiastically 'Like what?'

'Well, this one is quite good: *Why Women Shouldn't Be Slut Shamed For Promiscuity in the Search For Mr Right*. Oh, and I quite like this one, but the title needs work: *How to Explore Your Sexuality Safely Through Online Dating: The Man You Marry Will Thank You For It*.'

'Er, that's great, Aster,' says Mia, sounding slightly less enthusiastic. 'I'll add those to the "maybe" list. Perhaps we should stick to editing for the time being though.'

By the afternoon, I'm feeling a lot happier about things and I haven't thought about TJ for at least an hour. Even if he doesn't message me, I'm a strong woman, I'm a feminist. I practise some more affirmations: "I don't need a man to make me feel good about myself" and "I'm perfectly happy and able to live my life without ever seeing TJ again". I'm not sure I totally believe that last one, but perhaps if I say it enough, I'll start to.

Then Dee emails me her reference. Great, now I can start viewing flats without landlords looking at me like I'm a criminal.

To Whom It May Concern,
As her leaseholder and previous flatmate, I totally recommend Aster Daniels for any property she applies for. From the moment I met Aster, I knew she'd make a great flatmate, and I was right.

She's kind, considerate, and brilliant at cleaning, especially when there's a frightful mess in the kitchen after experimental cooking. We've lived together for two years, and in that time, she's become a beloved and trusted friend of mine. We've not had an argument even once. Anyone who gets her as a flatmate will be extremely lucky indeed (as long as they don't play Taylor Swift too loudly in her presence).

I hoped she might stay, but I understand her reasons for moving on, and I wish her all the best in her new flat. She is welcome to visit me frequently and she can always sleep over if we stay up too late talking.

Please don't hesitate to contact me at the email address below if you need any further information.
Yours sincerely,
Edie Crowley-Smythe
kikidee89@gmail.com

She rings me when I'm in the WeWork loo.

'Did you get it?'

'Mmmm.'

'Was it OK?

'Yahhh.'

'Why is your voice all funny?'

'Because you didn't have to say those nice things, it's set me off.' Tears course down my cheeks, and I sniffle.

'But they're all true. And I don't want you to move out. I want you to live with me, so we can keep having fun like before. You're my best friend.'

'Well, since you put it like that,' I say with a hiccup, wiping my eyes with a wad of loo roll. 'I guess I could move back in … but the first sign of any crazy shit, I'm out of there.'

'No crazy shit, I promise,' she says sounding relieved. But then, in typical Dee fashion, the planning begins. 'I'll get a new key cut today … and I was thinking, I might redecorate your room if you can last at Stacey's for another week? I'll make it all nice for you, like a fresh start. What about a shade of green for the walls, you like green, don't you? You can pick the colour, I've got some swatches.'

'I love green. Are you going to DIY?'

'God, no. I'll get the decorators in. Daddy can pay for it.'

A week later, I move back into my old bedroom at the flat. True to her word, Dee's had the walls painted in the shade I've chosen: Verdigris Green. The architraves are now snowy-white instead of a dull cream. She's flung open the window to air the space out and sunshine is pouring in. Calton Hill rises in the distance. It's glorious. *My room with a view …*

'It looks fantastic,' I say to her, dumping my bags by the bed and looking around. 'Oh, and the chair's been done too!' She's had it recovered in a satiny fabric of the same shade.

'Well, since I was redecorating, I thought I might as well do the job properly. I'm going to do my bedroom next, then the lounge and kitchen.'

'Your dad will balk at the decorating costs if you do the whole flat.'

Dee shrugs. 'Well, it's their investment. Besides, I'll tell him it's good practice for when I'm running his hotel.'

'Not … Manchester?'

'No, he's thinking—and Mummy is helping to convince him—that he needs to open a sister hotel in Edinburgh. It means I can live here and get to be the manager.'

'That's amazing.' I give her arm a squeeze. *Well played, Dee!* 'Just don't go entertaining men in the hotel rooms,' I tell her sternly. 'You need to be on your best behaviour.'

'Oh no,' she says with a mischievous grin. 'That was a one-off due to exceptional circumstances. Speaking of men, anything?'

I shake my head.

'Give it time. He's probably still processing.'

'How much bloody time does he need?' I mutter. But I can't fault Dee, she did her bit, whatever happens or doesn't happen, is in the hands of the Universe.

After I unpack and settle in, I decide to check Hearts of Fire on my laptop to see if there's any new blood. It never hurts to have a plan B.

I haven't been in there for a while and I've turned off my email notifications, so I'm surprised to see there are half a dozen date requests. I click on the most recent one. Lachlan, 36, into bag piping, imbibing and fraternising—hah. His profile photo shows a guy with a huge bushy beard, beetling eyebrows and massive shoulders. He's not my type looks-wise, but his tagline and bio are quite funny. Yet just thinking about sending off the questionnaire, waiting for him to reply, then arranging a date with him if he passes, makes me feel drained.

I force myself to click on the next one, sent two days ago. Thomas, 37, with Snoopy as a profile photo. *Cute*, I think. I read the bio:

I have particular requirements for the women I date. Please see the list below and only reply if you're a good fit.

OK, he's highfalutin; could be a psycho. But who am I to judge, when we've been sending out a screening questionnaire? I run my eyes down his list.

* Must be an expert hiker and not afraid to get feet wet.

* Must like energetic dogs that chew couch cushions.

* Must like mint and salted caramel chocolate.

* Must like soppy Bryan Adams songs.

* Must like lavender oil massages.

* Must be prepared to lose to me at Scrabble.

'Dee!' I scream, 'Dee, get in here!'

She comes bursting into the room. 'What? What's happened?' I gesture at my laptop. She reads the bio and starts chuckling. 'It's TJ! What I said to him worked!'

'It seems so.'

'But why didn't he just call you?'

'Because he likes to be clever, and he's trying to make a point.'

'Oh.' She reads it again. 'Lavender oil massages?' She sounds amused. 'What have you two been up to?'

'Don't ask. It's just a … thing.'

'Well, are you going to message him? He sent it two days ago. Some other lavender oil massage-loving woman might snap him up!'

I stare at the screen, my mind whirring. She's right. I need to reply pronto, but what do I say? I need to show I'm receptive, yet he hurt me so I'm not going to fall into his arms willingly either. He has to work for it.

The game is on …

Hi Thomas,

Your list is quite specific. So specific in fact, that it's almost as if you've been stalking me. I hope that's not the case. Just to let you know, I screen all my requests to ensure that I'm not wasting my time. So, if you want a first date, please fill in this questionnaire. This is non-negotiable.

Many thanks,

Aster

I slap the lid closed and look at Dee, who's been sitting next to me on the bed watching me type. 'There. Let's see what he does with that.'

'It's a bit unfriendly, isn't it?' she says 'Why couldn't you say "I'm into all that. I'd love to go on a date with you"?'

'It's called playing hard to get. It's a tactical manoeuvre. Like playing chess,' I reply.

'I'm so not a game player. Maybe that's where I've been going wrong.'

I refrain from rolling my eyes. This, coming from the woman who single-handedly outwitted me and brought me to my knees. 'Don't worry, I'll give you lessons,' I say, patting her hand. 'Five Easy Ways to Play Hard to Get.'

Shortly after we're in the kitchen. I'm sitting at the island drinking wine, munching on corn chips, and trying not to stare at my phone every ten seconds. Dee is happily chopping vegetables for some new recipe she's trying for our dinner tonight. She sings Taylor Swift's *This Love* softly under her breath; I won't let her have her Spotify up too loud in case I don't hear my phone, which I've turned up to full volume.

I'm about to ask her if she wants any help, when a church bell email notification resounds from my phone.

We stare at each other.

'That was quick, relatively speaking,' she says. 'He isn't playing hard to get.'

'It might not be him.'

Nervously, I check it and see that it is from TJ, though he's used a different email than his work address. There's a message: 'As you wish'. Ah, a Princess Bride reference, nice.

I read his answers. They pretty much align with what he gave Dee, including Maxie escaping his lead and chomping on the sausages in the park. It makes me chuckle every time. He's slept with one woman in the last month (I'm assuming it's me since he's added "three times"). For the 'What are you reading?' I note in surprise that it's the indie author I recently edited, the story about the aliens. Hah, my name will be in the acknowledgements.

Me

Thomas, your answers are suitable. You may proceed.

PS: Check out the acknowledgements when you finish the book. Yours truly is in there as the editor.

Thomas
Glad to hear it. Are you free this Saturday night?

PS: I flicked to the back, but you're not in there. Only kudos to his mother and his high school teacher for encouraging him to write.

Me
Yes. I'm free on Saturday night. What time?

PS: Damn. He didn't put me in. That's embarrassing.

Thomas
Does 7pm work?

PS: If it's any consolation I'm halfway through and I haven't found one typo.

Me
Yes, 7pm works.

PS: Thank you for saying so.

Thomas
Excellent. I'll pick you up.

PS: *No need to give me the address. I have indeed been stalking you, so I know where you live.*

Me
OK, *see you then.*

PS: *Very funny.*

Chapter 37

On Saturday morning, my nerves start to kick in. I've been fine up until that point, but after a quick rifle through my wardrobe I realise I have nothing to wear. There's been no mention of where we're going, but it's a proper date, so I get the feeling that we might be going to a nice restaurant. I can't turn up in cut-off jeans and a racerback tank.

I tell Dee over breakfast and she promptly says, 'We have to go shopping' in a matter-of-fact tone. This involves spending a painfully long time at H&M, where she flies around flicking through racks and throwing items into an ever-growing mound in her basket while exclaiming 'YES, I've been wanting one of those!' and 'THAT would go perfectly with my black skirt!'

'Do you ever shop anywhere else?' I ask impatiently.

'Not really. Oh my God,' she pauses in front of a dress. 'This is SO YOU.'

After purchasing half the store for her, and the dress for me, we traipse back to the flat. I'm looking forward to slumping on the couch with a cup of tea, but Dee has other ideas.

'Right, mani-pedi next.'

I look at my short, unvarnished, nails. 'I'll put on clear polish. Besides, will we even get an appointment?'

'I checked with my local before we went shopping. They had two spots at eleven, so I grabbed them. Come on, my treat.'

'Oh, well ... OK,' I say reluctantly. I've never been to a nail salon, it's always seemed a bit excessive when you can DIY, but if she's paying ...

When we're lying back in a cushioned booth, music is playing and my feet have been scrubbed, and are now being expertly massaged with perfumed lotion, I change my mind. This is the most relaxing thing ever! I might book in for one of these on a regular basis.

I wonder if TJ likes giving foot massages, I think idly. My stomach flips, imagining him sucking on my big toe. I've been trying not to think about it too much, but knowing I'm going to be seeing him in a romantic context in a few hours, is making me feel all fluttery, and kind of turned on. Will we be having sex? Surely, we will. Unless he's going to play hard to get in return. Give me a quick peck on the cheek at the door, and leave me gagging for it. Knowing him, it's highly likely. But that's OK, maybe it's best if nothing of a sexual nature happens tonight. TJ staying over could be awkward with Dee downstairs. Though, if we're quiet, will she even know? He could sneak out the next morning.

Feeling a bit guilty for planning a clandestine reunion with

TJ, I look over at Dee. She's got her eyes closed and a small contented smile is playing on her lips. I giggle to myself. I think she's enjoying my makeover more than me.

Fifteen minutes before seven, I'm putting the finishing touches on my eye make-up when the buzzer goes. I smile to myself. He's early. But I knew he would be. It's helpful to know the quirks of the man you're going on a first date with. It quells the pre-date jitters, and I've got those in spades.

There's so much we have to discuss, to reconcile.

Dee comes into my room and gasps. Her eyes start filling with tears.

I feel like I'm in one of those rom-com moments where the ugly girl walks out into the lounge after she's spent seven hours getting ready, and everyone is amazed.

She was beautiful after all ...

'You look lovely, that dress is perfect.'

'You have good taste,' I tell her. It's a strapless sheath of emerald silk that fits me like a glove and shows a decent amount of leg. With the gold hoop earrings, smoky eyeshadow, and stilettos, I feel like a starlet going to the Oscars.

'Have you let him in?

She nods. 'He's in the foyer.'

I let out a shaky breath. 'OK, let's get this show on the road.'

I pick my way down the stairs with Dee behind me. I'm concentrating on not falling ass over tit, so when a voice says 'Wow' it startles me.

I look over the railing and see TJ dressed in his suit, raking his gaze over my legs, then slowly up again. When his eyes meet mine there's an instant firework explosion and my ankles start wobbling, but I manage to make it to the bottom in one piece.

'Hello, Mr *Thomas*,' I say formally, inclining my head gracefully. I almost hold out my hand to be kissed, but stop myself since my palms have started sweating.

He plays along and inclines his head too. 'Miss Aster.'

'Bye.' I give Dee a quick hug. 'Don't expect an emergency text from the loo tonight,' I murmur in her ear.

She giggles and kisses my cheek. 'Have fun.'

When I walk outside, I see that TJ has ordered a black cab. 'Your chariot awaits,' he says, gesturing to it with a flourish and holds open the door.

In the cab, we're still role playing like we're in *Downton Abbey*. 'How was your day, Miss Aster?'

'Pleasant, thank you, Mr Thomas, and yours?'

'Adequate. The weather was inclement, so I got wet walking my masterful mutt in the rain'.

It's fun and it eases my nerves considerably. But with the way TJ keeps looking at me and pressing his thigh against mine, it's quite sexually charged, more like a scene from *Bridgerton*.

When the cab starts climbing up The Mound, I get curious and forget to role play. 'Where are we going?'

'You'll see.'

The cab turns right into the Royal Mile and I still haven't twigged. Then all of a sudden, I do. 'Not Witchery?'

TJ smirks, looking pleased with himself. Oh my God, I've always wanted to go there. No date I've been on has ever suggested it because it's too expensive. How did he know? An image of us standing together in the rattling snack car on the way to London pops into my mind; TJ enquiring what to buy Dee for lunch. *He's asked her where I'd like to go.*

Inside, I'm bouncing up and down with excitement ... Witchery! But I say nonchalantly 'I suppose that will do, Mr Thomas', making TJ chuckle.

At the restaurant, the waiter leads us to our table and I trail along behind taking it all in. It looks like a feasting hall in a castle. Intricately-carved oak panelling encases the walls and ceiling. There's red leather banquette seating, tables laid with white cloths, and polished silver cutlery. The sconce lighting and fluttering flames from the antique candles lend the room an intimate olde-worlde glow. I can almost hear the sounds of sixteenth-century life going on outside the deep-set window.

'It's *amazing*,' I breathe.

'You can sit down now,' TJ smiles up at me and I realise I've been standing there gawking like an idiot.

The waiter hands us thick leatherbound menus, and flicks

linen napkins over our laps, wow—everything is so elegant. I'm glad I dressed up.

Then, over TJ's shoulder I spot a group of girls in their twenties with ironed blonde hair. They're wearing luxe tracksuits, and sporting lipsticked trout pouts and spidery eyelashes. Like they've been lounging around the house then thought, hey, let's go to Witchery for dinner, I'll put on some Dior lippy and grab my Prada purse. All my dress shopping, nail painting and smoky eye shadow seems over the top. Should I have worn my trackies too? I drag my attention back to the menu, trying not to feel intimidated.

'I thought maybe the Caviar to start,' remarks TJ glancing at me.

When I see the price, I gulp. It's £185 for thirty grams. 'I'll pass. But you go ahead.'

TJ chuckles. 'Yeah, it's a bit expensive.'

Phew, I think, luckily he doesn't act like a millionaire, even though he is one.

'I might get the oysters as a starter though,' he adds.

It takes a concerted effort but I manage not to make an aphrodisiac quip. I've never understood why oysters are the food of love but watching TJ tilt his head back and slip oysters into his mouth, with a slight flick of his tongue as he does so, is pretty sexy. I shift on my seat and my thighs stick to the leather. 'Have you been here before?' I ask, to move the conversation away from my erotic thoughts. I take a careful sip of my shellfish bisque, trying not to spill any of the bright orange liquid on the snowy tablecloth.

TJ pauses his oyster consumption. 'Once—with Beth.'

'Was it a special occasion?'

'An anniversary I think, I can't remember.'

This reminds me that TJ is an old hand at long-term relationships, having them and breaking up from them, he knows what he's doing. I feel like a babe in the woods in comparison. But I hear Dee's voice in my head—*you've been on plenty of dates, you're the queen of dating, you got this.*

We're waiting for our mains to arrive, and I'm feeling surprised, and somewhat relieved, that a certain topic of conversation hasn't reared its ugly head: namely my dating history. I thought there would be a big deep and meaningful discussion about it, but it doesn't seem to be an issue anymore. Dee must've done an excellent job of pleading my case.

There's a lull in our pleasant chitter chatter, and I'm wondering if the loo has a medieval ambience, when TJ takes a sip of wine and looks at me intently over his glass in the candlelight. 'So, when did you know?'

There's a beat of confusion on my part. 'Know what?'

'That you were in love with me,' he says.

I suck in a breath. My carefully concealed ace of hearts flops onto the table and lies there—exposed.

I give a shaky laugh. 'What?'

Oh, she didn't. Please tell me she didn't.

TJ is staring at me with what I think is amusement. So

that's what this is all about. The two of them are in on it. Give Aster what she wants, expose her deepest darkest secrets, and then throw her under the bus. Hah bloody hah, what a joke. None of this makes the slightest bit of sense to my rational mind, but instantly I'm back in that playground again, surrounded by jeering … my breathing quickens.

'I, uh, I have to go to the loo.' I try to extricate myself, but the table has somehow moved forward and wedged me in on the banquette. I push at it fruitlessly with growing panic, tears of frustration welling. TJ's warm hand comes down over mine and grasps it tightly. 'Miss Aster … I feel the same.'

I stare at him. 'Seriously?'

TJ nods. 'Yes, indeed. Very much so.'

I inhale and let it out slowly. I squeeze TJ's hand in relief as the ghost of Christian Parker flickers for a moment, then dissolves entirely. 'But my dating history? You felt used …'

He smiles at me. 'When Dee said you loved me it changed everything. It's not my place to judge what you've done or who you've been with. All I know is that I love you, the rest is irrelevant. I don't want to miss out on something amazing because I'm hung up on the past.'

It's an inopportune time for our mains to arrive, but the server is waiting to place the dishes in front of us, and we reluctantly have to break our grasp. I sit there, gazing at TJ over my roast breast of Kype Muir duck hardly daring to believe it. *He loves me …*

Chapter 38

Near the end of the duck, which is delicious even if I'm having trouble thinking about eating, I summon the courage to ask the question. 'Do you want to come back to mine for tea and jaffa cakes?'

One stiletto is off and I've been rubbing TJ's calf with my toes for the last ten minutes under the table. I'm hoping that, plus all the oysters he's eaten, will have some effect.

He stretches back in his chair puffing out his cheeks. 'I don't know. Phew, I'm stuffed.'

'Oh,' I say, feeling disappointed and confused. Maybe the lobster thermidor with triple-cooked chips has overridden the oysters.

'Though if by "jaffa cakes", you mean what I think you mean, I'm sure I can fit in a few,' he adds smiling.

Declining dessert, and after one last sighing gaze at the beguiling Witchery on my part, we walk down the Royal Mile, attempting to flag a cab. TJ has to catch my elbow several times when I wobble into him before he gives up and holds onto my hand tightly.

'You're going to do yourself an injury in those things.'

'Oh, well, if I break an ankle, I know an awesome physio.

He'll whip me back into shape in no time.'

'Will he now?'

'I'm hoping he will, especially the whipping part.'

Perhaps the oysters kick in, or he's into whips, I'm not sure, but TJ veers us off the Mile and into a darkened close. His arms go around me and I nuzzle into his neck, lifting up his shirt to feel his smooth warm back.

'You're stunning,' he whispers, brushing his lips along my cheekbone. He leans against the blackened wall, pulling me to him. He cups my face in his hands and we kiss, his lips lightly pressing against mine. His tongue, which was recently flicking oysters, finds its way into my mouth and flicks urgently. My body starts quivering with want and I break away with a groan. 'Let's find a cab. Unless you want to do it here.'

'Yeah, good point. I'm not that limber.'

We flag a cab at last and manage to keep our hands off each other for the sake of propriety. Though, TJ drawing circles on my bare knee, is making my spine tingle. The passing street lights highlight the planes of his face. Perhaps love is giving my eyes a beauty filter, but he's definitely a strong ten, possibly even an eleven. I can't stop looking at him.

Of course, we get stuck at red lights all the way there.

'This is taking forever,' he mutters.

I kiss his hand. 'Patience, Thomas.'

When we reach the flat I have a moment of crisis. Dee's light is still on, and the thought of having sex in my room with TJ while she's down here reading feels a bit weird. I whisper to him to go up to the kitchen and put the kettle on and that I'll be there in a minute.

I knock softly and poke my head in. 'Hey, I'm back.'

'Hi! How was it?' She's got her hair up and her headmistress specs on. A book balanced on her knees.

'Fantastic,' I sigh, sitting on the edge of her bed. 'We went to Witchery.'

'Gosh, no way!' she exclaims in mock surprise.

'I know you told him I wanted to go there.'

'Yeah. I got the feeling he wanted it to be special. And since he's got cash to burn, why not?'

'I also found out you told him I loved him. Dee, seriously?'

'Ah.' She sinks down under the covers to get away from my accusing glare. 'Sorry, I had to do something drastic. He wasn't reacting too well to anything I was saying. Finally, I yelled 'For God's sake you plonker, Aster's in love with you!' and that seemed to do the trick. He said 'Is she?' in a surprised tone and got all misty-eyed. I didn't tell you because I knew you'd freak out and go all *High School Musical* on me. Did he say something at dinner?'

'Yeah.'

'But it's all OK?'

'Yeah, we're good.'

She smiles at me. 'Thank God for that. Is he here?'

'Yes, in the kitchen. We're going to have tea and jaffa cakes.'

Dee sniggers. 'Is that what it's called these days?'

'You don't mind if he stays over, do you?'

'No, I guess not.' She rolls her eyes. 'But keep it down. I need my beauty sleep.'

'Haha.'

'Dee?'

'Mmm?'

'Thank you.'

She gives me an air kiss. 'Mwah. Anytime.'

TJ's sitting at the island counter with two filled mugs of tea in front of him. 'I wasn't sure if you did want a tea. Or if "put the kettle on" was another euphemism.'

I laugh. 'I'm not sure either. But since you've made it, we may as well drink it.' I collect the biscuits from the pantry and hand him the packet.

'Oh, you actually do have jaffa cakes,' he says grinning.

'Of course.'

As I reach over to pick up my mug of tea, I notice a slim plastic object lying on the counter in front of him.

'What's that?'

'I don't know. It magically appeared.'

'It looks like a …' I pull it closer to see '… CD case.' I turn it over and **FOR ASTER** is written on the front.

'Oh.' *Oh!*

'Turns out I wasn't chicken where you're concerned,' TJ says, but I notice uncertainty in his voice, as if he's having second thoughts.

I grip the CD tightly before he can take it back. My heart is thumping. 'It's not Bryan Adams, is it?'

He shakes his head and laughs. 'It's not Bryan Adams.'

'Shall we go to my room?'

We sit on my bed side by side, sipping tea, the CD player lying between us with 1/1 displaying on the console.

'It's going to make me cry, isn't it?'

'Yeah.'

'Great. Just when I went to so much trouble with my smoky eyes.'

TJ grins and reaches into his suit jacket pocket. 'Luckily, I brought these along then.' He brandishes a small packet of tissues.

'You've thought of everything,' I say dryly.

'I wanted it to be the perfect date.'

'Fine, but you have to listen to it too. I'm not crying alone.' I give him one ear of the headphones.

I press "play", settle back against the pillows and close my eyes. It better not be bloody Bryan Adams. But it's not, it's worse. It's Muse's *Starlight*. Oh no, I'm going to be a wreck.

I'm doing well until the chorus, and then I lose it.

'The perfect song for my star girl,' TJ whispers in my ear, as he holds me in his arms and I cry freely into his chest, wetting his shirt.

'You've outdone yourself,' I sob.

He hands me a tissue. 'I'm just getting started. There are a lot more one song CDs where that came from.'

I give him a watery smile and wipe my eyes. 'Let's listen to it again.'

TJ chuckles. 'You're a sucker for punishment.'

'If this is love, then I guess I am a total sucker,' I say sniffing.

'It's gotta be love,' TJ says deadpan. 'No doubt about it, baby.'

From that moment, I'm unequivocally the happiest I've ever been. Everything seems to fall into place and I'm in a sanctum of centeredness.

I've taken on several new clients and I'm earning decent money for once, so I can save. Mia has also decided to interview me for her podcast. She says my "controversial topics" may cause a ruckus and I should expect a lot of comments, or as I like to think of it: a healthy discussion.

I'm staying over at TJ's three nights a week; twice during the week and on Saturday night. We're slowly working our way through the treat cupboard and *Outlander*. When we're not doing that, we're going on hikes, cooking international dishes together, taking Maxie for walks in the park, and getting to know each other better. It's lovey-dovey with mind-blowing orgasms; a win-win in my book. Since I've officially retired from the world of online dating, Dee suggested we delete the Trello board. I thought she might want to keep it for herself, but she said she was seriously thinking about getting a cat.

Speaking of Dee, she's fully supportive of my relationship with TJ now she's come to terms with it. There's been no bunny boiling on the hob or cutting up my green dress with the kitchen scissors. Not yet anyway. We've also started branching out socially, and having wine evenings at the flat with Stacey, Greer and Fleur, which are a lot of fun. Sometimes Rosie turns up too, depending on her schedule.

The jury is still out on whether Stacey and Greer are a couple. Dee thinks they are because she said she saw them having an intense discussion in the hallway one night when she went to get some more wine. But in front of us, they sit apart and barely speak to each other. I rather thought Greer was into me, but as Dee keeps saying pointedly when she sees her glancing my way, 'Aster is loved up. Look at her, she's glowing.'

'It's all the sex,' I say, but secretly I agree. I'm so loved-up, it's not funny.

One Sunday morning, after an energetic dawn romp, I leave TJ sleeping peacefully with Maxie cuddled up next to him, and head back to the flat. I'm looking forward to a healthy nourishing breakfast, a little light stretching, perhaps a post-sex nap. But, when I enter the kitchen, I find a dark-haired man clad only in Calvin Klein briefs, pottering about with the tea things.

'Hi,' I say surprised. For once, he isn't one of mine. At the sound of my voice, the man turns and I get the full-frontal experience. Hoo-wee, he's stonkingly hot with a body to match.

'Hello.' He smiles at me flashing beautiful teeth. 'I'm Dean, a friend of Kiki's.' His English accent is so posh, it's like his vowels have been clipped with a razor. 'I'm making tea and toast,' he explains, gesturing to the kettle and toaster. He doesn't seem at all concerned that he's practically naked.

'Um, nice to meet you, I'm Aster,' I say, trying to keep my eyes on his face.

'Have you found everything ...?' Dee comes swanning into the kitchen in a white business shirt à la *Risky Business*, with only a few buttons done up. It's obvious she's not wearing any underwear. 'Oh, Aster, hi. You're back,' she says, swiftly buttoning up the rest of the shirt. 'This is Dean.'

We both turn to look at Dean and I try not to ogle his abs, but fail miserably. 'Yes, we've just met,' he says, smiling pleasantly in all his muscled glory.

'How did you two become acquainted?' I ask. Oh no, Dean's posh accent is catching, my vowels are starting to clip.

'Camilla Sutcliffe,' mumbles Dee, moving to hop onto a bar stool when she sees me casting an eye over her thin shirt.

'Yes, Kiki and I were introduced at Camilla Sutcliffe's exhibition,' agrees Dean, continuing his ministrations with the tea and toast. 'Since I was in Edinburgh for work, I decided to look her up and see if she wanted to have dinner.'

It looks like it was a lot more than dinner ... Kiki.

'How do you have your tea?' he asks Dee.

'White with a half,' she says. 'I'm trying to cut back on sugar.'

'And you're sweet enough as it is,' he says, giving her a wink. He puts half a sugar into her tea as requested and stirs it with a flourish. Dee doesn't say anything but her cheeks are glowing pink from the compliment and she's playing with a lock of her hair.

Oooh, the hair fiddle, a dead giveaway that she likes him.

'Do you want to go back to your bedroom or eat here?' Dean asks.

'Oh, I think the bedroom most definitely,' she says, and he grins at her.

Whoop, go Dee, he's as keen as mustard.

Dean nods goodbye to me, then saunters sexily out of the kitchen carrying the mugs of tea. Dee follows him with a plate of jammy toast. She pauses beside me on the way past.

'Are you going to be around later? I may need a debrief.'

'Sure,' I say, grinning. 'Meanwhile, enjoy your *pre-debrief.*'

'Oh, we will,' she replies coyly. 'If you're not going out, you may want to turn Taylor Swift up loud for the next hour or so. Dean's quite vocal.'

She gives me a saucy wink and skips out of the kitchen. So much for getting a cat, or her "no sex until they're worthy" rule; Dee's gone rogue with Dean.

Shaking my head, I refill the kettle. There's never a dull moment in the house of dating disasters.

The End

Acknowledgements

Many thanks to my beta readers: Katie Griffin, Aimee Ferro and Lauryn Lambert for all your insightful feedback. A special thanks to Lauryn for her developmental editing.

More thanks go to Katerina Hristova for her beta reading and copyediting, my sister Tania Courtine for her proofreading, Kerry Ellis for her cover art, plus a shout out to the indie author community for their encouragement and support.

Thanks also to my partner in crime, Chris Lambert, who has encouraged my writing from the start, mwah!

Finally, thank YOU, reader, for giving this book a chance! If you enjoyed it, I hope you'll recommend it to a friend and consider leaving a review on Amazon, Goodreads, Instagram or TikTok. Indie authors rely on reviews and word of mouth to get our work out there. Thank you!

Angela Xx

PS: The Spotify playlist for this book is in my TikTok and Instagram bio link: @angelapearseauthor - please feel free to connect with me on there too!

Visit **angelapearse.pub to join my mailing list
for updates on new releases and offers**

About the Author

Angela Pearse is an indie author of quirky romantic comedies set in Edinburgh and European locations. She has an MA in English and splits her time between freelance copywriting and writing novels. When she's not tapping on her keyboard, she enjoys taking advantage of cheap travel deals, hiking around lochs, binge watching Netflix, and reading chick lit. Originally from New Zealand, Angela currently lives in Edinburgh with her partner who is also a writer. *The House of Dating Disasters* is her third novel.